I0554026

Every Month Original
Novels, Stories, and Articles

USA Today Bestselling Writer
Dean Wesley Smith

TABLE OF CONTENTS

SHORT STORIES

FULL NOVEL

SERIAL NOVEL

NONFICTION

POEMS

SMITH'S MONTHLY ISSUE #15

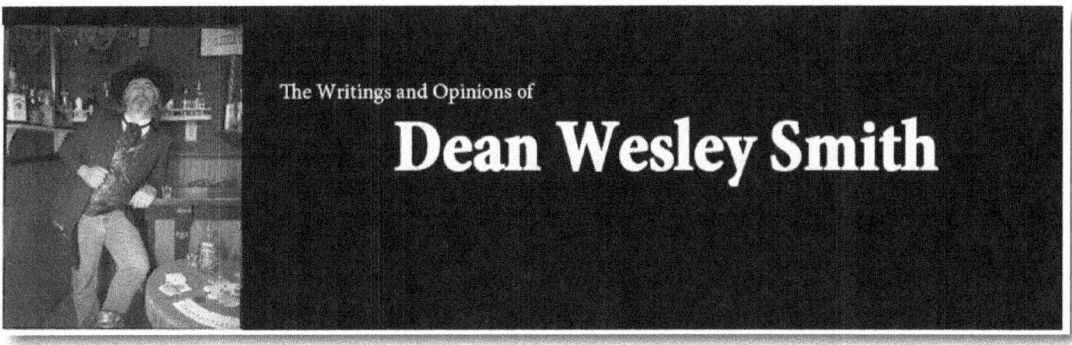

The Writings and Opinions of

Dean Wesley Smith

Introduction
THE NEW YEAR

EVEN THOUGH this is the December issue, it's going to arrive in most places in mid-January or later. And being January, that means some new stuff and some changes coming.

Nothing major.

But still some changes.

When I started this magazine, I had a series of nonfiction golf articles in it. Humor articles about my days as a golf professional. And those chapters were turned into a book last year that has sold some copies, much to my surprise.

So in the upcoming 2015 issues, I'll be bringing back some more nonfiction humor that will eventually be books.

Also, I decided to still keep doing poems, just not all the time. I did them in every issue for the first thirteen issues. That's enough poetry from anyone. But there will still be poems, just not all the time.

I will keep doing a full new novel per month. That will be the focus of every issue.

Plus there will be numbers of short stories every month as well. As I have been doing, the stories will be a mix of new stories, stories that were never published, and some stories that were published that I would like to bring to the present.

And the short stories will cover almost all major genres. This is a fiction magazine, not a genre magazine.

The serial stories will be here at times as well, but again not all the time. This issue has the second of four installments of the Poker Boy short novel *They're Back*.

Also, about the time the Poker Boy serial is done in these pages, WMG Publishing will be rebranding all the Poker Boy stories. And I'll write a new Poker Boy novel at that point. But until then, I'll try to have at least one Poker Boy story in every issue, plus the serial.

Thanks for the Support

Dean Wesley Smith

In this issue I have the second stand-alone novel in the Cold Poker Gang series called *Cold Call*. This series of novels are mystery novels where retired Las Vegas detectives solve cold cases. I hope you enjoy the novel.

As many of you have noticed, I'm writing novels inside a number of different series. I've put in these issues so far four of the time travel series novels called the Thunder Mountain series. The fifth novel will be next month.

I have also written two novels in a brand new series called Ghost of a Chance series. The ghost agents in those books are like a second superhero team in the Poker Boy universe. And, of course, they work with Poker Boy and his team to help save the world at times.

This coming year expect some novels that are not set in one of the main series.

That's the advantage I have of having a novel every month in these pages. I can do a lot of varied things.

So the focus of these pages will continue to be the novel of the issue and numbers of short stories. But there will be other features as well.

Thank you again, everyone, for the support.

And a huge thank-you to Allyson and the wonderful people at WMG Publishing Inc. who support this crazy magazine project. I couldn't be having this much fun without them.

Dean Wesley Smith
November 23, 2014
Lincoln City, Oregon

Coming Next Issue in Smith's Monthly
A return to the Thunder Mountain Series
in a brand new novel.

LAKE ROOSEVELT

Smith's MONTHLY

NUMBER SIXTEEN
JANUARY, 2015

Original Stories, Novels, and Articles

DEAN WESLEY SMITH

LAKE ROOSEVELT
A Thunder Mountain Novel

Dean Wesley **Smith**

USA Today Bestselling Writer

Daddy wants
her dead?
What's a girl to do?

**A POKER BOY
STORY**

Daddy is an
Undertaker

What's a girl to do when Daddy wants her dead?

Mortuary Dan, otherwise known as Death himself, just happens to be her father.

Poker Boy and his team must help the only daughter of Death understand that she might not really die as she turns twenty-one.

Even though she will.

Sort of....

DADDY IS AN UNDERTAKER
A Poker Boy Story

ONE

I USUALLY FIND the people I'm going to help by accident. Most of us superheroes do, or we are told to help someone by one of our bosses.

But this time, my sidekick and girlfriend, Patty Ledgerwood, aka Front Desk Girl brought me a person who really needed help.

And I do mean a lot of help if she planned on staying alive more than another few hours.

Actually, Patty sent my boss, Stan, the God of Poker, to get me.

It was a dark and rainy Oregon Saturday night in March. I was dressed and watching a rerun of an old Star Trek show starring the bald actor whose name I can never remember. In an hour or so, I planned on heading over to the casino near the double-wide trailer I called home. I never went near the casino too early on a weekend night, because the players were new and fresh and hadn't had enough drinks.

I always gave the Saturday players a few hours, and then went over to take the money that they were willing to give to me across the poker table. Even though I was a superhero, I still had to make a living, and playing poker was my way of doing it.

"Knock, knock. Poker Boy, need to talk," the voice-without-a-body said from the middle of the air in my living room, interrupting a scene with an alien with a forehead problem and some sort of sticky paste-like substance.

I knew the voice. Stan had only been to my home once before for only a second. It wasn't like him to be polite and actually knock.

"I'm decent," I said, standing and heading for my superhero costume on the hook by the door. I had on tennis shoes, jeans, and a white Polo shirt, but my costume was my black leather coat and black Fedora-like hat that I never took off in a casino. It helped funnel the power of the casino to me. If Stan was coming to talk to me, I knew I was going to need the costume very quickly.

Stan appeared in the middle of my living room and glanced first at the old television, then the remains of my T.V. dinner on the scarred coffee table, then around at the old 1970s furniture and green shag carpet that had come with the doublewide when it was new.

"We clearly don't pay you enough," Stan said, disgusted at what he saw.

"You don't pay me anything," I said as I slipped on my coat and hat.

"Oh, yeah, there's that," Stan said. "But I know for a fact you have enough in your bank accounts to buy a dozen mansions in every state in the country, with enough left over for a castle in Britain."

I shrugged. He was right. In about fifty accounts in fifty different banks, I had a vast amount of money. And a ton of investments that seemed to be doing real well when I bothered to check on them. I had won a lot of tournaments and just didn't spend much money after taxes every year.

"I like it here," I said. "Keeps me humble."

"Oh, yeah, Poker Boy humble," Stan said, laughing. "I bet Patty doesn't come over often,"

With that he had a point. We always stayed at her wonderful place in Vegas. She had only seen my home once and never come back. Maybe Stan was right, it might be time to upgrade some. When I had the time.

And besides, Patty thought I was a broke gambler. Maybe at some point I should get around to telling her about my money. Not a conversation I was looking forward to.

"To what do I owe this visit?" I asked the God of Poker.

"Just doing a favor for your girl-friend," Stan said. "She needs your help on a case and she asked me to come get you. Guess there isn't enough time for you to fly commercial." Stan just shook his head at my old doublewide. "You know, you could afford a few private jets as well."

"Or you could teach me the jumping-around-in-space skill," I said. "Or is that only for gods?"

He shrugged. "Maybe when you're done helping Patty."

I was actually surprised at that. I didn't know I might be able to actually teleport around the world. Of course, I still didn't know what half my powers were. I was still pretty new at this superhero stuff.

The next moment I was in the crowd-ed lobby of the MGM Grand.

The noise of the casino and the hundreds of guests in the lobby slammed into me. But at the same time I could feel the energy coming from the casino through my coat and hat, making me feel extra alive.

Patty was standing in front of the desk, talking to a woman with longish blonde hair. Patty glanced over, saw me, and smiled.

Like normal, her smile melted a part of me and got other parts all agitated in a very good way. She had the ability to do that to me with just a look. Her long brown hair was pulled back and she was dressed in the standard MGM front desk uniform of white shirt and black slacks and MGM vest. She made it look great.

She was a stunningly attractive woman. What she saw in me was anyone's guess.

I made my way through the crowd and luggage over to her and she gave me a hug. "Thanks for coming."

"Anytime," I said, and I meant it.

"Thanks, Stan," Patty said to the air.

"More than welcome," Stan said without showing himself.

The young woman with Patty sort of looked around for the voice, but before she could say anything Patty said, "Lisa, this is Poker Boy."

I turned on my what I called my "Charming Power" for lack of a better name. It helped put people I was trying to help in a more relaxed and talkative mood. I shook her firm hand. "Very nice meeting you."

Lisa looked like an odd imitation of an American flag, with a red, white and blue outfit that included a too-tight skirt. It really wasn't a flattering look on her. Up close I could tell she couldn't be more than twenty-two, and more than likely she would get carded everywhere she went in this town.

Plus she had on way too much makeup. Her eyelashes seemed to extend halfway into the big lobby.

She smiled, but the smile didn't reach her dark eyes. I could tell that something was very wrong in her life.

"Tell him what's bothering you," Patty said, patting Lisa's arm gently in support.

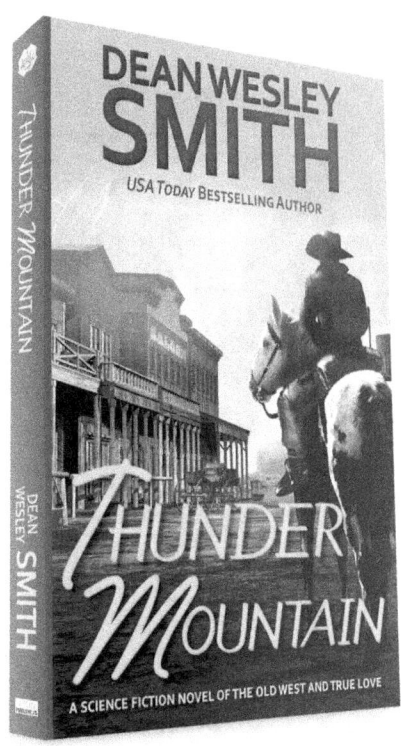

As a superhero in the world of hospitality, Patty could calm the most upset person and make them feel good about anything. It was one of her many superpowers.

Lisa nodded, took a deep breath, and then in a deep southern accent she said, "My daddy is an undertaker."

I waited for her to keep going, but she seemed to think that was enough explanation of her problem.

Finally I said, "Yes, go on. What's happening?"

"No, you don't see do you?" Lisa said, clearly about to break into tears that I was sure would run black from all the makeup. "I'm turning twenty-one in four hours, and my daddy is an undertaker."

I looked puzzled and was about to try a tell-me-the-truth power on her when Patty said softly to me, "Capitalize the word *Undertaker.*"

I opened my mouth to say something, then the realization hit me: the young woman in front of me was the child of an *Undertaker*, the most feared branch of all the deities.

That wasn't possible.

Undertakers never had children.

I had never heard of an Undertaker having a kid, and of all the rumors about Undertakers, the worst rumor was that their kids never lived past the first moment of their twenty-first birthday!

Now I saw the problem.

"Which one of the twelve is your father?" I asked softly, almost afraid to hear the answer. There were only twelve, one per month. It seems the twelve of them took turns being Death for the month.

"They call him Mortuary Dan," Lisa said.

Patty's face went white, and I felt like the chicken TV dinner I had eaten was about to make another showing in the lobby of the MGM Grand.

"I'm assuming you want to live longer than four more hours?" I asked, getting right to the point as I tried to get my stomach back under control.

The worst part of the kid rumor was that their own fathers took them.

The Undertakers took everyone at one point or another, except for maybe the gods, who seemed to live a very long

time. And some superheroes as well. Patty had been a superhero for about a hundred years before I became one. I'm not aging now and so far we've never talked much about what happened in those hundred years before I was born.

"I would like to live longer," she said. "Much longer. Can you help me?"

Usually I just say that I can help the person, give them encouragement, make them feel something positive. But all I said to Lisa was, "We can try."

But what Patty and I could do against an Undertaker was beyond me. Especially Mortuary Dan, the oldest of all the Undertakers. He was the worst, the nastiest of the twelve from what I had heard. All twelve were nasty people. Dealing with the dead and dying every day, day after day, would do that to a person. It was no wonder they only worked one month at a time. I had no idea what they did the other eleven months of the year. I honestly didn't want to know.

Somehow, to save this woman, we had to stop Death himself.

The big problem was that Death was her father.

TWO

I TOOK A DEEP BREATH and tried to pull my thoughts together. Somehow, we had to stop the tradition of not letting a child of an Undertaker live longer than the first moment of their twenty-first birthday.

I had no idea at all why such a stupid rule existed.

"Has your father ever talked to you about this?" I asked Lisa.

She shook her head.

"Do you have a place to stay here in Vegas?" I asked.

Lisa nodded. "I came here to enjoy my last night, then when checking in, I broke down in front of Patty and told her the entire story."

"Tell you what, Lisa, go ahead and go to your room, have a nice relaxing bath, then meet us down here in two hours if we haven't contacted you first. We need to do some work and you might as well enjoy the time it's going to take us."

"I'll upgrade you to a nice suite," Patty said, nodding to me and gently turning Lisa around toward the front desk before the Daughter of Death could object.

I pulled out my phone and called Screamer and had him meet us at our normal place downtown in fifteen minutes. Then I called The Smoke, the fourth member of my team, a human who could turn into a wolf when he wanted. He was out of town and working a case in the Canadian woods. There was no way he could make it in time, and I could tell he felt bad. I assured him that missing this one was a very good idea.

Then, as Patty got Lisa headed toward the elevators and turned to join me, I shouted into the noise and crowds of the large lobby, "Stan! Need some help!"

Around me the room froze except for Patty, as Stan took us out of time and appeared beside me. Everyone else just stopped in the instant of time. I had the power to do that as well, but Stan was better at it than I was.

"I thought I might be getting a call when I saw who needed help. You know the rumor is that she's going to be dead in a few hours by her own father's hand."

"That's what we need help with. We want to try to stop that."

Stan just laughed long and hard, choking before catching his breath. His laugh echoed in the quiet of the frozen huge lobby.

Patty and I didn't join him.

After a moment he said, "You two are serious, aren't you?"

Patty and I both nodded. "I don't even understand why a rule like that exists," I said.

"Because it does," Stan said.

"Why?" Patty asked. "How did it get started? Maybe if we knew that, we might be able to figure a way around it."

Stan shrugged. "I honestly don't know. It's just been a rule for the few children of Undertakers for as long as I have been around. Although, to be honest, no Undertaker has had a child except for Lisa in all my years. She's the only one."

I wanted to ask Stan how long that was, but decided it was a question for another time.

"Would Laverne know the reason behind all of this?" I asked, not really believing I had asked that question. Laverne was Lady Luck herself, one of the most powerful of all the gods. Patty and Screamer and I had saved her once, but that doesn't mean lowly superheroes like me and Patty and Screamer can bother her at every whim. But I was hoping that Stan might ask Burt, the God of Casino Operations; and if he didn't know, maybe Burt would ask Lady Luck.

"I don't know if she does or not," Stan said. "You meeting the rest of your team at The Diner?"

I nodded. "The Smoke is busy in Canada, but Screamer will be there."

"I'll see what I can do," Stan said. "I'll meet you at The Diner as soon as I get some information. You know, you

two worry me sometimes, screwing with things you shouldn't screw with."

Both of us nodded at that. What could we say?

He vanished, letting us slip back into normal time as he did. Around us the movement and the noise filled the air again, slamming around us like a stream moving around rocks.

"Sorry to get you into this," Patty said, looking worried as we turned and headed for the parking garage.

"Any excuse to spend time with you is great by me."

She laughed. "Silly, you never need an excuse, you know that."

For a moment I actually forgot that we were going up against an Undertaker, Death himself, to try to save Death's daughter.

THREE

FIFTEEN MINUTES LATER I told the problem to Screamer, a superhero with the power to read other people's minds and transfer thoughts.

We were sitting at a large table in The Diner, a hole-in-the-wall little restaurant decorated with pretend 1960s stuff. It was on a side street downtown, and a woman named Madge was our normal waitress. She always wore her uniform three sizes too small, and it was a chore to not stare when she had to pick anything up.

If you *did* stare, you ended up having nightmares for a week about exploding humans. Or at least I always did.

We had started going to The Diner when the team first formed and we had to fight the Slots of Saturn. And for every mission since, we met here to talk and plan and drink the fantastic milkshakes.

Madge had just set down our milkshakes when Screamer said he was very worried about even thinking of going up against an Undertaker. "Superheroes can live a long time, but we do die. We can be killed."

That was a thought I didn't want to think about at all.

Suddenly the sounds from the street stopped, and Madge froze in mid-stride back toward the lunch counter in the back.

A moment later Laverne showed up with a thin man dressed only in a loud-colored bathing suit and a white towel. I had no idea who he was, but he wasn't looking happy.

Stan appeared a moment later, smiled a sheepish grin, and sat down without a word at a nearby table to watch the fireworks.

"You know, Laverne," the man said, "I could have gotten at least two more waves in before sunset."

"Sorry, Dan," Laverne said, shaking her head.

Dan's bathing suit changed to a dark, silk business suit with his tie perfectly in place and a blue shirt under it that seemed like it belonged on a surfer.

Then Laverne said, "But after the month is over, you're going to have a lot of time to surf all you want."

Dan smiled, and an image of a skeleton face sort of flashed over his face. "You got that right."

All three of us at the table had slid back away from the front edge where Laverne and Dan were pulling up chairs and talking. I had zero doubt I was about to meet the most feared Undertaker of them all, Mortuary Dan.

Dan sat down and then glanced at us, nodding. "I see, Laverne, that you have your top superhero team together here, minus one. What can I do to help?"

Laverne glanced at the milkshake in front of Patty.

Patty nodded that it was all right for Laverne to take a drink and slid it to Lady Luck. After a sip, Laverne smiled, then turned to Dan with a serious expression. "You need to talk to your daughter."

"Why?" Dan asked. "I'm going to see her in just under four hours."

Wow, this guy was cold, even for Death.

"She doesn't know what's going to happen," Laverne said.

"That's silly," Dan said, taking Screamer's untouched milkshake and sipping it. "Wow! These are darned fine milkshakes. I can see why you guys meet here."

I think I nodded, but damned if I was going to say anything.

"She doesn't know, Dan," Laverne said, again sipping on the milkshake. "All she knows are the rumors handed down over centuries. You know she's the first kid of any Undertaker since the Dark Ages."

Dan nodded and made a large dent in the milkshake. "Yeah, those were tough times. It's been easier since."

The four of us just sat and listened to the two major gods talk and drink our milkshakes. As superheroes, what else could we do?

"She thinks she's going to die," Laverne said.

"Technically, she is," Dan said, slurping the milkshake and somehow managing to not get any on his silk suit.

"She contacted Poker Boy and his team to try to figure out a way to stop it."

Dan set the milkshake glass down hard, then turned and looked me directly in the eye. His face seemed to flash back and forth between skin and skeleton, and it had to be the most frightening thing I had ever seen. "What do you say to her?"

I sputtered, then dug down and managed to apply some calming skills from my years playing poker and said, "We told her we would find out what was happening."

He looked at me for a moment, than shook his head. "You don't know either, do you?"

Laverne laughed. "Dan, remember how long it has been since any of you had a kid. None of the younger superheroes or gods know anything more than the tradition of Undertakers killing their children."

He looked at Laverne, then back at me and my team. "So you are telling me, Lisa doesn't know what's going to happen in a few hours?"

"She believes she's going to die, sir," I said. "She's terrified."

Dan slammed his fist on the table, rocking all the milkshake glasses. If we hadn't been between time and frozen, that would have brought Madge running.

Dan's face went to complete skeleton, then he pushed his chair back and stood. "I knew I shouldn't have trusted her mother to raise her."

I desperately wanted to ask who Lisa's mother was, but smartly kept my mouth shut. When Death himself was pissed off, making him even angrier wasn't a good plan toward a long life.

Mortuary Dan paced for a moment, and even Laverne let him go, drinking the rest of Patty's milkshake with a slight smile on her face.

Finally Dan stopped and turned back to the table. "Anyone have any ideas what I should do?"

I didn't have a clue what the problem was, other than the legend that he had to kill his daughter in a few hours – and he didn't seem to be denying that at all.

I glanced at Patty. Her face was white and she was leaning back toward me. Screamer just seemed stunned.

Stan, in the other booth, had his God of Poker face on, and I couldn't even begin to get a read on what he was thinking or feeling.

"You need to talk to your daughter," Laverne said softly. "Before midnight. She needs to know and understand what's going to happen."

"Oh," Dan said, clearly disgusted as he started to pace again. "She's going to be so scared of me now, she won't listen. And she needs to know."

"Yes, she does," Laverne said, her voice softer and more compassionate than I had ever heard from Lady Luck.

I wanted to raise my hand like a kid in class and ask just what the adults in the room were talking about, but again my common sense got the best of me and I kept my mouth shut.

Dan kept pacing, clearly thinking, and after a moment Laverne looked over at me and Patty and Screamer. "I think Dan needs your help," she said.

Okay, at that moment you could have knocked me down with a slight breeze. Lady Luck just told us that Death needed our help.

Dan stopped and stared at the table, clearly as puzzled as I was, which made me feel only a slight bit better.

"Can you four," Laverne asked, nodding to us and Stan, "get Lisa and bring her here and help her father tell her what is going to happen tonight? She needs to be kept calm. Very calm."

Laverne just stared at me and Patty. After a moment we both nodded, starting to understand what we needed to do.

"And she needs to learn vast amounts of information from her father in a very short time." She glanced at Screamer who just turned white at the idea.

"I see where you are going, Laverne," Dan said, stepping back to the table and looking at me and my team. "Would you help me help my daughter through the transition?"

I couldn't take it any longer, I had to ask something, so I asked the most pressing question of the thousands I had spinning in my mind.

"What transition?"

"At midnight," Dan said, "Lisa will change from being a mere mortal to being an immortal god. An Undertaker. I'm retiring to surf in Hawaii. She's taking my spot, the first female Undertaker. I start her training at midnight tonight."

FOUR

IN MY FEW SHORT YEARS of being a superhero, I had never been so scared of an assignment. Somehow the three of us, with Stan's help, needed to link up a god, Death himself, and his daughter in an out-of-time link so that he could have the time to talk to her. And we needed to help her understand what was coming, and that it was all right that she was going to die.

Or sort of die, anyway.

If we screwed this up, none of us might live to see the end of the year.

If that long.

I had a hunch Mortuary Dan wouldn't think twice about just moving us on to the next place, wherever or whatever that was.

Stan gave me and Patty a lift to pick up Lisa.

When we appeared in her suite, she was still dressed in the same red, white, and blue outfit and was sitting on the couch. Clearly she had been sitting there since she arrived.

When she saw us, she jumped and rolled up over the back of the couch to get it between her and us.

I glanced at Patty. "She doesn't know anything at all about gods and superheroes, does she?"

"Not much I discovered," Patty said.

"How did you do that?" Lisa asked.

"I've been wondering the same thing," I said, glancing at Stan, who just shrugged. "We've got some good news for you," I continued, as Patty and I started working to calm her down with all the calming powers we had between us.

"You do?" she asked, clearly relaxing and even starting to smile, forgetting that we had just appeared out of nowhere in front of her.

"You're not going to die at midnight," I said, fibbing a little. She actually wasn't going to die. She just wasn't going to be mortal anymore.

A slight detail.

"But there's one condition," Patty said. "You need to talk to your dad. And your dad wants us there with you for support."

Lisa started shaking her head back and forth and I could feel the panic starting to gain intensity.

I dug deep and Patty and I joined hands and hit her with every calming power we had. And I have to say, that was considerable. We could have put a bull moose to sleep.

Lisa calmed some.

"It's only to talk," I said. "He needs to tell you where the rumor is coming from and why it exists. He said your mother should have taught you all of this."

"All she said was that my daddy is an Undertaker – the Grim Reaper."

"Well, he sort of is," I said. "And a pretty fine surfer, from what I gather."

"My father surfs?" Lisa asked, calming even more under the intense push of calming powers from me and Patty.

"Eleven months a year that's about all he does," Patty said, smiling.

Lisa finally stopped shaking her head and stared first at me, then at Stan. "Who exactly are you people?"

"I am known as Poker Boy. I am at the rank of superhero in the Gambling Gods universe, which basically means I do a lot of the chores the gods don't want to do."

She nodded, so I went on.

"This is Patty, also known as Front Desk Girl. She is a superhero working for the Gods of Hospitality."

I pointed at Stan. "This is my direct boss, Stan, the God of Poker. It is our boss, Lady Luck, known as Laverne, who convinced your father that he needed to talk to you and help you understand this different world before anything could happen tonight."

"But I still might die tonight?" Lisa said, the panic starting to build again even against the onslaught of calming that Patty and I were directing toward her.

"Oh, trust me," I said, "at ten minutes after midnight tonight, you'll be talking to me just fine. And you could talk to me any time you wanted after that. I promise."

"As do I," Patty said, nodding. "You just need to have a conversation with your father first, to understand everything that's going on."

Lisa clearly calmed with our promise. Then she laughed. "My mom hated what my dad did for a living, and never wanted him to come around. And she said his world was full of nutcakes. If I believe who you say you are, I guess she was right."

"Oh, trust me," I said, "as a person fairly new to this world as well, it's crazier than you can even imagine."

Lisa smiled and took a deep breath. "All right, let's go see my father."

A moment later the four of us were standing in The Diner.

Both Dan and Laverne were halfway through two more milkshakes, sitting in the booth with Screamer sitting in the middle looking slightly panicked. Madge was moving around, shaking her head as she sometimes did when she had to wait on us.

Mortuary Dan stood, his human face staying firmly in place, and stepped toward his daughter. "Hi, Lisa. It's wonderful to see you again. You've become a beautiful woman."

Lisa smiled and stepped into the hug of Death. "Hi, Daddy."

FIVE

WE LET LISA and her father talk.

After a few minutes, Dan turned to all of us, with Madge standing right there beside the table. "We need to start all this. Lisa has a lot to learn about her old man. Madge, would you put up the closed sign and keep those milkshakes coming for all of us? To do this right, we're going to need the energy."

Madge nodded. "I'll be glad to, Dan. Lisa, what kind do you like?"

"Chocolate," Lisa said.

"You got it, dear," Madge said, turning to close the front door as Patty and Screamer and I stared.

"Madge is a superhero in Food and Beverage," Laverne said, clearly trying not to laugh. "I thought you all knew that."

I shook my head and glanced around at Stan, who just smiled and shrugged. He had known, just hadn't bothered to tell any of the rest of us.

Laverne took one more long drink from her milkshake, then stood. "I'll be back a little later."

She vanished leaving us all alone with Mortuary Dan and his daughter.

Dan pointed to the spot where Screamer sat in the back of the booth. "Poker Boy, you and Patty sit back there. Lisa, you sit on one side of the booth, I'll sit facing you so we can talk directly, and Screamer, you sit on a chair at the head of the booth so you can touch both of us."

Dan glanced over at Stan. "Keep us out of time for about forty-five minutes the first time. We'll adjust from there. And help everyone with energy when needed."

Stan nodded.

I thought my heart was going to pound out of my chest. In the back of the restaurant Madge had the milkshake blenders going full speed, filling the restaurant with the whining sound. It didn't begin to cover the sound of my heart.

I could feel Lisa suddenly starting to get upset again, so Patty and I both sent calming powers at her as we slid into position, our legs touching for extra support.

I don't know how we could calm anyone down, as worried as we were ourselves, but for some reason our calming powers weren't hooked to how we were feeling. Luckily.

"What's going to happen?" Lisa asked, clearly afraid to take her position in the booth.

"Screamer here is going to hook our thoughts up so I can help you learn faster all the things your mother didn't teach you over the last twenty-plus years. And that way you can get to know me, the real me."

"You can do that?" Lisa asked, staring at Screamer.

"I can," he said, turning to face where she stood. "It's my power. You can trust me, it will be painless. Odd and a little confusing at times, but painless, I promise you. It will be exactly as your dad said, and the connection will help you learn very quickly what is a rumor and what is the truth."

"And I will be very careful to ease you into all of this," Dan said.

I was very glad he said that. I couldn't imagine suddenly knowing all at once all the things I had learned in my short five years being a superhero. But Lisa had no choice. She had to learn a lot and very quickly. There was only three hours to go until midnight.

"Ready, daughter?" Dan asked, smiling, and not showing his skeleton face at all.

Patty and I hit her with as much calming as we dared, and Lisa nodded. Then she slowly slid into position beside me in the booth.

I scooted closer to Patty to make sure I wasn't touching Lisa. Last thing I wanted to do was be included in the conversation they would have in their heads while Screamer held them together. But if I touched her, I would be automatically included, just as if Patty touched Dan on the other side.

The booth suddenly felt very, very small.

"I guess so," Lisa said.

Dan glanced at us and nodded, then nodded to Screamer.

Patty and I ramped up every bit of calming we could as Stan dropped us between time, killing all the sound in the restaurant and from the streets.

Screamer touched Lisa, then laid a hand gently on Mortuary Dan's arm.

For a moment, I thought we were going to have to calm Screamer down as well; but then he nodded and sat back and closed his eyes.

Lisa's eyes got huge and she was fidgeting some. I motioned for Stan to help, and he boosted both Patty's and my calming power.

Lisa calmed slightly. I was stunned she wasn't so calm she was asleep. The woman had a very, very powerful mind. No wonder Laverne wanted us all to help Dan with this.

And why Dan wanted the help. He and Laverne both knew how powerful the child of a god would be to deal with.

Screamer kept his eyes closed, and Dan and Lisa just stared at each other. I slowly motioned for Stan to back off and he did, then Patty and I pulled back slightly, only increasing when we could sense Lisa getting upset.

Forty-five minutes later in out-of-time time, Stan said, "Break."

Screamer pulled his hands away and Stan dropped the room back into real time. The sounds of Madge working on the milkshakes hit all of us hard.

Patty and I kept our concentration firmly on Lisa, who seemed to close her eyes, then open them and look at her father again as if she was seeing him for the first time.

No one said a word.

Then Lisa said, "So I'm not going to die, I'm going to become immortal at midnight."

Dan nodded. "For all intents and purposes, yes."

Lisa nodded, then said, "I have to use the restroom."

"I'll go with you," Patty said.

And wow was I glad she said that, since I had no idea how I was going to make it through more hours without visiting the restroom myself.

"I'll be right back," Dan said and vanished.

Stan also vanished.

"You all right?" I asked Screamer. I had no idea what it would be like inside of Death's mind, and I was very glad I didn't have to find out.

"I'm fine, actually. Dan is keeping me and Lisa blocked from most of his mind, just showing Lisa what she needs to see to get started. But this isn't going to be a short process."

"That slow?" I asked.

He nodded. Then he and I both headed for the rest rooms in the back, meeting Madge with a tray full of shakes.

"Don't tell me you all are leaving again?" she asked.

"Just a break," I said. "But I have a hunch that by the time this is over, you're going to wish we had left."

"Anything going on with both Laverne and Mortuary Dan, I suppose you might be right."

She went to put our milkshakes on the table as I just kept on, shaking my head at all the surprises I was getting on a simple Saturday night.

SIX

IT TOOK NINE HOURS of actual lesson time spread over six different sessions in just over three hours of real time before Lisa finally seemed to know what she was getting into and was ready.

It was five minutes until midnight.

Patty and I had stopped helping keep Lisa calm about three lessons back. Stan had asked me on the last break to help him keep up the out-of-time shield, since he was getting tired and Screamer needed some help with energy as well from him.

So for most of the last hour of lesson time, with Stan spelling me every ten minutes, I held up the shield that kept us out of real time.

As we dropped back into real time and Screamer moved away from the two he had kept connected for almost nine hours, everyone climbed out of the booth. I felt as if I had sat in that booth for most of my life.

Laverne appeared, smiling. She and Dan moved off to one side for a moment as Patty and I stayed with Lisa.

"Amazing stuff I was born into," Lisa said. "I wish someone had told me about this last year so I wouldn't have been so worried for so long, but thanks to all of you, this didn't catch me by surprise now."

"Good," Patty said. "Knowledge is far, far more powerful than rumors."

"But only slightly less scary," Lisa said.

Suddenly, around the restaurant, other people began to pop in, almost none of them anyone I knew, until the place was very crowded with only an open circle in the middle of the floor where a table used to be.

Stan stepped over beside us and whispered. "The other eleven Undertakers have arrived, plus a number of top gods from all the deities. This is a real event."

Stan and Screamer and Patty and I sort of moved back against the edge of the booth to allow the really powerful to take their places around the center.

"Are you ready to join me, daughter?" Dan asked, stepping into the circle in the center of the crowd.

Lisa smiled at us, then turned and stepped forward. "I am."

"Thirty seconds," Laverne said.

Dan indicated that Lisa should kneel in front of him and she did.

"Thank you all for joining this special occasion," Dan said, his face now a complete skeleton, even though his hands and business suit looked perfectly pressed and in order. "We are here to welcome to our ranks the first new Undertaker in centuries. And the first woman to ever hold that position."

"Five seconds," Laverne said.

Dan reached out both hands and placed them over Lisa's head. Then as the clock ticked midnight, Lisa seemed to slump slightly, then something bright and shining and very yellow filled the air around her.

After a moment the yellow light all went inside of her, like she was a giant sponge soaking up water.

After a long pause, she opened her eyes and smiled.

Everyone cheered.

I didn't know what to think. I didn't think I could feel so relieved in all my life.

"May I introduce you to the newest god?" Dan said, extending an arm to his daughter to help her off her knees. "My daughter Lisa. An Undertaker."

The entire room cheered, then calmed as Lisa looked around, smiling, nodding at many people she now clearly knew somehow.

Then she looked at us and said simply, "Thank you, Poker Boy, Screamer, Stan, and Patty. And most of all Laverne, who loaned my father such a wonderful team to help me through this transition. I will be forever grateful to you all."

Everyone cheered.

And I did as well, and just kept smiling.

Somehow we had managed to save yet another person. And that always felt great.

But it felt even better to have Death herself grateful to you.

It just didn't get any better than that.

Now Available
from all your favorite booksellers in trade paper and electronic editions.

Dean
Wesley Smith

USA Today Bestselling Writer

With a talking
oak tree,
adventure
and bad limericks
never end.

CUTTING DOWN FRED
A Buckey The Space Pirate Story

One fine summer night Buckey the Space Pirate takes his girlfriend for a little excitement to a local park. He hoped for a sexual adventure and ended up meeting Fred, a talking oak tree.

With a talking oak tree, adventure and bad limericks never end.

First published in Dinosaur Fantastic *edited by Mike Resnick and Martin H. Greenberg. The book came out from DAW Books in 1993.*

The origin story for Fred, the time-traveling and talking oak tree.

CUTTING DOWN FRED
A Buckey the Space Pirate Story

ONE

I TRIED TO MAKE LOVE under Fred for the first time on a warm October evening two years ago.

It was right in the middle of Big John's annual Halloween bash, the very same party that keeps three square city blocks of the city up all night. My current girlfriend, Annie, was in one of her moods, none of which I ever figured out. So when I suggested, after six very fast and hot dances, that we go somewhere cool, take off some costumes and really get hot, she laughed and said she would love to.

But she wanted to go somewhere new. She said she was tired of my apartment and "those old squeaky bed springs." She wanted to be daring. "Really live," was the way I think she put it.

So we ended up under Fred.

We left the party with a wave at Big John and headed downtown. I was wearing my Buckey the Space Pirate costume, with the white tights, white cape, lace shirt, saber, and plumed white hat. Most people thought I looked like one of the Three Musketeers, but what the hell did they know about space pirates, anyway?

Annie had on her Queen of the Alien Warlords' costume made up of black tights, high black boots, and lots of chains over a very open-necked blouse. On her head she wore this three-foot tall jeweled headdress that gave the entire costume a feeling of power. The only problem was that she kept forgetting to duck when going through doors.

I didn't exactly know what Annie had in mind when she said "daring," but I figured Russell Park might fit. And it was close by. I didn't feel like walking too far dressed as Buckey, especially in this part of the city.

Russell Park was the second oldest park in the city. I'd been there a few times, mostly passing through. It was one of those places where old people sat around on the benches and watched the young mothers ignore their children. It measured a half a block wide, a block long, and was filled with benches, small patches of grass, and big old oak trees. But it didn't smell much like a park because there just wasn't enough green to hold back the smells of the city.

We ended up under one of the biggest trees in the park, tucked off in one corner, near a hedge and a wooden bench that looked like no one had sat on it since the First World War. There I hoped we would have the least chance of getting seen, yet give Annie the thrill she needed.

To say Annie was thrilled would have been putting it lightly. She liked the idea of making love out in the open. In the two months we'd gone out she said we'd never done anything this much "fun."

"My dear Queen Annie," I said, taking my plumed hat off and bowing deeply at the waist while sweeping the hat along the grass. "Will this place of repose suit a lady of your stature?" She always loved it when I went formal on her.

"You have done well, faithful servant," she said, smiling. Then she reached up, took off her headdress, and sat it against the base of the tree. Then the chains came over her head, then the blouse. She was working on taking off the tights before I had enough common sense to start getting undressed too.

She was totally nude and lying on the grass by the time I had gotten my boots and saber off. So instead of finishing undressing, I went to work, kissing that soft skin, starting at her right ear and working my way down. I was doing my best to not miss a spot on that beautiful body, when this deep voice came out of nowhere.

*"There was a young lady from Hunt
Whose body could take a small punt.
Her mother said, 'Annie,
It matches your fanny,
Which never was that of a runt.'"*

I thought my heart was going to explode right out of my chest.

I expected to look up and see a policeman standing there with a big nightstick, slapping it into his palm as he smiled down at us. We were going to end up in jail. I just knew it. Mom would never understand.

So from between her legs I glanced quickly around. No one. At least in sight.

"What did you mean by that?" Annie said, pushing me away and sitting up. "That seemed like a pretty crude thing to say, especially when you were doing what you were doing. And just what the hell is a punt?"

"I didn't—"

"It's a flat-bottomed boat that is propelled by thrusts from a pole," the voice said.

Annie glanced quickly around, then stood up and stared down at me, hands on her hips. "I don't think I like you anymore," she said and pulled on her black tights.

"But I didn't say anything," I pleaded.

"Then who did," she asked. "And you know, if you were any bigger than a pencil, you wouldn't think I was so large."

"A pencil?" I said. "But—"

She pulled her blouse quickly on, grabbed the chains and headdress and stormed off with me still there on the grass trying to get my boots back on. "But— But— But—" I said over and over as she disappeared through an opening in the hedge.

"There was a young fellow of Buckingham
Wrote a treatise on girls and on fucking them.
A learned Parsee
Taught him Gamahuchee,
So he added a chapter on sucking them."

"Who's there?" I quickly turned around, but couldn't see anyone. The deep baritone voice sounded like it had come from right beside me. "Come out, damn you!"

I pulled on my boots and saber and checked behind the trunk of the old tree, then in the hedges, and then in the branches of the tree itself. No one. In fact, the entire little park looked completely deserted.

"Aren't you even curious," the voice asked. Again it sounded as if it was coming from right beside my head. I spun around, then checked my shirt for hidden microphones someone might have slipped in at the party. Nothing.

"All right," I said. "I give up. What's the joke?"

"Oh, no joke," the voice said. "But I wonder if you are curious as to what Gamahuchee means. Most people would be."

"Who's talking?" I shouted at the dimly lit park. This was getting damned annoying. It was going to take me a week to calm Annie down, if she would even talk to me again.

"I'll tell you who I am if you first ask me what Gamahuchee means."

"Oh, for hell's sake," I checked once more in the limbs of the tree, in the hedge, and around the trunk. Just one old oak tree. No one anywhere near.

Finally, I gave up and sat down. "All right, what the hell does Gamahuchee mean?"

"No one is really sure," the voice said.

"Great," I said. "You—"

"But it is thought to have a Japanese derivation, and in the context of the limerick, it refers to oragenitalism. Or, in more current terminology, oral sex."

"I could have figured out as much," I said. "If I really gave a shit. Now would you please tell me who the hell you are? And where you are so you can laugh and I can kill you?"

"I am the tree you now repose under. I refer to myself as Fred. I am sure you would not like to hear the story of how I came to acquire that name, even though it *is* quite interesting."

"You're right," I said, looking up into the thick green leaves of the tree. "I wouldn't. And I don't buy this for a minute. Where's the speaker hidden?"

"I am really the tree," the voice said, sadly. "Why don't you believe me? Dressed as you are, I had hoped you at least would believe me."

"Well I don't!" I shouted up into the tree. "And there's not a damned thing wrong with how I'm dressed." I felt immediately stupid for shouting. Somewhere, someone was laughing their fool head off and I was playing along. I stood and headed for the entrance to the park. A joke was a joke. But Buckey the Space Pirate had let this one go too far.

TWO

BY THE NEXT AFTERNOON, no one had come up to me and laughed at how much they had got me. And Annie didn't show one sign of talking to me no matter how much I pounded on her door. The only way she was going to ever speak to me again was if I proved to her that it wasn't me who had accused her of being able to do strange things with boats.

If I uncovered whoever the joker was, I could prove to her it wasn't me. So that evening I found myself back down at the park under the old tree.

"You look much more normal for these times dressed as you are today," the voice said as I walked up. I had on a tee shirt and Levi's. "Would you like to hear another limerick?"

"Whoever you are," I said as calmly as I could. "Please show yourself."

"I am showing myself. I'm shading you from the sun. What more do you want? Don't you like my limericks. I have one I made up for a young couple back thirty, maybe forty years ago. I was much smaller then and they were one of the first who used my shelter for the purpose that you were using it for yesterday. I feel it is one of my best limericks. And by the way, my name is Fred."

"Fred. Sure. You told me." I moved slowly around the tree trying to humor the voice while spotting exactly where the speaker was hidden. "You know you could have at least waited until we finished. And I'm not buying this talking tree line. I know someone's behind all this and when I find out who, I— I—"

"Do what you like," the voice said. "I won't be around much longer for you to believe or not believe."

"Sure." I searched through some high grass near a sprinkler head. "You're just going to pull up roots and walk away. Right?"

"Hardly," Fred said.

"All right then," I said and went back to searching the trunk, feeling for any loose bark. "Why don't you tell me, for starters, how you can talk. Some witch cast a spell over you or something?"

"I suppose it could be called magic," Fred said. "But I prefer to think of it as the miracle of life. Actually us trees are much more intelligent than you humans think and have very long memories."

"Sure. Sure. All from the miracle of life." I said, as sarcastically as I could make my voice sound. "So how'd that get you a voice?"

"I don't actually know. I don't actually have vocal cords as you do, but I can project my thoughts to make humans hear the thoughts as a voice. You see, ninety-seven years ago, a sailor visited a brothel here in this fine city. The man used a prophylactic. It was disposed of in the alley outside of the brothel and a very young girl found it a short time later. She took an acorn from my mother, put it in the sperm and planted the entire thing here. The young girl watered me carefully for the first two years until she died, ran over by a wagon right in front of me.

Poor child. Of course, there was nothing I could have done."

I had kept looking the entire time he had been talking and still hadn't found one hint of any speaker, microphone, or wiring. The voice seemed to come from everywhere around the tree and inside my head at the same time. "You don't really expect me to believe that?" I said.

"You asked," Fred said. "Would you like to hear another limerick? I know all of the good old ones."

"Not just yet." I had come to the realization that this stunt was so well done that I was going to get nowhere unless I played along. Eventually whoever was behind it would slip up. "Say, why don't you tell me how you came to do limericks?"

"If you stood in one place for almost a hundred years, you'd do limericks, too."

With that I granted he had a point. I studied the tree for a foothold. The speaker was probably hidden in the limbs somewhere and I was going to have to climb up there to find it. Best thing to do was keep humoring the voice while being quiet while climbing the tree. "What's this about you not having much longer?"

"Tomorrow, to be exact," Fred said. "That's why I decided to talk to you. Do you realize that I have only talked to seven people in one hundred years. I look back and find that fact most amazing."

"What's going to happen?" I picked my way carefully up the bark like a rock climber going up a sheer face. Finally I got my arms around the lowest limb and pulled myself up.

"See the stakes in the grass?" Fred said. "The ones with the orange ribbons on them?"

I looked back down through the branches. "Sure." They were scattered across this corner of the park. I hadn't noticed them last night with Annie.

"I overheard workmen talking about widening the road. I'm scheduled for the chain saws tomorrow."

"You're kidding?" I finished checking out the limb I was on and climbed higher where I could see the stakes better. They did show a pattern that looked like the street was going to be wider right through the big tree.

"I am afraid I am not kidding," Fred said, his voice almost too faint for me to hear. Then he got suddenly louder. "But, that is life. Or death. And please do be careful. I've had fifteen children and three adults fall out of my limbs. It is always so painful an occurrence. Actually, the first person who fell out of my limbs was killed by a dinosaur. It was a very sad experience since his wife was standing nearby in the park at the time and never really understood what happened."

"A what?"

"A dinosaur. Actually a Pterosaurs angry that he was there. You know that Pterosaurs were large flying reptiles that..."

"Now you have gone too far. First you expect me to believe you are a talking tree and then you expect me to believe that you have been around since the dinosaurs. There were no men during that time. That much I remember from grade school. And you said you were not even a hundred years old."

"You are quite right," Fred said. But we oak trees have family memories that go back, for lack of a better way of putting it, to our roots, which incidentally, were in the early Cretaceous period in this part of the world."

"Fine," I said, glancing down at the ground below, wondering when the funny farm wagon was going to come and take me away for talking to myself in a tree.

"I can tell you do not believe me."

"No shit," I said. "I am still looking for the microphone so I can get this joke over."

"Please hold onto a limb and I will take you back. Do you have a favorite dinosaur you would like to see?"

"Yeah, sure," I said and started down. "And next you will be telling me I can ride a Triceratops if I want."

Fred laughed softly. "Not hardly, but I can certainly show you why you wouldn't want to ride one."

THREE

AROUND ME the air suddenly shimmered and the branches of the oak seemed to move and sway, as if there was a slight earthquake shaking the roots. I grabbed tight around a limb and held on as I was suddenly hit by a wave of hot and very humid air that smelled of swamp and fresh greenery.

Below me there was a crashing of brush and again the tree seemed to shake. Through the shaking leaves I could see that the city was gone. There was nothing except trees and brush. And below me was the ugliest, most scarred-up Triceratops I could ever imagine.

"Hold on," the voice of Fred inside my head said as the dinosaur bumped into the tree and then started using it to scratch itself. I thought I was on a ride at a carnival.

The dinosaur bumped the tree and I bounced among the limbs. Then the Triceratops backed off, looked at the tree and hit it again.

As I held on for dear life I heard Fred's voice in my head. "See why you wouldn't want to ride one?"

Somehow, as the dinosaur took aim once more on the base of the tree I managed to scream, "Get me out of here!"

And I was back in the tree in the park.

A tree that wasn't moving.

I looked slowly around to make sure that I was where I seemed to be, then carefully pulled my fingers out of the grooves they had dug into the bark.

"Pretty amazing beasts, weren't they?"

I took a deep shuddering breath and let it out. "How did you do that?"

"How do you walk around and drink water without roots? It is just a part of what we are. We can move our conscious minds back and forth through our ancestors and through time. I guess it makes up for not being able to move in real time. You didn't actually leave the park, but I took your mind back with mine. Fun, huh? Now, would you like to hear another limerick now? I have one about a dinosaur."

"No. Thanks." I gave one more quick look to make sure the city was where it should be and there was no Triceratops lurking behind the hedge, then climbed down. Once I was back on the ground I walked quickly around the tree, then sat down.

"You seem upset," Fred said.

"That ride you gave me was really something. I am not saying that I believe you, but can you take me to any time at all?"

"Sure," Fred said. And to almost any place as long as the oak at the location is, as we say, in my family tree."

I groaned.

"Sorry," Fred said. "But," his voice suddenly sounding sad. "I am afraid that today will be the last day for you to experience any other time, so we should make the best of it."

I climbed back to my feet and walked along the line of stakes in the grass. They did start at the corner and go inside the edge of the tree. "Just for the sake of argument," I said, "is there something I can do for you? I doubt that I could stop the street from being widened, but—"

"Oh, my dear man," Fred said quickly. "It is so kind of you to ask. I was hoping you would. I have studied the problem at some length and I feel the only solution would be to repeat the process from which I came."

"What?" I asked. I had lost whatever Fred was talking about halfway through.

"In other words," Fred said, "get a rubber, ejaculate into it, put one of my seeds in the resulting solution, and plant it. Very simple, really."

"No way! You must think I was born yesterday?" Now at least I was starting to see the joke. I didn't know how they had pulled off the voice and the dinosaur schtick, but someone was having a great laugh on this one and I wasn't going to play along any more.

"I'm afraid I do not know when you were born," Fred said. "But I got here by exactly the method I told you. I have watched it happening. I have studied the event many times and I fear it may be my only chance of survival."

"Sure." I made one more quick check of the tree, then studied the stakes. I had to admit it was sure one elaborate gag. And it looked like the only way I was going to get to the prankster was go along

---

and get it over with. Then I could prove to Annie that I didn't say anything and get back on her "good" side.

"All right," I said. "I'll bring back the part of the deal you need from me. Where will I find a seed from you?"

"I will drop an acorn that is ready to sprout," Fred said. "And thank you."

"No problem," I said.

I made one more quick check around the area of Fred to make sure no one was hiding in the bushes laughing their fool heads off, then headed for Annie's house in hopes of her giving me a helping hand. She still wouldn't talk to me or even let me explain what I was trying to do. Not that I really blamed her. So I went back to my place and did it myself. I was back at the tree in an hour.

I checked quickly around to make sure no one was watching, then held the rubber up. "Here you go."

An acorn hit the grass right at my feet. I picked it up, looked at it, then stuck it inside the rubber. "Got any place special you think I should plant it?" I asked, checking the area of the branches it fell from to make sure there was no one sitting up there.

"Anywhere that will be safe," Fred said.

"I'll be back tomorrow morning early." As I headed for the park gate, I heard Fred start into a limerick about a girl from Troy.

THREE

I TOOK MY "PACKAGE" to mom's house in the suburbs and planted it off to one side in her back yard. She didn't care. As far as she was concerned,

I was always doing strange things. And she hadn't even seen me in my Buckey the Space Pirate costume.

I staked out where I planted the seed. I told mom it was a special seed for an exotic tree and needed really special care. She liked that.

I made it back to the park by ten the next morning, but I was way too late. The old tree was in a hundred pieces piled in neat stacks. I watched while the workmen used chain saws on what was left, but I couldn't take it for very long. Even though I knew the entire thing had just been a joke, I couldn't shake the feeling of pain and sadness coming from that wood.

I never did get back with Annie. She wouldn't have anything to do with me. And no one ever came forward and laughed at me about jacking off into a rubber and then planting it. If it was a practical joke, or a hidden camera stunt, I never found out about it. Seems to me that I would have, too. I don't understand why someone would go to all that trouble without pulling the final "gotcha?"

Since I never uncovered the joke, every time I visited Mom I found myself checking on the spot where I had planted the tree. Nothing. Over the winter I pretty much forgot about it.

It wasn't until the following May, while I was mowing Mom's lawn, that I almost ran over the little oak tree. I spent an entire hour cleaning the weeds and grass away from it, then putting up a solid, two-foot-high wire fence around it. It felt kind of funny to know that my sperm had worked as fertilizer for a tree.

I checked back on the little tree all through that summer and fall, telling myself I was crazy each time I did, but yet doing it anyhow. It became one of those little obsessions a person has that they can't explain. I sure in hell made no attempt to tell anyone. Mom loved it. Said she'd never had so much help on the yard.

It wasn't until the following May that something finally happened. I was carefully mowing around the now almost four-foot tall baby oak tree when I heard this high, child-like voice. At first I thought it was something going wrong with the mower, but after I turned the engine off, I heard:

> *"A bather whose clothing was strewed*
> *By waves that left her quite nude,*
> *Saw a man come along*
> *And unless I am wrong*
> *You expect this line to be crude."*

I sat down hard on the grass. I couldn't believe it. I was either going completely crazy, or it had worked. I had actually planted a tree with my sperm that grew and could talk. No way. That was just too stupid. Just like before, I figured it was either a joke or I had imagined it.

"You know," the little voice said from what seemed like the direction of the little tree. "I have this strange desire to do things to a woman dressed in a costume."

I stretched out on the grass with my face real close to the small trunk of the tree.

"Fred?"

"Hi, Dad," the little tree said. "You want to hear a limerick? Or maybe go see a dinosaur?"

~

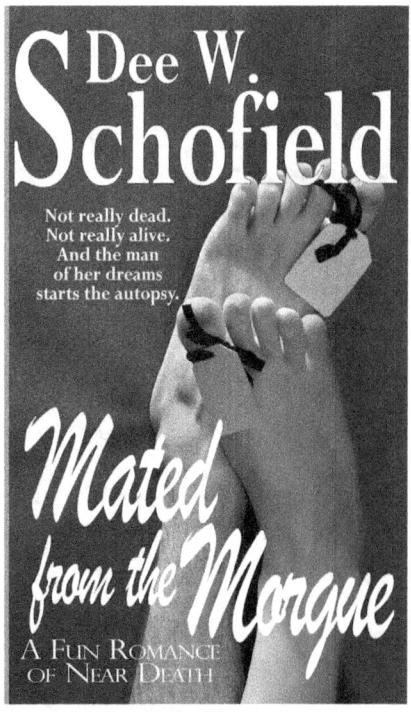

31

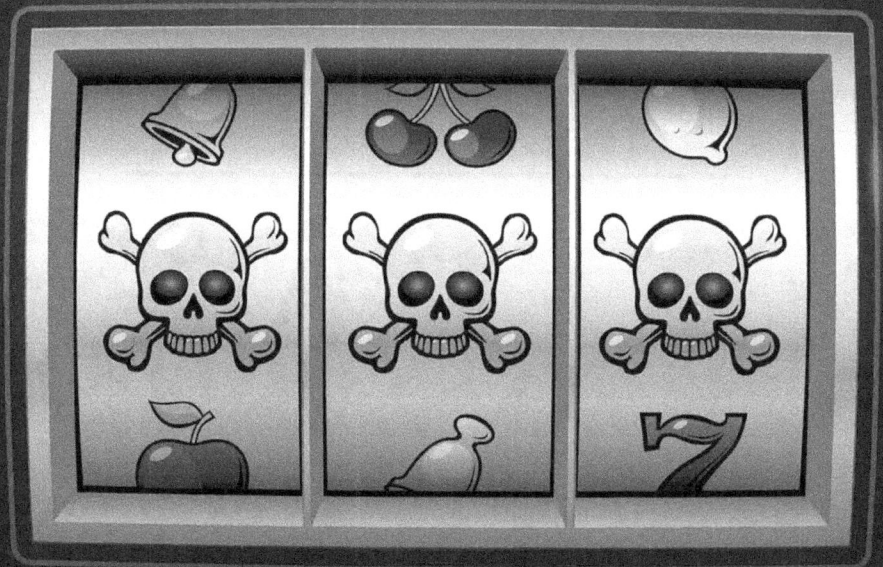

USA Today Bestselling Writer

DEAN WESLEY SMITH

THEY'RE BACK

A Poker Boy Short Novel

In the second of four parts, Poker Boy and his team must confront the worst enemy they ever faced. The dreaded Slots of Saturn once again.

But the Slots of Saturn died years before. How could they be back?

The sequel to the novel The Slots of Saturn, *this short novel appeared first in* Fiction River.

THEY'RE BACK
A Poker Boy Short Novel

Part 2 of 4

CHAPTER SIX
A Nightmare

I dozed, lying there on the bed.

In the dream, I was back in that old Standard Warehouse, and Patty and I and Screamer were madly trying to save people as the big machine spit them out, one per second.

Patty had slowed down time just enough that, as the people appeared, Screamer could shove them out of the way onto a big tarp. It had taken us a couple hours to get everyone out that way, with a few problems, but we had done it.

And then the memory dream turned to a nightmare as the ghosts of the people we had saved just wandered the old warehouse full of dead slot machines, not knowing where to go.

And no one would believe they were there.

I woke up with a jerk, sweating.

Patty had gone into the bathroom and was taking a shower.

I lay there, letting my heart slow down, trying to figure out what that dream was all about.

And coming up with nothing.

Ghost slots. Ghost people. That made no sense at all.

Then my cell phone rang. "Sherri's fine," Screamer said. "Meet in your office in an hour for dinner?"

"We'll be there," I said.

I took off my coat and hat and then the rest of my clothes. The nightmare had caused me to sweat right through them.

I headed into the bathroom and crawled into the large shower with Patty, who kissed me, then climbed out.

"What fun is that?" I asked, teasing her, even though I had no intention of fooling around.

"Lot of time for fun when we find those damn machines," she said. "And hurry up, I've got an idea I want to check out."

"Sherri is all right," I said as the cool water rinsed over me, chasing some of the nightmare away. "We're meeting in the office in an hour for dinner."

"Perfect," Patty said, heading out to get dressed.

Twenty minutes later I jumped us across town to a secluded spot near the front gate of an old wrecking yard.

The heat from the desert slammed in on us like a hammer. It always seemed hot in the city, but out in the desert, it always felt worse. And jumping from a comfortable air-conditioned apartment into the direct sun and heat wasn't fun. Especially wearing a black leather coat.

I looked around to make sure we hadn't been spotted. There was no one to see us. The place was acres of dead cars in a small valley to the east of Las Vegas, hidden from sight from just about anything. Sitting in long rows, the old and wrecked cars seemed to just be waiting patiently to be picked apart by car enthusiasts like vultures over dried bones.

A wooden building just inside the open chain-link gate served as an office. They were clearly open. Beyond the office was a huge machine that was in the process of crushing a car, making a noise I didn't want to really listen to for very long. At least not without some great earplugs.

We headed up the dusty gravel road and then into the wooden building that looked like it hadn't been painted since the area was settled.

The door creaked as we went in and a bell rang, as if the door creaking wasn't enough to shout that someone had entered. The cool insides of the office felt like I had dipped my face into a cold drink. We were greeted by an elderly woman who had to be in her seventies. She had on a nametag that read, "Denise" that looked like she was attending a convention more than working in a dusty office in the middle of nowhere.

The place smelled of auto parts and oil and grease, and there were pictures of racing cars on the walls and a large glass case full of trophies, some of which looked to be fifty years old. Some of the pictures jammed all over the walls were clearly of Denise in much younger and thinner days.

"What can I do for you kids?" Denise asked as she climbed to her feet and headed toward us from her cluttered desk.

"We're wondering if your smashing records still go back ten years," Patty asked, giving Denise her best smile and charm that was part of her superpower at front desks.

Patty could calm the most angry customer with a wave of energy and a smile. I could feel the waves of it coming off of her now.

"Oh, sure, dear," Denise said, her voice sounding like a grandmother's voice right out of the movies. "We have records back for forty years since we bought the Big Bully, as we call the noisy old thing."

"Any chance you might have records of crushing an antique three-chair set of slots ten years ago, almost to the day, give or take a few?"

"Let me check," Denise said.

She went to some huge metal filing cabinets that lined the back wall and stretched down one side of a hallway that led to a back office and bathroom.

I wasn't sure exactly what Patty was thinking, because if the slots never arrived here, we were still at the same spot. But I agreed with this search just to make sure they hadn't arrived here and then were sold from here.

Denise pulled open one drawer with a bang and thumbed through a few files for a moment, then checked a few more, and pulled one file, shaking her head.

"We only crushed one slot grouping that entire year," Denise said. "I remember they were really nice-looking old slots owned by Standard, but the guys from the shipping company insisted they help us put them into Big Bully themselves to make sure they were destroyed.

> *Patty could calm the most angry customer with a wave of energy and a smile. I could feel the waves of it coming off of her now.*

Something about them being haunted. It's in the notes here."

Denise shook her head again. "Can you believe haunted slots?"

Neither of us said a thing. I wasn't sure what I believed any more.

Then Denise slipped the manilla file folder across the counter toward Patty.

Patty looked at it and gasped.

I couldn't believe what I was seeing either.

Someone had taken a color Polaroid of the Slots of Saturn half crushed by two huge metal crushing arms of a big machine.

"We take a picture of everything we crush as it's being crushed," Denise said. "That way we're never accused of double-dipping like some crushing yards."

We said nothing. I was too stunned to say anything.

"That what you were looking for?" Denise asked. "Almost ten years to the day as you said."

"That's perfect, thanks," Patty said, pushing the file back to Denise. "Can you make us a copy of that?"

"Oh, sure," Denise said and took the thin file to a copy machine.

A couple minutes later we walked back out into the heat, Patty holding the copies of the file. The smell of desert and old cars hit me again as we walked down the slight hill on the old gravel road and through the big gate to get out of sight of anyone in the wrecking yard.

How could the slots have been destroyed?

I had just seen them at Binion's just a short few hours before.

"Are we dealing with real ghost slots this time?" Patty asked, her voice low and soft, as we walked through the heat.

"I honestly don't know," I said, feeling completely helpless as I jumped us back to my office overlooking Las Vegas.

I had no idea how to fight machines.

I really had no idea how to fight ghost machines.

CHAPTER SEVEN
A Silent Dinner

After Patty passed around the record from the wrecking yard and the picture, the dinner started off pretty silent. Stan, Ben, Screamer, and Sherri were there with us.

Screamer and Sherri were staying close and sometimes touching across from me in the booth. Ben sat in the back of the booth, saying little, and Stan sat in a chair at the end of the booth.

Madge came and went with food and drinks, but said little. That was normal for her unless she had some observation and like the rest of us, she didn't seem to have many ideas on this mess.

So finally I asked Sherri what exactly she felt when the machine jumped and knocked her out.

"Like I had grabbed a supercharged electrical fence," she said, shaking her head. "Hurt like hell."

Screamer touched her arm and she smiled slightly. Somehow his power and touch must have eased the memory of the pain some.

"Could you tell what kind of energy it was?" Patty asked.

"Human energy," Sherri said without hesitation. "The same kind of energy I can track long after a person goes by. Only multiplied by factors and focused."

"And any sense of the machine now?" Ben asked.

She shook her head. "Nothing. It just vanished."

"Do you think if it was here, you would be able to sense it?"

"I'm sure of it," she said. "And I think I'll know the instant it comes back anywhere in town."

"Well," I said, nodding to myself. "That's going to help."

And I really believed it might. I wasn't sure how, but knowing when it arrived, even if in a place the police didn't have protected, would help a lot.

Screamer smiled at Sherri. "That's what I said."

"I hope so," Sherri said.

At that point Madge brought everyone dinner. This was not the nice, quiet dinner Patty and I had hoped to have, but there were people's lives at stake. We could always go out to a better dinner on another day.

I had ordered deep-fried shrimp. Patty again had some kind of a salad, only with chicken on it.

We all ate pretty much in silence, and I was almost through my shrimp and baked potato when Lady Luck arrived and pulled up a chair next to Stan, who scooted over to give her room.

"Feeling better?" she asked Sherri.

Sherri nodded. "I am, thanks. Any leads?"

Lady Luck shook her head and a moment later Madge appeared and slid a salad similar to Patty's in front of one of the most powerful gods in the world.

We all went back to eating in silence.

I just kept running down everything I could think of, and I kept coming up blank. Then I remembered the Bookkeeper who had been trying to predict the machines.

"Stan, have you checked with the Bookkeeper?" I asked.

He shook his head. "Just makes him angry when I push him."

"Don't you think he needs to know the machines were destroyed ten years ago?"

Stan nodded and took out his cell phone, standing to move off to talk with the Bookkeeper.

Lady Luck looked at me with that stare of hers again, the one that could melt a normal person and pretty much did to me. I couldn't imagine what it must have been like for her daughters to grow up with that look.

"Destroyed?" Lady Luck asked.

I nodded and Patty took the copies of the file from beside her and handed them to Lady Luck.

"Son of a bitch," Lady Luck said after a moment of looking inside, then handing the file back to Patty.

I didn't know she swore like that.

Then Lady Luck took another forkful of her salad, stuffed it in her mouth, and vanished.

As we all sat there, sort of in shock at Lady Luck swearing, Stan came back over to the table and sat down. "The Bookkeeper was swearing at me when he hung up."

"Mom just did the same thing," Sherri said, shaking her head. "That's not a good thing when Mom swears."

When Mom was Lady Luck, there was no chance in the world I was going to disagree with that.

CHAPTER EIGHT
Another Encounter

Ten minutes later not a one of us could figure why both Lady Luck and the Bookkeeper were so upset about the machines having been destroyed ten years before.

"There's something none of us know," Stan said, "that they clearly do and don't really want to tell us yet."

I couldn't argue with that, but as a lowly superhero, I was sort of used to either being in the dark, or just flat uninformed. I didn't like it, but I had gotten used to the feeling. It was why I liked having Ben around. He helped me with the history.

I turned to him with that thought. "Any record of anything like this happening before?"

"Nothing," he said. "Nothing even close in thousands of years of my memory."

Suddenly, Sherri tipped forward and grabbed her head.

Screamer instantly held her, clearly working to help her in some fashion, his eyes closed.

After a moment I asked softly, "Need help?"

"Patty," he said.

Patty reached across the booth without hesitation and touched Sherri's arm and then closed her eyes.

At that moment I knew all three of them were linked up for some reason. And I had a hunch I knew what the reason was.

The machines were back in town from wherever they went.

And Screamer and Patty were helping Sherri set up some mental shields against the intense energy.

Finally, after what seemed like a very long time, but must have only been fifteen seconds, Patty sat back and released her touch on Sherri.

"Machines are back at Binion's again," Patty said.

Sherri sat up straight and opened her eyes. They looked a little haunted, but not bad.

"Thanks," she said to Screamer and Patty. "I can deal with them now if I don't get too close."

Screamer's phone rang and he answered it. Then after a moment he said, "Make sure no one goes near them."

"Police still have the area surrounded," Screamer said. "So we won't lose another person this time."

"Think from this distance you might be able to follow the machines this time when they jump?" I asked Sherri.

She nodded. "With Patty and Screamer's help I can try."

Patty slipped out of the booth and slid in on the other side with Sherri and Screamer. I watched from across the expanse of empty plates and used drinking glasses as the three of them got ready.

I felt helpless. But I knew that sometimes a leader of a group was best left observing. I didn't like it, but I knew that to be the case now.

All three of their minds were going to be linked.

"It's powering up to jump," Sherri said.

Screamer held her shoulders and Patty reached over and held onto Sherri's arm.

All three of them closed their eyes, clearly no longer mentally in the booth.

After four or five seconds, all three of them jerked as if shocked. Then they slumped.

I wanted to shout to see if Patty was all right, but somehow I held my panic under control slightly.

Finally Patty opened her eyes, looking at me and smiling at what must have been a panicked look on my face.

"Could you trace them?" Stan asked.

Patty shook her head and took a deep breath.

"We should have been able to follow them," Sherri said, opening her eyes as well and looking at Stan. "Anywhere on the planet. But it was as if the surge shut them off as they vanished."

Screamer nodded agreement and handed Sherri a glass of water.

"We never saw them shut off ten years ago," I said. "So is there any place on this planet you couldn't trace them to?"

"Nowhere," Sherri said, and beside her Screamer again nodded in agreement. He had been inside her head, he knew what she felt and saw as well.

Suddenly Lady Luck was back at the end of the table.

She pulled up a chair, still clearly upset. "You are both right and wrong, daughter. There is no place on this planet you could not have traced them to with your power and the help of your husband and Patty."

"So where are they?" I asked.

"They are on this planet," Lady Luck said, looking at me. "Just not in this timeline."

Lady Luck took a forkful of the salad still sitting in front of her. And before putting it in her mouth she added, "and not in this time period either.

CHAPTER NINE
A Time Headache

I hated any thought of time travel. It always gave me a headache.

And now just mentioning it again felt like it might give me one again.

Patty stood and stretched and then came around and slid back into the booth beside me. She touched me and I could feel she was tired, drained from her experience with Sherri and Screamer.

I focused some energy in her direction through our contact and she smiled, letting the energy in so that she could regain some strength. I liked that about our relationship. Together we were a lot, lot stronger than alone.

Before I could even formulate a question for Lady Luck, Stan's phone rang.

"Bookkeeper," Stan said, and answered the phone without leaving the table.

"Yeah," Stan said. "We know that."

Then he listened for a moment and I watched his face. It wasn't easy to get a read on the God of Poker, but sometimes when Stan wasn't aware, he let down his guard. And this was one of those times.

His eyebrows seemed to creep up his forehead toward his receding hairline as he clearly got news he didn't want to hear.

Then he asked, "How long?"

"Thanks," Stan said after a moment. "Anything else, call me."

He clicked off his cell phone and looked at the silent group around the table.

"We have fourteen hours," Stan said, "to solve this."

"I was afraid of that," Lady Luck said. "That's what Kronos told me as well."

Kronos, the God of Time, was the only one allowed to travel in time. He controlled it and if he thought this was a problem, it really was a problem.

"What happens in fourteen hours?" Sherri asked.

Some Classic Jukebox Stories
Available at your favorite booksellers.

"This timeline we are in is permanently separated from our original timeline," Stan said.

Lady Luck and Ben were both shaking their heads, clearly understanding what that meant.

And knowing what he meant.

I had no clue. Not one.

And I could tell the other superheroes at the table had no idea what the gods were saying or thinking, since there were blank looks on the faces I could see. I could feel my look was as puzzled as the rest.

"What happens then?" Screamer asked.

"This entire timeline drops into a time loop," Lady Luck said.

"A what?" Screamer asked a moment before I could get out the question.

"Think Groundhog's Day, the movie," Stan said, "only we won't have a memory of anything repeating."

"This timeline would just repeat the last few days," Lady Luck said flatly, "plus the next fourteen hours over and over and over. We would never know it and never escape."

My stomach clamped up so tight I wasn't sure if I could even swallow. And my lungs seemed to expel every ounce of breath they were holding.

That was the worst kind of jail I could ever imagine.

"How do we know," I asked, afraid of the question, "that we didn't fail and are already in a time loop?"

"We don't," Lady Luck said. "So let's not fail, because I don't want to eat this salad for the rest of eternity."

CHAPTER TEN
A Ticking Clock

After we all sat there for a few long moments in silence, thinking about our possible eternities having dinner together, the same dinner, and not knowing we were doing it, I finally managed to get a thought in my brain and let it come out my mouth.

"What caused this in the first place?"

"You did," Stan said.

"We all did," Lady Luck corrected. "None of us knew. We were just glad Poker Boy and Patty and Screamer saved the gambling industry, remember?"

"I'm not following," I said.

"We saved people the machine had taken from this timeline and just left them in the past," Patty said.

Now I knew that didn't sound good.

Stan nodded. "So to get those same people again, the machine has to jump to another timeline and take the same people again and again and again. Jumping from timeline to timeline. A time loop creating new alternate realities off the same event."

"So we already saved everyone who is in the machine the first time?" I asked.

"You did," Lady Luck said, nodding. "Now we have to save all the rest of us and everyone in this timeline."

"So the main timeline actually got split back ten years ago?" Screamer asked.

Lady Luck nodded.

"So to stop this," I asked. "Will Kronos allow us to go back in time and fix the mistake?"

"He will," Lady Luck said. "I already asked him and he agreed if I went along.

We can bring the victims back to the future and that will reset all the timelines."

I could feel my stomach starting to unclamp. "So what's the problem?"

She looked at me. "Do you know which people you saved were from that past time and which were from this time?"

"Oh," Patty said, slumping slightly beside me.

"We don't have a lot of time to figure that out," I said. "We can do that, can't we?"

Lady Luck nodded. "We can, but if we miss one, we're into the time loop and will always miss one."

She was so full of good news I couldn't stand it.

She stood. "I've got some things to set up, and I need to talk with Kronos again."

She vanished.

I took a deep breath and pushed the headache back. We needed to get moving and move fast. I turned to Stan. "Can you get the Bookkeeper on this?"

"He said he would start the computer searches for them when I talked with him. He should have a list for us shortly."

I nodded. "We don't want to trust it, though." I looked at Stan again. "Can you talk with the gods in charge of the police and get a full list of names we rescued?"

"I'll get it," Stan nodded and vanished.

"So what do we do?" Screamer asked.

I sat there staring at the four left around the table that was still covered with our dinner dishes. Then it suddenly dawned on me that we had yet another way of getting information.

We could travel back without actually traveling in time.

"Screamer, when you pushed those people out of the chair, you touched them."

"I did," he said, frowning at me. "Do you really think after ten years that I can remember flashes of who they all were just from touching them for an instant?"

"I do," I said, smiling at my friend. "With help. Whatever we get can work as another check-point to make sure the lists we get are 100% accurate."

"I don't know how I could do that," Screamer said, shaking his head.

"It won't just be you," I said. "Remember, all three of us were hooked up and thus all three of us caught a glimpse of the mind of each person you touched."

"Good point," Patty said, "But I don't think I remember much either."

"I remember us being a little busy," Screamer said.

"But we have a secret weapon."

I looked directly into the wonderful brown eyes of the love of my life. It took her a moment, but then she laughed, clearly understanding what I was getting at.

She smiled at me and then turned to Screamer. "Remember how I slowed the time down so we can get the people out of the chairs?"

Screamer nodded.

"I can slow the time down even more in memory. A lot more."

I looked at Ben, who just smiled at me and nodded his agreement.

"Ben can remember what we all only caught a glimpse of in each person," I said, "if he's linked to us when we go back into the memory."

Screamer nodded slowly. "You know, Poker Boy, that's a hairbrained scheme like most of your schemes, and it just might work."

I was sure hoping it would.

"And what am I going to do?" Sherri asked.

I looked at her and then at Screamer. "Keep all of us calm and focused, since that few hours we spent getting those people out was very traumatic for all of us, and will be hard to relive."

She looked at her husband and nodded. "I can do that."

"Ben," I said, turning to him, "are you going to be able to remember all the details we each see with each person we rescued?"

He laughed. "I promise, I won't miss a detail, no matter how small. But I suggest we do nine at a time, stop, and I relay everything I got to see if it matches what everyone remembers from the experience."

"Very good idea," I said. "That way we won't be totally stressed."

"Oh, we'll be stressed," Patty said. "I never thought I'd have to relive those hours of sheer terror again."

"I didn't either," Screamer said. "I had nightmares for years about bodies materializing inside of each other."

"We got to do this," I said, shuddering at the memory of that exact same nightmare. "And we have to get it right."

"Because if we don't," Screamer said, "we're destined to relive what we are about to try over and over and over inside a time loop."

"That's not a time loop," I said. "That's hell."

"I've been down on a visit to hell," Sherri said. "This would be worse."

Everyone but Screamer looked at her. I think I had my mouth open.

She looked around and smiled. "What? An old boyfriend is all. You know how kids are."

"Before my time," Screamer said, shaking his head.

To be continued...

Now Available
from all your favorite booksellers
in trade paper and electronic editions.

USA Today Bestselling Writer

DEAN WESLEY
SMITH

Playing Golf
with a Ghost
Can be a Problem

GUS

Imagine the past masters of the game of golf getting a chance to play the top players of the 1980s.

Imagine a ghost golfer gag getting a little out of hand.

There's all that and more in this crazy story. This is the first publication of "Gus" anywhere.

GUS

July 17th, 1986

Dear Bill,

Thought I'd better write you real quick like and tell you what's going on. Since it was your crazy idea that started this mess, I figure you just might have a way to get rid of Gus.

You remember Gus, don't you? That was the name you suggested. You know, the idea for the invisible golfer?

Gus?

I'm sure you remember. It was in your Christmas letter. You said, Wouldn't it be funny if someone got one of those new remote controlled golf carts (not the ride-in kind, but one like a pull cart, only with a quiet little motor and a remote control switch) and hooked up a tape player in an empty bag with all the sounds of a golfer pulling a club out of the bag, hitting a ball, and putting the club back in the bag?

Then, from a hidden spot, someone could drive the empty bag and cart up near some unsuspecting golfer, stop the bag and start the tape. After the imaginary shot was hit and the imaginary club put away, the bag would head up the fairway as if pulled by an invisible golfer chasing an invisible ball.

That's exactly what you said because I went back and got your Christmas card.

"Funny as hell," you also said.

Well, like a damn fool, I agreed with you. I've got to stop doing that. Every time I've gone along with one of your crazy ideas, it's gotten me in trouble.

Remember that belly dancer? I'm still sending her checks.

Anyway, stupid old me followed your instructions and rigged up one of those remote controlled carts with a tape player in the bag. It took me a good month to learn how to steer the thing so that I wouldn't run it into trees. Did all my practicing in the back yard so no one would know about it over at the course. I'd stand up in the kitchen window and steer it around and around the back yard. Even chased my dog with it once. Scared hell out of the poor thing.

Alice thought I had flipped totally until I told her it was your idea. Then she just shook her head.

Mostly she wasn't real happy with me spending that much money. Just the empty bag alone cost sixty bucks. She's on one of those kicks lately about saving every penny for retirement. She scares me with that kind of talk. Hell, I'm only forty. I got a few good years left in me, don't I? Besides, I'm still technically recovering from "the accident." You spend all your accident money, yet?

Anyhow, it was two Saturdays ago that I finally had enough courage, matched with good weather, to give the cart its first run on the course. I picked hole number fifteen.

You know, the par five that runs along the edge of the river. I figured I could hide down in the trees alongside the fairway and steer Gus from there. My intended first victim was Carl Stevens, a new member at the club, just down from Boston.

I think I introduced you to Carl last time you were here. Tall guy, skinny, bald, always wears yellow. He usually gets a real early start and plays alone. I figured he'd be out on fifteen by about eight-thirty. So I was there at eight.

I hid the cart over behind the pump house and got down in the trees where I could see the tee. Old Carl came off fourteen green ten minutes later, walking fast, head down, not looking real happy.

Just as he reached the tee, I sent the cart in motion, bringing it around from behind the pump house and up toward the tee box. Carl didn't even see it coming until it was almost up to the tee.

I guess I didn't tell you. I added one little feature to your idea. Instead of just having the sounds of the clubs, I added a few lines of talking.

You were right about one thing. The entire gag was damn funny.

The look on Carl's face when that empty cart pulled up and stopped beside the tee box was almost more than I could stand. I bit my lip to keep from laughing and started the tape. I had used my own voice on the tape and talked through a tennis ball can to disguise it.

Sounded really strange.

Almost spooky.

"Excuse me," my tennis can voice said, "Would you mind if I play through?"

At that point I had recorded the very clear sound of clubs rattling and then one club being withdrawn.

"Nice weather, huh?"

I could see Carl's head nodding in stunned agreement with the voice on the tape. He just stood there and listened to the sound of a ball being hit. He even glanced down the fairway to see if he could see the ball. I damn near fell over laughing, let me tell you.

"Damn slice," the tape said, followed by the sound of a club being put back in the bag. I started the cart just as the tape said, "Thanks again."

I steered the cart down the fairway to the right and then off into the trees like the owner of the thing was looking for a sliced ball.

Poor Carl. He looked almost white, standing there.

Finally, after I had the cart and bag out of sight, he teed up his ball and topped it down the fairway. I waited until he was completely out of sight around the dogleg before I moved the cart from where I had steered it behind the maintenance shed.

As fast as I could, I got the cart back in my car and headed up toward the clubhouse. I wanted to be there when Carl came in and had his usual breakfast in the coffee shop.

I've got to hand you one thing. At that point, I was laughing. In fact, I didn't know if I was going to be able to keep a straight face around Carl.

I got myself a stool at the lunch counter just as Carl came in from the back nine. He dropped down into a chair at an empty table and just sat there shaking his head. Besides Carl and me, there were only about a dozen other men in the coffee-shop.

Perfect for part two of my plan.

"What's the matter," Doris asked Carl as she slid a glass of water in front of him. "Bad morning?" Doris is the normal Saturday waitress in the coffee shop. All the guys like her, even though she talks too much and doesn't know a thing about golf.

Carl shook his head no. "Just saw the damndest thing," he said, almost to himself. "Out on fifteen."

"Oh oh," I said loud enough for Carl to hear, "Gus is back."

"What?" Carl said, looking over at me.

"Oh, nothing," I said, waving off his question as if it didn't matter. "What'd you see?"

I swung around on my stool to face him.

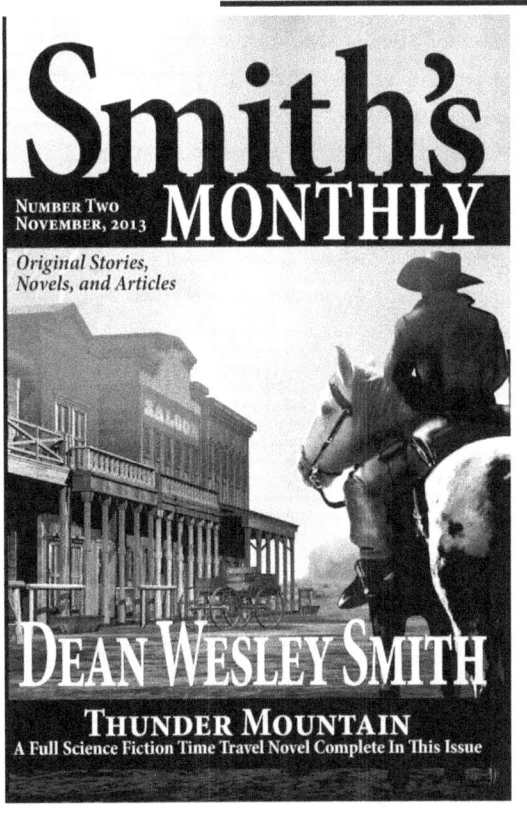

At this point five or six of the other men were listening, but Carl was now talking to both me and Doris.

"This pull cart with an empty bag on it came up on the tee and—" He shook his head. "No, this sounds so stupid, I can't even tell anyone."

"And this voice asks to play through," I said, acting real serious.

"Yeah," Carl said, nodding his head like a toy in the back window of a car. "That's exactly right. How'd you know?"

"That's Gus, the course ghost. You fellows remember hearing about Gus, don't you?"

I turned to the table of three Saturday morning regulars. I had learned a long time ago that if you directly ask a group of men a question that puts them on the spot and has a yes or no answer, they will usually nod their head in a vague yes.

I suppose it's just easier than looking stupid in front of their friends by not knowing some obvious sounding piece of information. This time, two of them nodded while the other just looked at me blankly.

I turned back to Carl. "You just had a run in with the course ghost, that's all. I'll even bet he sliced his shot into the right trees. Right?"

"How'd you know?" Carl's face was again white.

"He's been hitting that same shot for eighty years," I said. "Ever since the course was built. I've seen him twice. Lucky for you he didn't ask you to play along."

"No, he just asked to play through," Carl said.

"Lucky for you, right guys?"

This time five men in the room nodded, and one even said I sure was right.

"Why?" Carl asked.

"Well, the last time Gus was around a lot was back in the middle thirties. Almost exactly fifty years ago, now that I think about it, since this is nineteen-eighty-three. The stories go that he usually just did what you saw this morning. But one Saturday, he asked to join this twosome. They both knew about Gus and the story goes that they said yes just for the hell of it."

Carl nodded so I went on.

"The three of them played off down the fairway and no one has ever seen those two men since. Of course, there have been lots of reports of people sighting them playing early in the morning when the dew is still fresh on the greens. In fact, you know when you're out there real early and there's footprints already in the dew around the flag?"

"Yeah," Carl said. "Happens all the time, but I never see who's ahead of me."

"Take a guess," I said and took a long sip of the coffee Doris had brought me. I didn't want to tell him those footprints were really made by the green's keeper changing the pins every morning. What he didn't know wouldn't hurt him.

"Oh," was all he said.

"You think maybe this means Gus is coming back?" one of the other men asked.

I shrugged, fighting like hell to keep a completely serious face. "Maybe. All I know is that I'm certainly not going to get near that empty bag if I see it."

I tossed Doris some money for the coffee and headed out the door before I exploded trying to contain myself.

And the rest of the week I just kept laughing. Gus was the talk of the club. Most of the members didn't really buy into the tall tale. But people talked about it. Carl even got invited to join a regular group on Saturday mornings so he wouldn't have to play out there alone.

For me, I couldn't leave well enough alone.

The following Saturday, I got down to the course real early, had Gus hidden behind the pump house, and me down in the trees way before anyone was around.

Forty minutes later, Steven Forbes and Franklin Jones came off fourteen green and headed for fifteen tee. You haven't met them. They work for a law office downtown and play golf a few times a week. I had heard them laughing about Gus Wednesday afternoon in the bar. I also had heard Thomas Sullivan, a regular member, warn them to stay away from the ghost cart if they saw it. Just in case.

Well, Bill, your idea worked twice. I ran the cart up beside them just as Franklin was teeing up his ball. Startled him so much that he stepped back and tripped over the tee marker.

I ran through the entire tape and had the cart headed down the fairway before either of them even thought to move. Damn that was funny. My side hurt from laughing without making a sound.

Again, I hid the cart over behind the old maintenance shed. That's where I think I made my mistake. You see, I left the cart there while I went up to the clubhouse to listen to the fun. And when I went back down an hour later to get it, there were just too many people around to get it over to the road and into my car without being seen.

> *I ran through the entire tape and had the cart headed down the fairway before either of them even thought to move.*

So I had to come up with something fast or blow the entire gag. I don't know if you noticed the old white house sitting off to the side of sixteen, way back in the trees. It's been abandoned for years and there was talk at one time among the men's association about turning it into a club, but nothing has ever been done.

I decided to hide Gus there until there were fewer people on the course. I put him down in the fruit cellar of the house and tossed some old newspapers over the bag. No one had been down there in years. A great hiding place. In fact, at the time, I was really happy I found the spot. Beat hell out of lifting it in and out of the trunk of my car.

Monday I was sitting in the coffee shop, after playing with my usual group, when Hector, the assistant pro, came in. He'd been about three groups behind us. He started in about how he and three guys had just seen Gus. Only this time Gus was playing sixteen and had hooked the ball.

Let me tell you, I scrambled out of there and down to the old house faster than I had moved in years. I sure didn't like the thought of just anyone messing around with Gus. I planned on using him for my own golf cart when the joke was done.

Well, you guessed it.

Gus was gone.

I searched everywhere, but couldn't find a clue as to who took him. I even walked the golf course and sat out beside fifteen for a few hours in hopes that whoever had taken him would strike again.

I looked all day Tuesday, too.

Nothing.

Wednesday (yesterday) Gus found me.

Gus and his friend, Horton, that is.

This is where I'm hoping you might have an idea or two. You see, normally on Wednesdays I have my match with the "Cold Crew." That's what we call those of us who play golf most of our lives instead of working like our wives think we should.

I was playing with old Doc Rule, Howard Erickson, and Scott Golden. We were out on twelve, the short par three, when Gus and this other empty bag come up onto the tee box. Let me tell you, I was one scared fellow right at that moment. And trust me, I wouldn't have believed it if I hadn't seen it myself.

Why?

Because the other empty bag was a carry bag. And some invisible person or thing was carrying it about three feet off the ground and the shoulder strap was full of something that I could see the trees through.

Gus excused himself and asked very nicely if they could play through.

Bill, it wasn't my tennis can voice that asked. No sir. It was just as spooky as my made up voice, but it wasn't mine. And it didn't come from the bag.

At that point the empty carry bag dropped to the ground with the sounds of clubs rattling.

After a moment there was a sound of a golf ball being hit.

"Nice shot, Horton," a voice said from the area of Gus.

"Thanks, Gus," a slightly higher voice said from the tee box.

You could have knocked me down with the old proverbial feather.

All four of us just stood and watched, or listened would be a better way of putting it, as Gus hit his shot and then the two bags headed up toward the green.

Just before they reached the green, though, both bags just sort of faded away.

Now I'm not kidding.

Remember, twelve is a short par three. Those two bags vanished not more than eighty yards in front of me, right out in plain sight in the middle of the fairway.

One moment they were there, the next, bingo, they were gone.

Well, we waited an extra long time just to make sure they were off the green, then tried to finish our round. Ruined the day, though.

And back in the clubhouse, I learned that we weren't the only ones to see Gus and Horton. They had played through three other groups as well.

Bill, any idea as to just what the hell is going on?

Or any ideas as to what I might do to get rid of Gus and Horton and maybe even get my cart back? You know more about this stuff than I do. I've really gone and gotten the club and myself into a mess, this time.

People are getting scared and if word of this gets out, it will close down the course. If that happened, there would be no way I could talk Alice into letting me buy another membership.

Please send any ideas you might have as soon as possible. Hope you are well.

Say hello to that beautiful wife of yours for me.

Desperately,
Fred

———————————

Dear Fred,

I looked up the name Horton in one of my golf reference books and it just so happened there was a great golfer back in the early part of the century named Horton. Horton Smith, to be exact.

Track Gus and his Horton friend down and find out if it really is the same Horton. If it is, I've got an idea or two that just might work.

In response to your question, my "accident" money is holding out just fine. But in about five years we might have to try that again.

What do you say?

Say hi to Alice for me.

Keep it hooking,
Bill

————————————

Dear Bill,

Are you kidding? Just how the hell am I supposed to find out the last name of a ghost?

The situation is getting worse. Gus and Horton were seen three times yesterday. And this morning I heard that they played through a group of women, and on women's day, to boot. And there was a third bag with them. They called that bag "Harry."

Hoping for help,
Fred

p.s. Repeating the "accident" might just get some folks a little suspicious, don't you think?

————————————

Dear Fred,

Simply walk up to the ghosts and ask them.

And while you're at it, ask Harry if his last name is Vardon.

And if it is, see if you can get me some lessons.

Slicing is part of life,
Bill

————————————

Dear Bill,

Damn it, I'm serious. This is a real mess down here.

Now a forth golfing ghost has joined the group. At this rate, they're going to be holding tournaments. So be serious, would you?

I need help.

I figured that it wouldn't hurt to try your suggestion about finding out their names, since they do seem to talk a lot between themselves and they do ask everyone very politely if they can play through, even though no one has ever seen them finish a complete hole.

I told Hector, the assistant pro, your idea about talking to the ghosts, but I didn't mention the names. He thought it might work and agreed to play a few rounds with me to see if we could spot the invisible foursome.

They found us on the seventh tee. Gus, plus three carry bags, all floating three feet in the air as if slung over invisible shoulders.

"Mind if we play through?" a voice said from the direction of Gus.

"Not at all," I stammered out after a moment of shock.

And let me tell you, seeing those four empty bags and hearing the normal sounds of four golfers on a tee box, is a shocking thing.

"Wondering if you'd answer a question or two?" I said after a moment of swallowing hard to get the courage.

"Sure thing," Gus said. "Harry, you're up."

"Is that the Harry Vardon?" I asked.

"Sure is," a voice laughed from between the tee markers.

"Harry's reputation always did beat him to a course," another voice said from near one of the carry bags laying on the ground.

I waited for the laughter from the four invisible men to subside slightly before I asked my next question.

"Is Horton Smith also here?"

"Sure am," a high voice said.

"Who's your fourth?" I asked.

"Well, you know me," the voice said from beside my trick pull cart. "So I guess you must mean Bobby."

"Bobby?" I asked.

"Not Bobby Jones?" Hector blurted out.

"That's right, son," another voice said. "Now can we stop all this gabbing and let Harry get on with his shot. We don't have all day, you know."

Hector and I stood there in silence and listened to the sounds of four men laughing and hitting shots.

"Thanks again," the voice said from beside my trick cart after they had all hit. And with that, all four bags started off the tee box and down the fairway. They vanished about a hundred yards off the tee.

They had played through three other groups that we know of by the time we got into the clubhouse.

Bill, the course just can't take much more of this. People are afraid of going out to play. Men's league has been canceled this week. And sooner or later, someone at some newspaper is going to start believing all this and then where will we be? I'll be without any place to play, that's where. And that means staying home with Alice all day and you know how I'd feel about that.

I don't see how knowing they are the ghosts of three great golfers does any damn good at all. We sure can't stand around and watch them. But send any ideas you might have. It was your idea that started all this mess.

Besides, no one here can seem to come up with anything other than shooting at the bags. And so far, calmer heads have held those trigger happy fools off. Luckily, very few really staunch Catholics have seen the foursome so far. Otherwise, we'd have priests doing exorcisms on the putting green.

Damn. Why do I ever listen to your fool ideas?

Although, I must admit, the accident idea worked out real well.

Waiting impatiently,
Fred

———————————

TELEGRAM

Fred STOP Tournament brilliant idea STOP Will solve your problem and make us rich STOP Flying in tomorrow at ten STOP Please pick me up STOP Bill

———————————

Article from the local Monday newspaper.

MODERNS WIN BIG
IN MATCH OF THE CENTURY

For years, golf historians have asked the question, "Who was better? The great players from the past or today's super-stars?"

Yesterday, in one of the most bizarre golf matches ever played, that question might or might not have been answered by the resounding victory of Nickalas, Travino, and Palmer over the supposed ghosts of Bobby Jones, Harry Vardon, and Horton Smith in the controversial tournament billed as "The Match of the Century."

"Thrilled," Nickalas said, when asked how he felt after the match. "How else could I feel?"

Travino and Palmer seemed equally excited to be taking part.

When asked if he thought the entire match was serious, Travino replied, "Would I be here if I didn't?"

But to many, the question of the day was, "Is this all a giant hoax?" Three of today's great players didn't act like it was. All three dropped commitments to the Greater Sunshine Open and put on an exhibition of golf at its finest.

Consequently, "The Match of the Century" between the modern day greats and history's finest was never even close.

Travino led the elite field with a superb eight under 64. Nickalas followed with a brilliant 66 and Palmer with a 69. Harry Vardon led the "Ghost Team" with a 72, followed by Smith with a 74 and Jones with a 75.

When asked by reporters near the last hole why they were having troubles, Harry Vardon answered, "The courses are tougher today. I haven't been back long enough to get the feel of them. Back in my day," he said, "the greens were like post-age stamps and hard as rocks. Different kind of golf."

Horton Smith, said to be the best put-ter ever in the game, had trouble even getting to the greens. "The holes are a lot longer. And there's a bunch more sand," he said. "Makes it more interesting, that's for sure."

Horton Smith found sand traps an even dozen times in the eighteen-hole match.

The match, the brainchild of Fred Henning and Bill Addison, was set up on the Shadow Acres Country Club after the sudden unexplained appearance of the three golfing greats. Or, more accurate-ly put, the appearance of their bags and voices.

Hundreds of unanswered questions surround yesterday's match, such as why the bags appeared, but not the clubs or the men. Or how could the ghosts hit visible new balls with invisible old clubs? When asked just exactly what they were playing for, and why, all six contestants stuck to "No Comment."

And all six just laughed when asked if this would become an annual event.

However, they had no trouble talking about everything else, so the gallery and the viewers at home were treated to an eighteen-hole history lesson on the early days of golf.

It seems that most of the questions will never be answered. It doesn't seem to matter. "The Match of the Century" now joins the three ghosts as part of history.

But one thing is for certain, regardless of whether you believe in ghosts or think somehow the entire day was a setup, "The

Match of the Century" at Shadow Acres Country Club was a day the game of golf will not soon forget.

––––––––––––

Dear Bill,

Thought you might be interested in the enclosed article. It came out in the morning paper the day you left. Didn't know if you saw it or not, as busy as you were.

You know, over the last few weeks I've been thinking a lot about what happened. And the more I think about it, the more amazed I become. The best way to describe what we pulled off was a miracle.

No, a serious of miracles.

For example, in all the craziness those three weeks before the match, I never did ask you just how you got Lee Travino to fly in and meet the ghostly foursome.

But somehow you did. Amazing.

And the way you talked the club into putting up perpetual memberships and complete playing right-of-way as prizes for the ghosts is beyond me. Who else but you would realize that the one thing the ghosts would enjoy more than anything was never having to ask to go through another group again.

And then talking the ghosts of three of the top players in history into wagering that prize versus finding a new place to play in a match against the three best players of modern times.

Brilliant.

Nothing short.

But we forgot one thing. Gus. He was seen yesterday down on sixteen again. He's still got my bag and cart and now he seems to not be real happy. He even

yelled at one woman to get the hell out of his way so he could play a decent round of golf.

Did you talk to him while you were here? I sure didn't. Hell, I still don't know who he is. Or was. I'm going to go down and try to talk to him. But I don't know exactly how that's going to work.

Any ideas this time?

Let me know if the movie deal goes. Always can use more money. Alice is happy about what we got from television rights and stuff, but she's still clamping down hard on every penny. I suppose someday I will thank her for that.

Someday.

At least the match keeps us from thinking about another accident for a few more years.

Your friend in the money,
Fred

––––––––––––

Dear Fred,

Just got back and opened your letter. The movie deal looks like it's a for sure. We'll make another bundle on that when it happens. And there's talk about a book. Not bad, huh?

Sorry I didn't tell you about Gus. I feel sort of bad about this, since I forgot all about Gus. There were just so many details that had to be looked after. Sorry.

I did get a quick chance right at the beginning to talk to Gus. Remember that first day after I arrived when we walked down seventeen fairway with them. You were talking to Horton about the match and I was talking to Gus. I found out his real name was Lawrence Meadows. He used to own the old white house down off sixteen that you stored the cart and bag in. In fact, his body is buried in the fruit cellar.

And he was the one who brought back Smith, Jones, and Vardon. He said he just wanted someone to play a few rounds with.

I did promise him a few things, but now I think it might be too late. You had better get down there and talk to him if you can.

Again, sorry I forgot.

Happy digging,
Bill

Dear Bill,

Not damn funny.
Not by a long sight.
Me and the sheriff found the skeleton in the mud and clay in the old fruit cellar. Right exactly where you said it would be.

I told the sheriff you told me where the body was, and he now wants to know if you would please tell him exactly who killed the poor guy and buried him there sixty years ago. There was a bullet hole in the skull.

Leaving that fun little "chore" up to me would have made me real mad at you if not for the fact that in the same mail as your letter I got a very, very large check.

Alice likes you more every day.

Maybe next week she might even let me phone you instead of write.

However, I still got Gus, or whatever his name is, to contend with. The members are not real happy he's still around and some of them are starting to blame me. I finally caught up with him down on number three yesterday and he said I was supposed to play with him and had gone back on my side of the deal.

Just what the hell is he talking about? I'm not going to go around playing golf with any damn ghost. No way. Even if the entire PGA tour does it.

And if you told him I would, you get your ass down here right now and play with him yourself.

Waiting with muddy shoes,
Fred

Dear Fred,

Glad you found the body.

Gus, or I guess his name was Lawrence, never told me he had been killed. But you could always ask him who done it next time you play with him. You see, that really was the deal.

Sorry I forgot to ask you, but you're supposed to play golf with Gus every Monday morning or he's going to bring a bunch more golfers back. He said he'd just stick his invisible old clubs in your bag so no one has to know he's there.

I feel really bad about mentioning this before, but you know how busy it was. Besides, what could be wrong with playing golf with Gus? He told me he was a pretty good player in his day. He just might give you a run for your money.

Just be careful with what you bet.

Money from the movie deal should be heading your way this next week.

Have fun,
Bill

Dear Bill,

Go to hell.

There's no damn way I'm going to play golf every Monday with a ghost. You better think of something fast. If I get booted out of this club because of you, I just might think about telling a few certain people about your little "vacation" last year.

You remember the one, don't you?

Think quick,
Fred

————————————

Dear Fred,

I don't understand why you are so upset. You play golf all the time, anyway. I sure didn't think anything would be wrong with playing just one round a week with Gus.

Give it a try. You might like it.

And it certainly will solve your problem with the club.

By the way, I got the money for the movie deal. Your half is enclosed. Now, wasn't that worth it?

Wishing you luck,
Bill

————————————

Dear Bill,

Boy was I mad when I sent you that last letter.

Wow.

In fact, I was so mad, I came up with an idea all my own.

I went marching down to the club and spent the entire afternoon looking for Gus. Finally spotted him on ten tee, getting ready to go out on the back nine. I told him my idea and he liked it. So now I have played twice with Gus.

And you know what, you were right. Gus is a pretty good golfer.

Today I got your letter and the check. Made Alice real happy. We even went out for dinner tonight. I don't know if my heart can take many more shocks like that one.

She even suggested it. Thanks.

That much money means we don't ever have to think about another accident. I like that.

I still haven't been able to talk Gus into telling me who killed him. He said it just doesn't matter anymore. It was a long time ago. For some reason, the sheriff still thinks it matters. He's going to send someone to talk to you next week.

You know, that money you sent calmed me down some. I'm not anywhere near as mad at you as I was.

And that brings up a problem I suppose I should tell you about. Maybe you, since you got me into this mess, can help me with it. You see, I think Gus cheats.

That's right, I think a ghost cheats at golf.

Think about it. With an invisible ball, it's damn hard to tell exactly what his score is on any given hole. I'm not always close enough to hear every shot. And who the hell knows if he's improving his lies. He might even be kicking the ball. I tried to get him to use some of my balls, like you had them do for the match, but he says he doesn't want to take the chance anyone will see them and discover he's still around. He says that's part of the deal I made with him.

He's right.

It is part of the deal. And it's got the Country Club off my back. You see, for me to play with him, I figured it had to be worth my while.

So I made him a little side bet. You know, just like all golfers do. Just like you had them do in the Match.

What are we playing for? Good question. Remember now, I was really mad at you when I made this deal.

I feel bad about this, especially after all the money you made us. But after all, you did tell Gus I would play with him without asking me first. So I feel bad, but not too bad.

If I win, it's simple. Gus tells me where some buried treasure is. He says there's lots of it around the area. In fact, he hinted he even knew where the Lost Dutchman Mine is. He said ghosts just know those sorts of things.

What am I giving him if he wins? He made me promise I wouldn't tell you. Just trust me that it is very important to you that I win.

Very, very important.

Remember, I was really mad at you when I came up with this idea. And I'm sure I would win, too.

If Gus wouldn't cheat.

You'd better think fast.

Losing, but smiling, your friend,
Fred

Dean Wesley Smith

USA Today Bestselling Writer

Sometimes
You Just Have to
Let One Fly
to Find Your Future

THE LAST BURP
OF A VERY GOOD WOMAN

Mary did her best in her small restaurant to keep everything just perfect. She swept and cleaned constantly and didn't much like crude behavior near her.

And everyone knew of her bad stomach.

But now even a handful of Tums couldn't help Mary do what she needed to do to move forward.

THE LAST BURP
OF A VERY GOOD WOMAN

Mary, the owner and only cook at Mary's Cafe on the old highway, was a prude, plain and simple. No one in Idaho City, the closest town to the north, would ever think of swearing or saying anything crude at all in Mary's. No one who actually knew Mary was sure just how often she cleaned the place, but bets were that it was at least three times a day. She always wore a plaid dress, proper shoes, and a towel tucked into her white apron. Mary seemed to constantly be wiping her hands on that towel.

People in the valley liked Mary's place, and liked Mary, but in the backwoods Idaho valley there just weren't that many people. Not anywhere near enough to support a restaurant. Yet somehow Mary kept open Mary's Cafe, selling a sandwich or soup to the occasional tourist who stopped there thinking that the pristine little place with wooden booths, table cloths, and the ancient cash register were all just part of some "local mountain charm."

When I first met Mary, more than fifteen years ago now, she was a thin woman, with clear blue eyes, a wide, welcoming grin, and a temper that flared into a frown and nothing more. Normally her skin was pale, accentuated by the bright colors of the plaid dresses she always wore. But when she got angry a bright red flush took over her face and made her skin splotchy, like she had some bad sickness.

I was about Mary's age, pushing the wrong side of sixty like it was a heavy wheelbarrow too full of my life to move. Why I thought of her as a friend I'll never know, but I did, and she sometimes beamed a little when she saw me. My wife had died eight years ago of the cancer, and her husband was long gone and she never mentioned him. Just like me she had had no children, and considering what a prude she was, that didn't surprise me.

Up here in the Idaho wilds, where the snow was six foot deep in the winter and the dust three inches thick in the summer, we sort of leaned on each other. And to be honest, I liked that. And I liked her.

The last day of July started out just like any other day, with the highway running logging trucks off the Sand Creek section down to the mill below Idaho City. All of the drivers knew Mary, knew Mary's place, but just never had the time or the thought of stopping. Those big trucks, even loaded, roared by at upwards of forty, leaving large clouds of dust to cover everything in the narrow valley behind them. After a few weeks of no rain and dust from the trucks going and coming, everything around Mary's place looked gray.

Even when I went through the front door and banged it closed, I sent a thin cloud of dust into the air.

Mary during the summer was always in a constant battle with the dust, and since the logging started, this summer was even worse. Since there were no cars in the gravel parking area, I expected her to be madly dusting some part of the restaurant.

But when I went in Mary was sitting at the counter, her head down, like it was too heavy for her neck to hold up right. I moved up beside her and sat down. I hadn't seen her sit at the counter in all the years I had known her. Usually when she rested she sat at the table near the old jukebox, waiting for a customer to come in, or trying to get up enough energy to clean something.

She always tried to keep a fresh pot of coffee going to keep the smell nice in the place, but today the restaurant just felt hot and dusty.

Mary's Cafe never felt hot and dusty. I knew right then that something was wrong.

"You need to kick up the air conditioning a little," I said.

She didn't move or even say anything, so I asked, "You all right?"

She still didn't move so I did something that never would have occurred to me with Mary at any other time. I touched her shoulder.

She sort of tipped real slowly and went over sideways.

Now at my age I don't move real fast, and I didn't move fast enough to catch her as she tumbled to the floor, hitting with a sick thumping sound.

I went to one knee and moved her gently over so I could see into her face. The moment I touched her I knew it wouldn't matter. She was cold and dead, her eyes open and staring at nothing.

"Shit, Mary," I said, swearing in a place that I had never spoken a swear word in before. "What happened?"

I wasn't expecting an answer, but I half expected Mary to sit up and just scold me for using foul language.

But I think she might even find it in her heart to excuse my one swear word. I was seeing the only friend I had in these damn woods laying dead on the old tile floor. The idea of Mary being dead just sort of took my breath away.

I made her look a little more comfortable even though I knew it made no difference at all to her. And I felt odd not taking her off the floor, because Mary would have never spent any time on the floor. But I left her there anyway, because I would have felt even odder touching her to pick her up and move her.

I went into the back and got her best tablecloth that she kept stored there for special occasions. I figured her passing on was about as special as it got.

As I put the tablecloth over her face I heard her voice from behind me. "Real nice of you."

I spun around to see her sitting there at her table by the old jukebox, just like she always did.

I stared at her, then back at the body under the tablecloth on the floor. My old brain was just not working today it seemed.

"Wish you hadn't used my good tablecloth though," she said. "One of the old white ones would have worked just fine. Now you've gone and got that one dusty from the floor."

This time I slowly looked up at where she sat at the table. She was there all right. Or more likely, her ghost was there. The ghost was wearing the same exact thing the body was. And the ghost was talking to me.

At that moment, to be honest, I thought my old heart might just up and stop.

"You're dead," I said.

> *As I put the tablecloth over her face I heard her voice from behind me. "Real nice of you."*

Not a real bright thing to say, but under the circumstances, it was the only thing I was thinking about.

"No kidding," she said, sort of smiling at me like she always did when she humored me. "Hurt like all get out for a minute. I must have burst a few blood vessels in my head."

She pointed at the counter. "The headache came on so fast that I sat down there at the counter and don't remember another thing until you started covering my body with my best tablecloth."

I glanced at the body, then back at her sitting at the table.

"So," I said, glancing once more at the body and then moving over and sitting at my normal spot at the counter on the end where I could talk to her sitting at the table. "How come you haven't, you know, passed on yet?"

"I don't honestly know," she said, shaking her head and looking very puzzled as if I had asked the most difficult question ever thought up. "Maybe it takes a while for the next life to find me way up here in the mountains."

"Could be," I said. No chance I was going to argue with a ghost, so just agreeing seemed to be my best choice.

She smiled at me. I always enjoyed when she smiled at me. I missed the companionship of a woman, and Mary was the closest thing I ever got to that now. Or had been.

"Maybe I'm doomed for all eternity to sit and talk to you."

She was still smiling, letting me know she was joking. Mary's jokes were always light and very seldom funny.

"So you're not upset at dying?" I asked, glancing back to make sure her body was still right there on the floor where I'd left it.

"Of course I'm upset," she said, shaking her head at me. "I had been looking forward to cleaning up after another day of dust from the logging trucks, and sitting in this place for ten hours without more than five or six customers."

"Oh," I said. I said that a lot with Mary, especially when she tried to be sarcastic.

She patted her chest lightly with her age-worn right hand. "I think I have heartburn. And my stomach's acting up again."

I stared at her for a moment, not really understanding what she had said.

"Would you mind getting me that bottle of Tums back there by the Coke machine. For some reason I don't think I can leave this spot." She shrugged. "Not sure why I know that. Just do."

I got up and grabbed the bottle of Tums and sort of eased myself toward the table where Mary's ghost sat.

"Don't be worrying about me biting you," she said, smiling. "I have never heard of a ghost biting anyone, have you?"

I couldn't say that I had, but I still didn't much like taking any chances. I slid the bottle onto the table and moved back to my stool.

I needed to be calling Sheriff Andrews about Mary. It would take him a good half hour to get up here from Idaho City as it was, but instead I sat down. Even though she was a ghost, talking to her was a lot better than not talking to her, especially when this might be the last time I could ever do it.

Mary tried to pick up the bottle of

Tums and her hand went right through it. She tried twice more before saying, "I suppose that's not going to work."

"Heartburn that bad?" I asked.

"Like a bad case of chilly," she said, pressing her chest. "I don't know what I'm going to do if this gets any worse."

Suddenly she just up and burped.

A good one, too. It echoed around the empty restaurant.

I stared at her in complete shock as she turned bright red and covered her mouth. In all my years I could have never imagined Mary letting out a belch like that.

I started to laugh and she just got redder.

But she was also lighter, more see-through, more ghost-like.

"Oh, please pardon me," she said. "I don't know what's come over me."

"You being dead might be a fairly large part of the problem."

I didn't tell her the burp had changed her as well. She was just too embarrassed to stand any other news. And clearly, from the way her hand pressed against her stomach, the heartburn was still bothering her.

"I need to be calling the sheriff," I said. "Mind if I use your phone?"

She pointed to the antique dial phone on the back wall. "Be my guest. I don't think I'm going to be worrying about the bill at this point."

I moved around the counter and toward the phone as she burped again.

I pretended not to notice, but when I glanced back at her she had gotten a little lighter, a little more see-through.

I spent the next minute telling the sheriff about finding Mary, and promising I would stay right where I was until he got there.

I hung up the phone and looked back at Mary, who was considerably lighter still. She must have been burping those little hiccup-like burps that tight women like Mary used in polite company.

Just as I was sitting back down she covered her mouth and gave out another little one, her face getting even redder.

"I'm really sorry I'm burping like this," she said. "Guess death just isn't good on the stomach, and you know how uneasy my stomach can be at times."

Everyone in the valley, and even some of the tourists who stopped by, knew about Mary's stomach, and all her problems with the doctors down in Boise, and how they wouldn't do anything for her to help. The worst fear many locals in the valley had was being trapped in Mary's place for dinner when she didn't have a tourist or two. Then all you heard about was her stomach problems.

She covered her mouth again and burped lightly. Again she sort of faded a little.

Finally, after a few more small burps, she sort of stared at her hand for a moment and then shrugged. "Guess I'm slowly going on to the next life."

"One burp at a time," I said.

She frowned. "What do you mean?"

"Every time you burp you get a little lighter."

"That's not possible," she said, shaking her head. "I just have a horrible case of heartburn is all."

"You want to say anything about impossible?" I asked. I pointed at her body on the floor. "I'm sitting here talking to you while your body is stretched out on the tile. I know for a fact *that* isn't possible either."

She nodded. "I suppose that's true, but I just don't see how my burping is moving me any closer to heaven."

"A good belch can sometimes be heaven," I said, then instantly regretted being so crude to Mary.

"I suppose," she said, actually seeming to think about what I had said.

I could tell she was in some pretty intense discomfort, and no matter how hard she tried, after a moment she covered her mouth with a see-through hand and burped softly again.

Again she faded a little more.

"You know," I said, "maybe this burping is just God's way of having people get the last of their earthly bodies out of their system before moving on. Sort of a letting go of the pressure thing."

Mary looked at me and then half nodded. "I suppose, but it just doesn't seem right that the stomach problems I had all during my life would go with me into the next."

"Maybe they're not," I said. "Maybe that heartburn you're feeling is the old problems wanting to leave you. Maybe a few more good belches and you'll be free to move on into the next world."

As crazy at it sounded, I actually seemed to be making sense to Mary.

"So you think I should just go ahead and let it all out?" she asked, clearly uncomfortable with the idea.

"I'm the only one here, and I won't think any the less of you if you do. A couple of good belches and off you go to heaven."

Even as a ghost, Mary's face turned bright red with my comment. But I could tell the pain in her stomach was getting worse and she was thinking about it.

Finally she nodded and took a deep breath and looked at me. "You've always been a wonderful friend. If this works and I move on, I just wanted you to know that."

I could feel a little moisture sort of building up in my eyes with her statement. I swallowed and then said, "You've been a great friend to me. The valley is going to seem empty without you."

She nodded, a tear in her eye.

Then she sort of squared her shoulders, took a deep breath, and without even covering her mouth, let out the longest and loudest belch I had heard outside of the army.

I wanted to cheer her.

For an instant there, before she disappeared completely, while that huge rolling belch came out of her mouth, she seemed so free, so unencumbered by all the rules she had lived by.

She had finally let go.

As the last memory of her belch echoed through the insides of her diner, I suddenly understood that she was gone.

Really gone.

Only her body remained behind me on the floor.

I put my head down on the counter top and just sat there, trying not to think about how empty my future was going to be. She had been my best friend, a prudish woman who strived to always do everything just right, keep everything clean, keep me on the straight and narrow, yet she was still a good friend.

I had to admit that it was ironic that Mary, a woman who had owned and run a restaurant her entire life, went out in a burp.

Granted, it was one hell of a burp.

I stared at the empty chair at the table where Mary always sat. I was going to miss her more than I could imagine. She had been a very good woman.

Not a great woman, just a very good one.

But I still had no doubt they had heard that burp all the way to heaven.

~

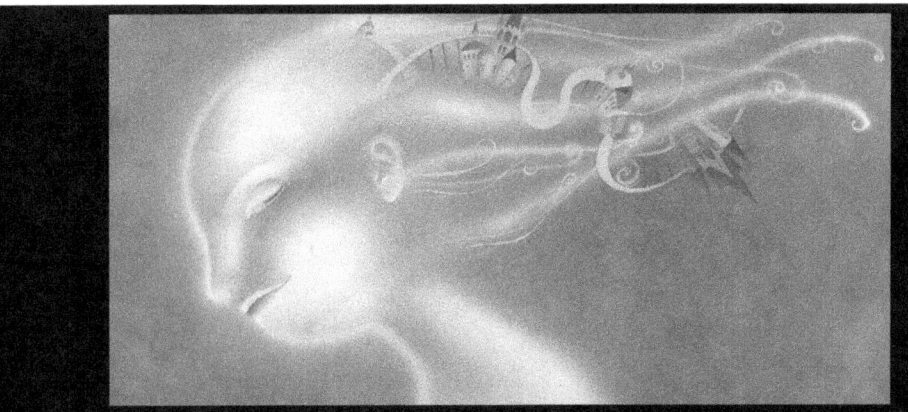

Poems by DEAN WESLEY SMITH

Gutter

Her sunglasses hang
from her ears directly under her chin
like a gutter
to catch and filter
through dark glass
any stray word
or stray crumb.

She slips them on
to look back in time
shocked by
all the wrong words
she said
or unhealthy food
she ate.

She would be better served
carrying the sunglasses
in her purse in the dark
tucked away from the reminders
of bad food and slipped words.
It would also look better.
Less stupid.

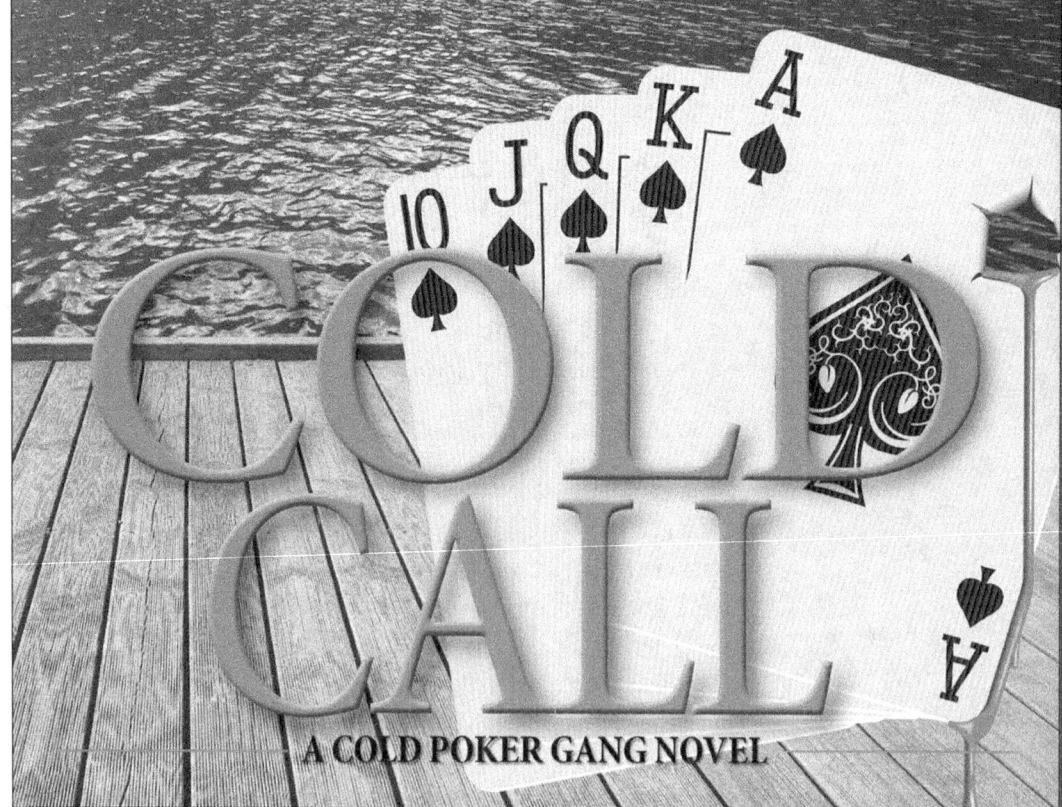

USA TODAY BESTSELLING AUTHOR

DEAN WESLEY SMITH

COLD CALL

A COLD POKER GANG NOVEL

When Retired Detective Bayard Lott offers to help Retired Detective Julia Rogers search for her lost friend in a remote Idaho lake, they find clues that might lead them directly to the most dangerous serial killer in Las Vegas history.

A twisted mystery that pits the Cold Poker Gang against a master criminal.

Set in the rugged mountains of Idaho, this mystery will grip you until the last plot twist.

COLD CALL
A Cold Poker Gang Novel

AUTHOR'S NOTE

The town of McCall, Idaho, is real and a wonderful place to visit, but all people, businesses, and locations in this novel are simply figments of my overactive imagination and are not based on any person, living or dead.

Part One
THE SET-UP

CHAPTER ONE

May 21, 2002
9:30 P.M.
Lake Mead, Outside of Las Vegas, Nevada

THEY'D COME TO THE EDGE of the big lake to celebrate.

It was Danny and Carrie Coswell's first wedding anniversary, and since the night was so warm and both had just finished another long semester at UNLV, they had decided to go back to the place they used to go while dating.

It seemed right. Danny had loved the idea when Carrie suggested it over great steak dinners at the MGM Grand Hotel. They had gone home and changed clothes after the fancy dinner, changing back into their jeans and t-shirts and carrying sweatshirts in case the night cooled.

Danny loved how Carrie looked with her long blonde hair pulled back and her trim figure. Both of them ran for exercise and at times their class and study schedules allowed them to run together.

Danny really enjoyed being out at the lake, but Carrie liked it even more. She had told him that being along the vast expanse of Lake Mead made her feel part of the world. The silence and the wild of the shores of the lake were a sharp contrast to the constant motion and noise of Las Vegas.

He and Carrie were what some called childhood sweethearts. He knew he had loved her since the very first time he had seen her walking the halls of their high school, her books clutched against her chest, trying to find her locker. They had both been in the tenth grade and he offered to help her find her locker and they had became friends, then dated all the way through school after that.

They had wonderful memories of all the dances together, graduating together, and two years later getting married.

Below them, the lake was calm, its black surface spread out to the outlines of the hills on the other side. The faint moonlight shimmered across the water, making the night feel just a little brighter.

When dating, they would often go down the gentle gravel slope to the edge of the water, maybe even do some skinny dipping. But tonight they were content to

sit on a blanket on the slight bluff, holding hands, leaning into each other, just talking about their first year of marriage, and their plans for the future.

Danny had called it their private place because they were tucked into what felt like a fort of brush and small scrub trees on the bluff. No one could see them, even down along the shore. And it was on a blanket in this private place that they had first made love in their senior year of high school.

The shelter in the brush with a view of the lake was a perfect place to dream about the future, and they had used it often to plan everything from their wedding to which classes to take.

Then a dark Mercedes eased slowly down the gravel road toward the edge of the lake, its lights off, its wheels making cracking noises on the rocks, its engine muffled by the tall, thick brush that lined the top of the bluffs along this part of the lake.

There was just enough moonlight to see the worn gravel road used during the day by fishermen and at night by kids like Danny and Carrie. Danny had parked their Toyota Camry in some brush about fifty paces back up the hill. It couldn't be seen at all from the gravel road.

The Mercedes was the wrong kind of car for a lake adventure. Danny could clearly hear the beautifully engineered chassis scrape against the rocks and bumps of the rough gravel and dirt road.

The only reason Danny could get his Camry this close to the lake was because he knew every bump and large dip. Clearly the Mercedes driver did not.

"What's a car like that doing on a road like this?" Danny whispered.

"I just want to know when he's going to leave," Carrie whispered back. She smiled at him. "I have plans for you, and I don't want an audience."

He laughed. Even after all the years, they still had a good time out here along the lake.

"He can't see us," Danny said. "More than likely just some rich daddy's kid on a date with his dad's car."

"Dad's not going to be happy if he notices the scrapes under the car," Carrie said, laughing softly.

The driver of the Mercedes stopped ten paces short of the edge of the bluff overlooking the water on the other side of the road.

Danny watched as a tall man got out. In the faint light from the Mercedes interior, Danny couldn't see the man's face, but Danny could see that the man had on a suit nearly as expensive as the car he drove.

"Not a date," Danny whispered.

Carrie grasped Danny's hand and said nothing as they watched.

The man opened the back door of his car and dug out a pair of dark coveralls. He pulled them on over his suit, put a dark hat on his head, and dark gloves on his hands.

With one final movement, he put on plastic boots over his shoes, the kind that golfers wear over their golf shoes on a rainy day.

Given that the night was perfect, not a sign of rain in sight, Danny had no idea what the man was up to with all the protective gear. But Danny's stomach was telling him it wasn't good.

Then, whistling a faint tune that seemed to just drift on the slight wind, the man moved around to the trunk of his car and opened it.

Since Danny and Carrie were just above the man and the trunk light came

on, it was clear there was a human body in the trunk.

Carrie inhaled, about to scream, but Danny put a hand over her mouth before she could make a sound. He could feel her trembling beneath his touch.

Or more than likely, that was his own hand shaking.

With a swift motion, the man in the expensive suit and coveralls yanked a woman's body out of the trunk and slammed her to the ground on the rocks and gravel.

Danny wanted to be sick. Beside him, Carrie was grabbing his hand hard and trembling.

The rich guy pulled out the plastic sheet the woman had been on in the trunk, spread it out beside her, and then rolled her body onto the plastic like it was so much garbage.

The dead woman seemed young, with long blonde hair and nice clothes. She might have been pretty because she had a thin body, and she seemed very, very stiff. Nothing about her seemed to bend.

Danny still couldn't see the man clearly enough to pick him out of a crowd.

The man was whistling a little louder, clearly enjoying himself. The whistling sent chills through Danny's back. He knew they were witnessing pure evil.

The man pulled the woman and the tarp toward the edge of the bluff over the water. Then, with a strength that surprised Danny, the man picked up the woman and tossed her into the water below.

The sound of her body splashing in the black lake water carried through the night air like a death knell.

"We've got to get out of here," Danny whispered to Carrie. "If he sees us, he'll kill us."

She nodded, still staring at the man on the edge of the bluff as he took a couple

of rocks, wrapped the plastic around them, and then tossed the plastic into the lake as well.

"Wait," Carrie whispered. "Let's try to get the plate number. He hasn't noticed us so far. Maybe we're better off letting him leave first."

Danny nodded. He agreed with that now that he thought about it. They would not be able to be silent moving through the brush back to their car. They were in their hidden secret place. If they stayed still, the man wouldn't see them.

They waited and watched until the man took off his protective clothing, boots and all, wrapped rocks inside of them, and tossed the clothing in the water as well.

Then, still whistling, he climbed back into his car and shut the door.

The sound of the high-powered Mercedes engine cut through the night air. He quickly turned the car around in a wide area and went back up the road slowly, without lights or parking lights on.

It surprised Danny that a modern car could even move without at least some running lights on, but this car was nothing more than dark ghost moving along the narrow gravel road in the faint moonlight.

Danny thought his heart was going to pound right out of his chest. He was terrified the killer would see them, make them his next victims.

As the car headed slowly up the rough road, Danny eased out to see if he could read the license plate number.

Nothing but a faint dark outline of the car disappearing into the night.

When it vanished into the distance, Carrie let go of a long, shuddering breath, then burst into silent tears.

Danny let out a breath he didn't know he was holding and they both sat there, holding each other, shuddering.

Danny could see no evidence of what had just happened in the lake below.

He and Carrie had both been born and raised in Las Vegas. They heard about crime on the nightly news, but never had been this close to anything like this.

After a few minutes, Danny figured enough time had passed. He couldn't hear the Mercedes at all.

They moved as silently as they could to their car and then sat there for another few minutes.

Nothing moving in the dark night.

Danny finally started the car and faster than he had ever driven the gravel road, he headed for the main highway.

Within minutes, Danny and Carrie were speeding back into town along the old Boulder Highway, Danny driving as fast as he could do safely.

Next stop: the Las Vegas Police Department.

He just hoped they would get there alive.

CHAPTER TWO

May 21, 2002
9:48 P.M.
Near Lake Mead, Outside of Las Vegas, Nevada

WILLIS WILLIAMS sat behind the wheel of his Mercedes, his engine off, the car tucked back into some brush along the side of the road, watching the entrance to the dark road that led down to the lake. Danny and Carrie Coswell had watched him from a spot on the bank above the lake. They would show up soon enough.

Of that he had no doubt.

He was impressed. It took almost fifteen minutes before the Toyota that had been parked off to one side of the dirt road screeched out onto the highway like the devil was chasing it.

Fifteen minutes must have felt like an eternity to them, making sure the big bad guy in the Mercedes was gone.

That made him laugh.

The Toyota headed down the two-lane highway toward town.

He couldn't see them clearly, but he laughed at how they must be feeling. He knew it was Danny and Carrie's first wedding anniversary. It would be one Danny would remember for a very long time and Carrie for her very short life.

He had enjoyed them watching his little play down near the lake. And he knew exactly where that Toyota was going now. Straight to the Las Vegas police, who had already been sniffing around him as a suspect for three disappearances.

The police had nothing solid, and even now he knew they would have no more, but he had better get home and get ready for a visit from the police.

He loved taunting his victims and the police almost as much as he loved killing.

Maybe even more.

He was careful, very careful, with every detail.

And the police were stupid and too bound up by their own rules to ever get to him.

He waited until the Toyota was completely out of sight and then turned on his lights and pulled onto the highway, making sure to stay right at the speed limit on the way back into town.

It took only one pass near the main downtown police station to see the Toyota parked on the street. He laughed, then turned for his home, a beautiful gated, ten-acre estate overlooking Las Vegas.

He had a stage to set and details to take care of before his police guests arrived. He was going to enjoy their visit, of that he had no doubt.

He always loved a good game.

Especially when the cards were rigged and the wager not even known.

Part Two
THE STAKES

CHAPTER THREE

Thirteen Years Later…

May 12, 2015
5:45 P.M.
Las Vegas, Nevada

RETIRED DETECTIVE Bayard Lott hummed softly to himself as he unpacked the supplies he had just bought for the poker game this evening, spreading them out over his light granite countertop in his kitchen. Chips, soda, pretzels, and a bag of peanut M&Ms for "The Sarge" as everyone called him.

Lott had never imagined four years ago when Carol, the love of his life and wife for thirty years died, that he would ever be happy again. But he honestly was and mostly didn't feel guilty about being happy anymore either.

On his wooden kitchen table, smelling like heaven sent to tempt him, was a large tub of Kentucky Fried Chicken, original recipe. Damn he loved KFC and his daughter, Annie, accused him of living on the stuff. He had to admit, many meals during a regular week were KFC.

Once a week, he hosted from four to six retired detectives in his basement poker room for a friendly game, depending on who could make it each week. The group called themselves the Cold Poker Gang. Besides playing cards, they also worked on cold cases for the Las Vegas Police Department.

They used the poker games to discuss process on different cases and brainstorm ways to break the case open.

They had been so successful over the last two years solving old cases that the Chief of Police had given members of the Cold Poker Gang special status. Not active and paid, but not fully retired and shunned.

The Chief allowed them to carry their guns if needed and keep their badges and act on behalf of the department as long as they stayed inside the regulations.

Lott loved being part of the Cold Poker Gang. When he had retired five years ago to take care of Carol in her last year of cancer, he felt like he still had a lot of years left to give the city.

So now the Cold Poker Gang allowed him to do just that, only in a much more relaxed fashion, and without all the annoying paperwork.

He had just filled a large plastic bowl with peanut M&Ms when there were two quick knocks on the back door and Retired Detective Julia Rogers walked in. She had her long brown hair pulled back and tied and her face was slightly red. She had on jeans and a light-tan blouse that he could see a running bra through.

He and Julia weren't really dating, but he thought of them as a couple and so did she. They were getting closer to making their dating status official.

"Isn't it early in the year to be getting this hot?" she asked, clearly enjoying the cool air-conditioning of his kitchen when she came in.

Lott had to admit, outside it did feel hot, especially after the fairly cool spring they had just had. But this was Las Vegas. It got hot.

Julia was retired from the Reno Police Force because of a bullet that had shattered her leg and caused her to walk with just a slight limp. The two of them had been getting closer and closer since they had solved her husband's cold case murder (actually fake murder) six months before.

Compared to Lott's six foot frame, sixty-four years of age, and tight gray hair, Julia was five-three at best, had no gray that she let show in her long brown hair, and was only fifty-five years old.

They both spent hours each day exercising. He walked and lifted weights, she ran and did aerobics to stay in shape. He really loved the shape she was in, that was for sure. He considered her the most attractive woman he knew.

Because they both wanted to have a healthy relationship when they finally allowed it to happen, both of them were getting professional counseling help. He needed it to help him deal better and accept Carol's death.

Julia said the counseling was to help her get past what her husband had done to her and her daughter when he faked his death and left them before her daughter was even born.

He and Julia had agreed that to have anything solid between them that would

last, they needed to move their pasts into the past.

So in six months, they had been slowly becoming a couple, but had not yet brought sex into the relationship. But they both seemed to know that was all right. They wanted to build something good, without too many ghosts from their pasts getting in the way.

And honestly, Lott enjoyed the teasing and flirting they did. It made him feel really young again.

Every week, Julia came over early before the game to help him set up. And they often went out to dinner after the game either with other players or on their own.

A few nights a week they had movie night, either here or in her home near the university. And a few other nights a week they both played together in a poker tournament down at the Golden Nugget.

Julia was a fine poker player and often he hung around to watch her win money in the end.

They were becoming friends, close friends, before ever moving forward with any relationship. They talked and saw each other every day and spent a lot of time together. They were a couple. They just hadn't called it that yet.

And Lott liked that as well.

Lott had a hunch that Carol would have been glad he was slowly healing as well. His not moving on was her biggest worry in her last days of life. He had promised her he would, because she had made him, but he never thought he actually would.

Him not moving on with life had been his daughter Annie's worry as well for a couple years after Carol died. Annie had got him to build the poker room downstairs and start to remodel some of the house. Lott had still not touched the living room, where Carol had spent most of her last year sitting and watching television, covered in a blanket. But eventually he knew he would even remodel that.

Eventually.

Annie loved Julia, and half the time they would laugh about something that Lott just missed. Lott figured that if his really smart daughter liked Julia, he couldn't be far off in his own taste.

Julia went to the fridge, got out a bottle of cold water, and drank a third of it before turning to him while leaning against the fridge.

He glanced back from where he was opening packages of snacks for the game and realized in her wonderful green eyes that something was really wrong.

She was pretending to smile, but after six months he knew her well enough to know that was just a show.

He quickly grabbed some paper plates, some napkins, and a few forks, and pointed to the table. "Sit and tell me what's going on."

"That obvious, huh?"

"Everything all right with Jane?" Lott asked as they sat down.

Jane was her daughter and a grad student at UNLV. Lott liked her a great deal, and so did Annie.

"Jane's great," Julia said, waving away any suggestion of something wrong there as she dug into the tub and grabbed a wing.

Lott took one of the legs and bit into the wonderful taste, letting the oil and tender meat from the chicken melt in his mouth. Wow, he had been hungrier than he had thought.

He quickly finished off the leg, putting the remains on the edge of his plate.

Julia didn't like legs and he didn't like wings. Somewhere in their first month

together, he had teased her once about that being enough to base a relationship on and she had agreed, then laughed at his shocked look.

Licking his fingers and then using the paper towel to wipe off his face, he looked at the woman he was falling for more every week. "So what's the problem?"

"Remember I told you about my friend Trish Vittie?"

Lott remembered clearly. In fact, he and Julia had talked about her a number of times because Julia so often got worried about Trish. Julia called worrying about Trish one of her hobbies.

The two had been friends in high school and stayed friends, at least e-mail and call friends. From what Lott remembered of the conversations about Trish, she was very different than Julia. Trish was a floating free spirit that liked to bounce through husbands as well as adventures.

"I do," he said, staring into the worried green eyes of Julia. "What's happened?"

"She was supposed to contact me last week and didn't," Julia said. "So I tried to contact her in all our normal manners and nothing. No internet, no phone, nothing."

Lott nodded and waited for Julia to finish.

"So I called the friends she has set up as contacts when she moved back into the mountains in Idaho a year ago and they haven't seen or heard from her in two weeks either. And I tricked someone at the post office to see if her mail had been picked up and it hadn't been picked up."

Lott sat back, worried, and not really knowing what to say. "Isn't she living in a remote part of Idaho? Somewhere up in the mountains?"

"She is," Julia said. "About three hours out into the mountains from McCall, Idaho."

Lott sat forward as if his chair had been wired with electricity. "Is Trish wearing her hair long and blonde?"

Julia nodded, now looking really worried.

"Shit, shit, shit," Lott said, grabbing his phone. He had a hunch that chilled him to the bone. More than likely, Julia's friend was fine.

More than likely.

In fact, probable.

But if his hunch was right, this wasn't good.

Not good at all.

CHAPTER FOUR

May 12, 2015
6 P.M.
Las Vegas, Nevada

LOTT QUICKLY DIALED Andor's number as Julia sat there stunned at his sudden outburst and movement.

Andor was his old partner and a member of the Cold Poker Gang as well.

When Andor answered the phone Lott said, "Check out The Phantom files from downtown on the way here."

Across the table Julia had a deep worried look on her beautiful face.

"Going to take me an hour to get copies," Andor said. "Worth being late for the game?"

"Worth it," Lott said.

"On my way," Andor said and hung up.

Julia stared at Lott as he put his cell phone back in his shirt pocket.

"One of the great unsolved cases in Las Vegas," Lott said, "is called by the name The Phantom. Actually it's a string of unsolved cases. All disappearances. No bodies ever found."

Julia frowned. Clearly she had never heard of it.

"In Seattle, they call him, The Wind. In Boise, they call him The Ghost."

"Him?" Julia asked.

Lott nodded, remembering the smirking face of maybe the greatest and smartest serial killer of all time. "His name is Willis Williams."

Julia shook her head. "Never heard of him."

"That's because he doesn't have a home in Reno," Lott said, trying to keep the anger at the man out of his voice. "He has an estate here, a huge mansion in Seattle, and his estate above Boise covers acres in the hills. Plus he has another mansion in McCall, Idaho, on the lake."

"You think Trish's disappearance might have something to do with this guy?"

Lot shrugged. "I honestly don't know. I doubt it, to be honest. But since 2000, women with long blonde hair have vanished without a trace in all three major cities."

"You think this Williams guy is to blame?" Julia asked.

"Clues, but no evidence linked Willis Williams to almost all the disappearances. He has never even come close to being charged or even named a person of interest, though every cop in all three cities knows he did the crimes. He loves taunting us. Takes pleasure in it, actually."

"That bad?" Julia asked. "Really?"

Lott nodded. "One night he dumped a female mannequin with a long blonde wig into Lake Mead while two kids watched him. He did it just to drive us all crazy. Then two weeks later one of the kids, a girl named Carrie Coswell disappeared while out for a run. She also had long blonde hair."

"Oh, no," Julia said. "When was this?"

"Carrie disappeared in 2002. Andor and I were lead detectives on the case."

"You think Trish might have become part of this?" Julia asked, clearly trying to give herself some strength after what Lott had just told her.

"No woman has disappeared from the McCall area before, so more than likely Trish is fine. But it was the first thing that came to mind and we need to go find out."

"Go?" Julia asked.

He smiled and took another piece of chicken, this time a breast. "You up for a trip to Idaho to see if we can find Trish? I'm sure she's all right, but let's go find out."

Julia hesitated for only a moment, then said, "Very much so. I was thinking of doing that myself as it was."

Lott licked off his fingers, wiped off his mouth and hands, and then grabbed his phone again to call his daughter.

He knew Annie and her boyfriend, Doc Hill, were in a poker tournament down at the Bellagio, but Lott also knew that on this topic Annie wouldn't mind being interrupted at all, even as slight the chance that this might be related to Williams, she would want to be involved from the start. Annie had been on a couple of the cases involving Williams.

Doc Hill, Annie's boyfriend, was the best tournament player on the planet and with his partner, Fleetwood Kort, had built a very large empire of investments and real estate. Lott had decided he flat didn't want to know how rich Doc and Fleet were.

Fleet had once said they were up in the scary-rich neighborhood.

Annie used to be a Las Vegas detective as well until she met Doc on a case and retired to make a fortune playing poker with Doc. And from what Annie had said one night in passing, Fleet was helping her with investments with the winnings to shelter some of it from taxes.

Lott also decided he didn't want to know just how rich his daughter had gotten in the last few years either.

When Annie answered, she said, "Hold on, Dad." He could hear her excuse herself from the table and walk out into the casino area, since cell phones were not allowed in the poker room.

"How's it going?" he asked.

"I'm hanging on, trying to make it into the money," Annie said. "Doc is just powering over everyone as he does. We're down to just two tables, and luckily Doc is on the other table at the moment, so I might have a chance. So what's happening? Thought you had a poker game yourself tonight."

"We do, starting in about an hour or so," Lott said. Then he quickly detailed out that Julia's friend had gone missing up around McCall, Idaho. We're thinking of going to look for her tomorrow."

"I hope she's all right," Annie said.

"More than likely she is," Lott said. "Her name is Trish and she has long blonde hair."

"Damn it all to hell," Annie said, instantly knowing what Lott was talking about. And she had jumped to the exact same hunch he had jumped to. She had worked two of the Phantom's missing person cases while a detective, and she had taken both very personally, which Willis Williams seemed to take a joy from.

"Let me get Doc out here," Annie said.

Lott could hear her going back into the poker room.

He smiled at Julia's worried expression across the table, but said nothing.

A moment later Lott could hear Annie explaining to Doc what had happened and what the background was. He also heard Annie tell Doc that chances are nothing had happened, but they needed to make sure.

Then Lott heard Doc say, "Tell your dad and Julia we'll put all our resources behind their investigation. I'll get hold of Fleet. Tell them to be at the airport before 5 a.m."

Annie spoke back into the phone. "You hear any of that, dad?"

"I did and we'll be there. Thank you both."

"Let's just hope this doesn't involve Williams," Annie said and hung up.

Lott had a hunch he had just ruined Annie's chance of hanging on in the tournament.

He put his phone away and smiled at Julia. "Our ride has been arranged."

Julia reached across the table and touched his arm. "Thank you."

"You are welcome," he said. "But thank Doc and Annie. They are putting anything we need behind us."

And both Lott and Julia knew that meant vast resources, far more than any regular detectives could ever ask for or take legally while on the job.

Then Lott pointed to the tub of chicken. "Now eat before others get here and we have to share this with them. I want to save some for the plane tomorrow."

She shook her head and laughed, digging into the bucket of chicken looking for another wing.

Lott watched her, smiling. There was no doubt he was smitten with this wonderful woman.

No doubt in the slightest.

CHAPTER FIVE

May 13, 2015
4:30 a.m.
Las Vegas International Airport

JULIA STOOD with her jacket pulled tight around her, shivering slightly in the cold predawn air. Even though the day would be warm, at 4:30 a.m. out on an open runway, it could get pretty darned cold in early May. She had brought the jacket for the Idaho mountains, but was very glad she had it at the moment.

Behind her was Doc Hill's private jet hanger, now standing open and empty since the large private jet sat on the taxi-way about fifty paces in front of her. It looked like the two pilots were going through a pre-flight-check in the cockpit.

Lott had picked Julia up at her house a half hour ago. Annie had met them inside the hanger and Lott was now briefing her on what some of the plans were and where they were headed exactly in Idaho. While he was doing that, Julia had gone out to get their bags from Lott's Cadillac.

She couldn't believe Lott had jumped in so fast to help with her friend Trish. His willingness to help was one of the many things she loved about him.

And she had to admit, she was falling in love with him.

He seemed to be falling for her as well. They didn't talk about it, but it seemed they both knew and were just going slow. She liked that.

During the game last night, on Lott's prompting, she had told the other three players about her friend Trish going missing.

The moment she had said Trish had long blonde hair and lived outside of McCall, Idaho, the other three had instantly jumped to the same conclusion Lott had come to. But they all agreed that chances are they were overeating.

They said that chances are Trish was fine.

And their initial reaction scared Julia more than she wanted to admit. She did not want to lose her old friend Trish.

Andor, Lott's former partner, was the oldest of the Cold Poker Gang at seventy. But he was very spry and walked like a bull, always seeming to storm forward when he moved. Lott towered over him, since Andor barely made five-five. But with his brown sports jacket and pants that never matched and his shining bald head, he seemed far more intimidating.

Julia had really come to like Andor, even though they seldom said much to each other.

Sarge was ex-military from Nam and never talked about it. He was mid-sixties and had some scars on his face from different fights. Lott had full gray hair he kept cut short. Sarge had thinning hair with a large bald spot in the center of his head that always looked sunburned.

Julia had never been able to get a real sense of him, even though he came to the games every week since his wife had died. He seemed very closed up.

Benson was the fifth member of the Cold Poker Gang that had showed up for the game. Besides Julia, he was the youngest of the bunch, but looked older than Lott with a large gut and a limp. He had taken early retirement to work on real estate investing and gotten bored enough to want to do more detective work at times. He was married with two grown kids and only made about half the games since his wife liked to travel.

Julia liked Benson because he had a mind that could fit unrelated details into patterns. They had solved a few cases because of Benson's skill at that.

They cut the game short and all five of them pored over the files Andor had brought from the department. Lott said he never thought the Cold Poker Gang would ever think of tackling Willis Williams. But now they had a connection and couldn't not go after him.

Julia was glad they were all so willing to help.

She just really, really hoped they would get to Trish's home up in the mountains and they would find her there, well. But her gut told her that was not going to be the outcome.

After they had finished going over the files on the various disappearances linked to Willis Williams, they divided the nine Las Vegas cases up among the three staying behind in Vegas.

While Julia and Lott were in Idaho, the other three were to go over the cases again, trying to find anything at all someone might have missed, some sort of similarity they could tie together.

And Andor had suggested that he work with a detective from both Boise and Seattle and get their files. "Call it an "old person's task force.""

"Think they would go for that?" Julia had asked.

"I'll get the Captain to call them. The least they can do is send files."

"My gut sense," Lott said, "with Willis Williams, they'll do more than send files."

She had headed home at ten right after the game instead of going out to dinner with Lott as was their habit over the last few months. Since he was picking her up so early, she wanted to at least try to get a little sleep and pack.

She had managed the packing, but the sleep had mostly eluded her.

Now the cold wind was waking her up and she was ready to go.

She really needed to find out what had happened to Trish.

CHAPTER SIX

May 13, 2015
7:15 A.M.
Boise, Idaho

THE SUN was just coloring the mountains above Boise when they touched down. He and Julia had tried to nap some on the flight, but mostly they had ended up talking about Trish.

From what Julia said, Trish was like a wild sister she never had. They had been friends in college and while Julia didn't date much and studied too much, Trish partied all the time and was married the first time by her sophomore year.

It seemed she had six marriages after that one, tossing men away after she got tired of them.

Julia and Trish were exact opposites and that had kept them in touch and talking over the years. Julia valued the wild side of Trish and the friendship and Trish seemed to value the stableness of Julia.

Julia said Trish had planned to calm down and just read and relax after the last divorce, which is why she rented a house so far from anything. Julia said Trish was going into Boise twice a month for supplies and to go to counseling sessions. Otherwise, Trish claimed she was staying home most of the time.

Lott had asked Julia if she believed that Trish was trying to change.

"I believe she is, yes," Julia said, nodding. "Is she succeeding, I doubt it. Stripes and a zebra sort of thing."

As the jet taxied up to Doc's private hanger at the Boise airport, Lott caught a glimpse of Fleetword Kort standing just outside the building, waiting for them.

Lott was surprised that Fleet was there to meet them. It seemed Fleet had a Jeep SUV for them gassed up and ready to go.

Fleet was a tall, lanky man who towered over Lott. Lott had never seen Fleet out of a silk suit with his hair combed perfectly. This morning was no exception.

He was Doc's closest friend from high school and college, but the two were about as opposite as they came. Doc seldom wore anything but jeans and button-down shirts with the sleeves rolled up. And while Doc was solid and muscled and tanned from guiding rafts on the River of No Return in the summer, Fleet looked so thin that lifting a weight might break something.

After they put their luggage in the back seat of the Jeep, Fleet showed them that he had stocked the back of the Jeep with all sorts of equipment they might need while up in the mountains, from extra food to flashlights to sleeping bags and tents.

Then he handed both Lott and Julia special satellite phones. "These should work in most areas, depending on the terrain and height of the mountains. Think of them for emergency use only. I'll have a helicopter standing by here if you need something."

"Thank you," Lott said, tucking the phone in his bag in his car.

Julia nodded and looked puzzled at Fleet. "Is where we are going that remote?"

Lott knew Julia had sent Doc and Annie directions to Trish's rented home on the edge of a lake in the mountains. So no doubt Fleet had looked it up.

"About as remote as it gets in the lower forty-eight states," Fleet said. "That you can actually drive to."

Lott was not sure he liked the sounds of that in the slightest. Julia only nodded, but clearly didn't like that either.

Then, as they were about to head out, a State Police car pulled up next to the Jeep and an officer got out, leaving his hat in the car, and came toward them, smiling.

It took Lott a second before he recognized Ben Stephens, a former Las Vegas detective and one of the nicest men Lott had ever known.

Ben had reached detective status about ten years before Lott retired and Lott and Andor had taken him with them on numbers of cases as he got his feet under him. In essence, they had trained him.

Five years ago, just about the point that Lott and Andor both retired, Ben had taken a job up here in Idaho to be closer to family. He still had the military flat top cut to his dark hair and shoulders that looked like he could play pro football.

Lott gave Ben a big hug, then introduced him to Julia, who shook his hand.

Before Lott could introduce Ben to Fleet, Fleet said, "Ben, glad you could make it."

"Anything for you and Doc," Ben said to Fleet.

Then Ben turned to Lott and Julia. "We're going to have extra State Police patrols in and around the McCall area, in case you need backup. I know this isn't official business, but considering what you are doing, we felt it only logical to be close."

"Thank you," Fleet said. "And you have told no one of the reason for all this?"

"In this state," Ben said, "only the four of us really know what you are suspecting. Too dangerous any other way."

Lott was too surprised to even say anything quickly.

"In fact," Ben said, "I'm going to be up there on patrol myself over the next week. I'll be staying with a cousin in McCall, but can scramble to help at any moment, day or night."

He handed Lott a piece of paper with a private cell phone number and the Idaho State Police phone number on it.

"Did Fleet tell you there is an outside chance we might have another Willis Williams problem?" Lott asked, folding the paper and putting it in his wallet. "Chances are she's fine."

"Andor called last night, right after Fleet called," Ben said, nodding. "We don't want you two walking into a hornet's nest without some resources."

"Thank you," Julia said. "With luck, we'll find my friend alive and well."

"That's what we are all hoping," Ben said, nodding. "And expecting, actually. But better to be safe on this."

"How are the county and local police in the area up there?" Lott asked.

"Small town slow and decent," Ben said, shrugging, "at least from what we can tell over the years. Nothing that would make them suspects in anything.

But I wouldn't trust them with much of anything."

Lott and Julia both nodded.

Ben wished them both well and headed back for his patrol car.

Lott turned back to Fleet. "Looks like we have a lot covered. Thank you."

"Yes, thank you," Julia said.

Fleet nodded. "We have tried to think of as much as we can. Now it's up to you two."

"We'll try to stay out of trouble," Lott said.

"Well, as much as we can considering who we are," Julia said, winking at Fleet.

Fleet blushed and shook his head and then turned for his car.

All Lott could do was laugh.

CHAPTER SEVEN

May 13, 2015
1:30 P.M.
McCall, Idaho

WITH ONLY ONE STOP for lunch, they had reached the small resort town of McCall in the early afternoon and checked into Shore Lodge, right on the edge of Payette Lake. Fleet had made them reservations there for the night because he had said it was too far to drive into Trish's home in one push.

After the smooth, but winding drive from Boise up through the mountains, Julia was glad they had decided to do that.

The road was only two lanes wide and barely that in some places. She was tired from lack of sleep last night and didn't want to take a chance of having to drive any road in this area after dark. Neither her nor Lott's eyesight was good enough for that kind of strain at their age. And she could tell the drive had tired Lott out some as well.

Shore Lodge didn't look like much from the highway, but it stretched three stories tall along the white beach, with long docks and ski boats tied up in neat rows in the blue water. The May afternoon air had a bite to it and some of the mountains around McCall still had snow on them, which worried her as they got their bags out of the car and headed up the concrete steps and through the massive log front doors.

Inside the high ceilings and huge polished old logs just stunned her. She had seen fake interiors like this one, but never something genuine and really made out of logs so large she could barely imagine the size of the trees they came from.

A middle-aged clerk was at the long wooden front desk that looked out over the calm blue waters of the lake. He told them the lodge had been built over a hundred years before out of massive pine trees and except for a short period as condo units, had been a hotel the entire time.

Julia was flat impressed. The furnishings in the lobby were warm and cozy patterned cloth, the bases also made out of logs, and there was a wonderful smell of fresh steak in the air coming from a restaurant nearby. A crackling log fire in the massive stone fireplace to one side of the huge lobby looked wonderful and welcoming.

Julia felt instantly at home.

The hallway to their rooms was narrow and like walking down through history, with old black and white photos on the walls of the last hundred years of the area.

Life in these mountains had clearly been rugged. Far more than Julia could imagine.

Their rooms were side-by-side on the second floor and as comfortable as the main lobby. The beds were even feather-beds, which she couldn't believe.

What hotel had featherbeds anymore?

Lott stored his bag and came over into Julia's room as she moved out onto her room's deck that overlooked the bright blue waters of the natural lake.

The air smelled so fresh and cool, it seemed almost fake.

Pine-covered mountains towered into the sky around her far higher than she had imagined possible. She had lived in Reno for years and had been used to the mountains going up to Tahoe, but these mountains dwarfed those by factors.

The crisp air smelled of summer pine. Around the lake she could see hundreds of homes built into the trees, each had a dock sticking out into the dark blue water.

Just standing there staring at the natural beauty seemed to drain the tensions from the worry about Trish and the long drive. Here, Las Vegas seemed like a distant dream. She had a hunch this was the dream and the city was reality.

Lott stood beside her, leaning on the wooden railing and looking out over the lake as he took a deep breath of the cool mountain air. "Doesn't get much better, does it?"

She looked up at him. "It doesn't."

His dark eyes looked at her and they held that gaze for a moment. She almost reached up and pulled his head down to kiss him, then decided now was not the time. Not with her worrying about Trish and them both being so tired.

"I'm going to take a two-hour nap with the this patio door open and that

wonderful air flowing in here," she said, "then take a shower and meet you for an early dinner in three hours in that restaurant off the lobby. How does that sound to you?"

"Perfect," he said. "He glanced at his watch. "Two p.m. local time now. See you at five in the restaurant."

With that he turned and headed out of the room, pulling the large, wood hallway door closed behind him with a solid thump.

That could have gone another way very easily. She knew that. But there would be time.

And clearly Lott understood that as well. One of the many things she was growing to love about him.

He understood her.

CHAPTER EIGHT

May 13, 2015
5 P.M.
McCall, Idaho

THE DINNER that night had been fantastic, sitting at a table against the window looking out over the lake. The chairs were solid wood with comfortable cloth padding and the wooden table was covered in a tan tablecloth with a single candle to one side.

Lott felt a lot better after a nap and a shower and clearly Julia did as well. She seemed to be almost beaming and enjoying every detail around them.

Both of them had tried the pan-fried trout on the recommendation of their waitress, a young college woman with short brown hair working the summer between semesters.

Lott couldn't believe how the trout just melted on his fork and in his mouth. He could never remember eating any fish that fresh before, and the buttered potatoes were perfect as well, accented by steamed spears of asparagus.

After they shared a piece of key lime pie, they headed out and down toward the dock in front of the lodge. The sun was already behind the mountains and the air had turned cool, but neither of them seemed to care as they walked along the narrow shoreline as the small waves lapped at the coarse sand.

They walked in silence for a few minutes, then turned back.

"You up for a movie to relax?" Lott asked. "I saw they had some old classics to rent at the front desk."

He didn't feel like sleeping after the nap just a short time before, but he knew they needed to rest. Who knew what tomorrow was going to bring. With luck, nothing but finding Julia's old friend alive and well.

Julia shook her head. "Actually, I was thinking about a drive. Let's cruise around this area a little bit, go past William's estate, get the lay of this small town just in case."

Lott stopped and looked down into the green eyes of the woman he cared about. She clearly was focused and worried.

"A good idea," he said, nodding. "Then we come back and relax with a movie."

She smiled. "Deal."

Two hours later, they were watching a classic Fred MacMurray movie in Julia's room. She fell asleep on her bed about halfway through and Lott shut the movie off, told her to get ready for bed, and headed for his room.

He really wanted to just curl up with her, but the time would come for that. After they found her friend.

CHAPTER NINE

May 14, 2015
8:45 A.M.
McCall, Idaho

THEY HAD a great breakfast in the lodge of eggs, bacon, and homemade bread as they sat looking out over the smooth blue waters of the lake. The weather was crisp and there was frost on the ground, but the day promised to be sunny. Lott had watched the weather and knew a small storm was scheduled to come through during the night, but nothing bad, and the next day was to be clear and sunny as well.

Then they filled up the gas in the Jeep, got some snacks from a grocery store, and called both Fleet and Annie to tell them they were headed out.

"Drive carefully," Fleet had said.

Lott had assured him he would and they set up a time to contact Fleet and Annie the next afternoon, since they planned on staying at Trish's house for the night, even if she wasn't there.

The road that headed east toward Trish's place turned bad almost from the start. The moment they left McCall, the pavement ended and the road turned to gravel. It was wide and Lott could make good time on it, avoiding the chatter bumps where he could.

There was some traffic, but not much after they were twenty miles out of town.

For the first hour the road kept climbing gently up a valley with mountains that towered over both sides of them, mostly covered in pine trees. As they got higher, the road got narrower and narrower as the valley narrowed down. They crossed back and forth over a fast-moving stream with spring runoff coming off the mountains.

Snow still clung to areas of shade under the trees and in the ditch along the road. And ahead they could see snow-covered peaks. Lott had no idea if they were traveling into trouble or not.

Just after two hours, the road peaked over a tall summit with a sign that said, "Road Open."

"Good to know," Julia said, shaking her head with a worried look.

They were so high, Lott could feel the thinness of the air.

From the sign, the road stayed along the top of the ridge of rock and scattered scruffy pine trees for a short while and then started down a cliff-face, far, far too steep for anything but brush to grow on.

The road, if that was the right term for the goat trail they were on, was barely wide enough for their Jeep and there were no guardrails at all. The road seemed to be cut out of the cliff face and twisted in and out of any tiny crevice in the hillside.

Once Lott had started down the road, there was no place to stop or even think of turning around.

Talk about feeling trapped.

He wasn't sure if he was up for this kind of stress, but at the moment they clearly had no choice.

On Julia's side, the drop had to be a good two thousand feet down into a tree-covered valley floor, the trees so tiny below they looked like kids' toys.

She was holding on to the door handle beside her so tight, her knuckles were white.

Lott gripped the steering wheel in the same fashion. He had no memory of ever driving something like this road, and he was more worried about meeting another car coming up than anything else.

After the longest forty-five minutes he had ever spent, he had managed to creep down that excuse of a goat trail to the valley floor where the road widened beside a mountain river.

Neither of them had said a word the entire time.

Julia managed to pry her fingers from the door handle and took a deep breath. "How about we stop and let me just kiss the ground a few times."

Lott laughed, feeling more relieved than he wanted to admit. "My driving that bad?"

"Great driving," she said as he pulled over. "Shit excuse for a road."

With that he could only laugh and agree and not say anything about the fact that he was pretty certain they needed to go back out that way as well. When Fleet had said this was remote, he hadn't been kidding in the slightest.

And if Fleet had warned them about that stretch of cliff road, neither Lott or Julia would have driven in here. Or at least Lott hoped he would have been smart enough to not try it.

They rested in a wide area beside the loud, rushing river before moving on. The sky up through the mountain peaks was bright blue, but the air felt very cold.

The side road to Trish's home cut off the main road about ten miles of winding gravel road farther down the valley.

Her road was back to a one-way dirt goat track and it wound up a narrow canyon until it topped over a small summit. The climb wasn't that far and thankfully, with mountains on both sides, it didn't feel that bad.

Much better than driving along a cliff face. Nothing could match that cliff drive in pure terror factor.

Just over the summit, in front of them was a deep blue mountain lake that seemed to almost sparkle in the afternoon sunlight. It was fairly large and filled the bowl between two tall mountains covered in pine and rock.

From where the road came over the top of the hill, the water was only about a hundred feet below the edge of the gravel.

Lott could see that the road wound down along the lake to a large log structure on the far side of the blue water. A long dock stuck out into the water at the end of a path from the building.

"Wow!" Julia said. "No wonder Trish wanted to live up here."

Lott had to agree. It was stunningly beautiful.

And isolated.

Very, very, very isolated.

CHAPTER TEN

May 14, 2015
2 P.M.
High Mountain Valley
Near the Central Idaho Primitive Area

LOTT PARKED below the log-framed lodge, tucking the Jeep back under some trees and out of the way so it wasn't obvious. He wasn't sure why he did that, but as he realized just how iso-

lated this place was, his little voice started shouting at him to go carefully. And after all the years of being a detective, he had come to trust that little voice.

They climbed out into the cool afternoon air. The intense silence was the first thing that Lott noticed. No sounds at all, not even a slight breeze through the pine trees that formed walls on the hillsides above the log building.

The sun had already disappeared behind one ridgeline, leaving the valley floor in shadow while the tops of the mountains around them were in bright sunlight. Drifts of bright white snow covered those peaks and around Lott snow still hadn't melted under the nearby trees.

"Beautiful, isn't it?" Julia said, standing and taking deep breaths and looking around.

"More than I could have ever imagined," Lott said. "We're going to have to visit her more."

"Fine by me," Julia said. "As long as we stay in Shore Lodge coming and going. That fish last night was amazing."

"Deal," Lott said.

To one side of the wide parking area there was a wood-plank garage and Lott moved over and pulled open the side door. As he feared, the garage was empty except for a few tools and two large snowmobiles. Julia had told him that in the winter this was snowed in and Trish used snowmobiles to get out to a trading post twenty miles along the main valley.

"No car," he said to Julia and she nodded, again looking very worried.

Besides where he had tucked the Jeep in under some pine trees, there was nowhere else a car could be parked that they wouldn't see. A wide gravel parking area in front of the garage looked large enough to hold ten cars.

They climbed the fifty or so log steps up to the large log building. It had clearly been designed and built by someone with money, as it had the look of a mansion more than a log cabin.

The steep, towering roofline seemed to pretend to mimic the pine trees around it and the building itself was tucked back into a hillside.

From what Lott could tell, this place would be buried in snow in the winter and impossible to get to. Trish would have had to shovel to just get down to the garage and the snowmobiles.

They banged on the door a few times and looked in the windows, but no sign of Trish at all.

Julia found a key under the front door mat and opened up.

"Trish!" Julia shouted, but only got an echo.

The house had an empty and cool feel about it.

It was clear she was not here.

And that had been their biggest worry.

Lott nodded to Julia and they both moved inside, clearly acting more like detectives in a crime scene than friends looking for another friend.

The inside of the big log home was as impressive as the outside. Most of the inside was a massive main room showing all the log beams. The logs were polished to a golden brown, and a smooth stone fireplace dominated one side, surrounded by soft furniture. A log staircase went up one wall to what looked like bedroom and bathroom doors along a walkway above the big room.

Lott used his sleeve to flick a light switch and could hear a generator kick in from somewhere behind the home as the lights came on.

They spread out, he looking in the downstairs rooms and kitchen and bathroom while Julia went upstairs. They were both very careful to not touch anything.

He saw nothing that set off alarm bells.

Nothing.

A woman had clearly been living here. No sign of anything to do with a man.

And no sign of struggle at all in any fashion.

"Nothing seems wrong or out of place," Julia said as she joined him in the kitchen area that was open off the large room. "Three bedrooms and two baths upstairs, one clearly Trish's. The other two made up for guests, but clearly not used in a long time."

"So what do you want to do now?" Lott asked, glancing at his watch. It was just after two in the afternoon. He wasn't sure they could get back over that cliff road before it got dangerously dark.

"We look around the grounds first some and then we stay the night," Julia said. "Just as we planned.

Without talking they did a quick walk around the outside of the building, again seeing nothing at all out of place. Trish had clearly locked up and just left in her car. Where she had gone from there was going to be the big question.

They went back to the Jeep and unpacked their things, bringing them in and each claiming a guest room upstairs. Lott volunteered to cook an early dinner and Julia built a fire in the fireplace.

By the time the lake was being sheltered in darkness, they had finished the two steaks and sliced potatoes in butter he had cooked them, eating mostly in silence at the dining table that looked out over the dark water.

Finally Julia said what they had both been thinking. "Something's happened to her."

Lott nodded. "But not here."

"I agree," Julia said. "But where?"

Lott had no idea. More than likely her car had gone off the road somewhere. It was going to take a pretty massive search to find her if that was the case. And after this long, if she had survived the initial wreck, Lott doubted they would find her alive.

But he felt like he needed to do something, so he put his hand on Julia's. "Let's wash these dishes and get a couple of flashlights and go out and look around the lake a little and the shed down by the dock."

She nodded. They both knew her car wasn't here, so any kind of search like that would be pointless, but better that they did it anyway.

Fifteen minutes later they were both bundled up with down parkas and thick gloves. Not at all what two Las Vegas detectives looked like normally.

Outside, the air bit at Lott's face and surprised him that the temperature had plunged so quickly. No wonder the snow hadn't melted yet.

They first headed down the main path toward the dock. A lawn chair sat alone just above the dock. Clearly Trish had sat there alone at times, staring out into the water.

Above the lake on the right, Lott could see the cut in the hillside where the road wound down from the top to the home.

"We've got to find her," Julia said, standing with her hand on the back of the chair.

Lott said simply, "We will."

Seeing that single chair stabbed at Lott. He could only imagine what it was doing to Julia.

They had moved past the chair and down toward the water when Julia stopped and pointed to something floating in the dark water out near the end of the wooden dock.

Lott felt his stomach twist into a knot.

He knew what that looked like. He had seen it far too many times over the years and he didn't want to think about it now.

Quickly, the two of them went out onto the dock just as a slight rain started to fall. Very light, very cold rain.

Lott could feel it against his neck as he bent over the end of the dock and stared into the black water.

A woman's naked body floated facedown, rubbing against the dock like it was a hard-up lover. The bluish-white skin on her leg was streaked by the green moss growing on the wooden pilings and her long blonde hair seemed to appear and disappear in the water around her making it seem like she was getting closer one moment, then farther away the next.

Lott glanced over at the shocked expression on Julia's face, then got down on his hands and knees and leaned over the edge of the dock, trying to get a closer look without really wanting to.

Beside him Julia did the same, her breath coming hard and fast as she struggled to control her emotions.

"See the distinctive star pattern of moles on the left shoulder?" Julia asked. "Trish always called it her star on her shoulder and considered it good luck."

It clearly hadn't been, but he said nothing.

Lott stood, helped Julia back to her feet, and forced himself to take a deep breath and let it out slowly. The night around them suddenly seemed a lot darker, the rain suddenly harder than it had been just a few minutes before.

A spotlight on the back of the main lodge of the building was aimed at the dock, but it wasn't nearly strong enough to cut through the rain and illuminate much of the water. And the beams from their flashlights seemed to be sucked into nothingness.

However, the light was enough for them to see Trish, a white, ghost-like figure floating against the blackness.

"Damn it," Julia said to herself, her voice swallowed by the tapping of the rain on the water. She turned and moved away from the edge of the dock a few paces, then came back.

"Damn it all to hell."

Lott couldn't have agreed more.

Lott eased his arm around Julia and the two of them stood there, on the end of the wooden dock, saying nothing more.

The cold rain pounded his head and the back of his neck as they stared out over the water, not looking down at what was floating near their feet.

Lott knew they were both hoping something would happen.

Anything but what they had found.

Julia shuddered and hugged him with one arm.

He hugged her back.

There was little either of them could say.

It was now time for the detective training to take over. Something had happened to Trish and they had to figure out what.

Lott forced himself to move.

He left Julia standing in the middle of the dock again stepped closer to the edge to study the body. He couldn't think of that body as Trish, Julia's friend. He had to think of it as just a body for the moment.

The white body's up and down rubbing against the footing of the dock was hypnotic and after a moment Lott made himself look away so he wouldn't get dizzy.

He was glad he couldn't see Trish's face. He had seen pictures of what she had looked like alive, and keeping that image in his mind was enough for the moment.

He looked back at where Julia stood, staring out over the dark lake.

He knew that soon they would have to get around to pulling Trish out of the water. Considering how she was floating, Trish must have been in the cold water for at least three days.

Lott had no doubt that living image of her face was going to be forever replaced by a white, bloated one, with black, empty eyes. He had pulled far too many people out of swimming pools to not know that look.

"What the hell happened?" Julia asked, her voice raspy, her head shaking back and forth in clear disbelief.

"Maybe drowned while skinny-dipping," Lott said, without looking back at the body. "Hit her head or got too far out in the cold water to make it back. An accident. Logical as anything else."

Julia nodded, her eyes clearing some. Lott could tell that the detective training was coming back to her as well.

Lott turned and stared down at the floating body of one of Julia's best friends.

This was not the outcome he had hoped for, but one he had feared.

CHAPTER ELEVEN

May 14, 2015
7 P.M.
High Mountain Valley
Near the Central Idaho Primitive Area

JULIA JUST COULDN'T get her mind to accept that the white form floating there in the black water was her friend Trish. Yet she knew it was.

Trish could not be gone. She had been a part of Julia's life forever. Trish had always been this wild element that Julia loved to watch and talk to and laugh with.

Now Julia would never hear Trish's wonderful laugh again. How was that even possible?

She stood there beside Lott in the rain, staring out at the black lake.

She had to get her brain back.

As a detective, she had seen a lot of death. Right now she needed to figure out what happened. She would mourn Trish when the time was right.

"So you think it was an accident?" Julia asked, taking a deep breath of the cold night air to make herself try to think.

"There doesn't seem to be obvious marks on her body," Lott said, "from what I can see in this light."

Julia was glad he didn't shine his flashlight on Trish again.

But then something bothered her about Trish's body.

Something didn't look right.

If she had been in the water and was floating, her body would be bloated, at least enough to make it float. Trish didn't seem to be bloated at all. Maybe the cold water of the mountain lake had kept that effect down.

Julia had seen enough three- and four-day-old-bodies pulled from the water to suit her for a lifetime. She had hated it worse when it was kids.

Suddenly the way Trish was floating there just didn't seem right.

She took out her cell phone and took some pictures of how Trish was floating. Both down close and back a ways.

Lott nodded and did the same on his phone, making sure he got Julia in the picture as well. They needed to document anything they did here.

"Help me look at this," Julia said to Lott after they finished with the pictures.

Once again they both moved so they could see Trish's body.

The rain was easing some, so their flashlights were clear on her naked back.

"See something wrong with this?" Julia said

"Her arms seem to be tucked up under her chest," Lott said. "That's not the way a body floats."

He was right.

She knew that.

Floating bodies mostly float face down, arms out, not tucked under as Trish's arms seemed to be.

Suddenly both of their years of training as detectives seemed to kick in full force.

"Help me turn Trish over," Lott said, his voice soft, yet firm, "I need your help to turn her over."

Julia nodded and both of them got down on their hands and knees on the wet wood of the dock.

Then together they slowly reached down and grabbed Trish, Lott on her left shoulder, Julia just below her left knee.

"Pull up and roll her over," Lott said. "On the count of three."

Julia only nodded.

Julia took her grip on Trish's cold, almost slimy-feeling leg. For an instant she was surprised. She had expected to feel the soft, almost pulpy flesh that she had felt with many bodies after days in water, but Trish's flesh was almost hard and waxy.

"One. Two. Three," Lott said. "Pull up."

Like a canoe, not wanting to right itself, Trish fought them for a moment, then finally flipped over.

Both of them let go at once, drawing back as if they had been shot at. Julia almost felt as if she had been.

"What the hell?" Julia asked, staring at her friend's body floating there.

Lott just stared, shaking his head.

In the dim light it was clearly Trish's face, only drawn and almost mask-like. Not bloated at all.

Trish was smiling slightly, her eyes closed, her face peaceful in the faint light as water washed over it. Far more peaceful than Julia had ever remembered Trish being in life.

Trish's hands were clasped across her stomach, almost as if she were asleep there in the water.

"Not possible," Lott said softly.

He had his phone back out and taking pictures. Both down close and back.

It took Julia a moment to pull her gaze away from Trish's face, then she glanced at Trish's neck, then down her body until Julia found what she was looking for.

"She's been embalmed," Julia said, standing up and turning away.

For the first time in a few minutes, she noticed the pounding rain, the cold mountain air, and the remoteness of the valley.

"Embalmed?" Lott said softly. "What the hell is going on here?"

Julia forced herself to take a deep breath and think.

They were a good hundred-plus miles of winding mountain roads from the nearest funeral home. They hadn't seen another car in the last seventy miles of road. Trish had no neighbors and no one was in this valley but the two of them.

And the house was completely clear of any struggle or signs of something like this being done.

"Embalmed," Lott said, climbing to his feet. "It can't be, but it is clear she is."

Julia turned around and stared at her friend's white body, shaking her head in disbelief. Then she looked up at Lott.

There was a haunted look in his eyes.

"Someone embalmed her," Julia said. "That means she was murdered."

"Looks that way," Lott said. "But the real question is what is she doing in the lake?"

"And why?" Julia said softly.

"Exactly," Lott said. "Why?"

Part Three
PLAYING THE HAND

CHAPTER TWELVE

May 14, 2015
8 P.M.
High Mountain Valley
Near the Central Idaho Primitive Area

THEY HAD COME to find Julia's friend Trish and they had done just that.

And everyone had been worried she had been murdered by Willis Williams. Well, if she had, this was the first body of any of his victims that had ever been found.

It didn't seem like Williams to just leave a body floating in a mountain lake. That seemed far, far too careless for a serial killer flaunting his actions to three major police departments.

But something was nagging at Lott and he couldn't remember what.

Lott kept trying to put pieces together, but none of this made any sense at all.

They had come afraid they would find Trish missing. Lott wasn't sure if this was worse.

He stood on the short dock and stared at Trish's white skin as her body floated face-up in the dark water. Light rain roughed the surface of the mountain lake, and a gentle wind formed waves that rocked Trish up and down against the wooden pier.

Trish's face had a gentle smile on it, her hands were folded below her chest, and her legs appeared and disappeared into the black of the water. She was nude, missing rings and all other jewelry.

Julia stood beside him on the dock, her back to the body of one of her best friends. Lott had no doubt that Julia was managing to hold her emotions in check by sheer will and years of training as a detective.

In all his years as a detective, Lott had never seen anything like this. There was no doubt it was going to be difficult to tell how long Trish had been dead, let alone how long she had been in the cold water.

And the biggest puzzle was why, and how, she had ended up embalmed, floating in a small mountain lake in the primitive area of central Idaho, a hundred plus miles of dirt road away from the nearest funeral home.

Lott stepped toward Julia and touched her arm lightly. "You can go back up to the house while I get her out of there."

Julia shook her head, still not looking at the body. "No, you're going to need help."

Lott had to admit that she was right. He wasn't young anymore, and moving bodies around was never an easy task even when he had been young. But they had to get Trish out of the water to at least attempt to preserve what evidence might be found on the body.

Lott knew this was going to be rough on Julia, but they both knew they needed to do it.

"Take pictures of this every step of the way," Lott said.

Julia nodded and got out her cell phone.

Lott got down on his hands and knees and shoved Trish's body along the dock toward the shore as Julia recorded each move.

After he got Trish's body close to the shore, he sent Julia to get a tarp or a quilt or something from the lodge. She moved off without a word.

He stood there in the dark looking out at the lake, at the embalmed body, at the log home lit up behind him, at the road down the side of the hill.

Nothing made sense. Nothing.

Julia started back down the trail from the log home with a quilt in her arms, so he forced himself to move. He waded into the water, the coldness shocking him.

His legs went numb almost instantly.

Julia stretched a plastic sheet on the ground just above the water line and then put the quilt over that. Then she took a couple quick photos of him standing in the water with Trish.

Then Lott watched her as she took a deep breath and came into the water. She took Trish's legs while Lott lifted Trish by the shoulders.

The body seemed heavier than it should have, and the skin was hard to the touch.

Somehow, they managed to get Trish's body on the quilt in the dim light and rain, take more photos, then wrap Trish in the quilt.

The plastic sheet that Julia had laid down first would make it easier for them to slide Trish along the ground. No way could they carry her.

It took them three rest stops before they got Trish's body stored in the maintenance shed. Lott was sweating about as hard as he could remember sweating and he was out of breath.

Julia was panting as well.

As hard as it was to do, both of them knew it was better to have the body stored than leave it in the water where it might sink and never be found again.

After a few more pictures, Lott locked up the shed and rolled a large stump against the door so no wild animal could dig at it, then they turned and headed back up toward the lodge.

Neither of them had said a word since the dock.

All Lott could think about was how lucky they were that Trish didn't smell like most bodies found floating. Some of the ones he had helped get out before had been in the water for so long that he had had to soak a rag in gasoline and cover his nose with it to even get near the rotting mess.

But not Trish.

No smell at all.

He had no idea what that meant.

They hung their coats up near the door to dry and then went upstairs to change into dry clothes.

"Get your satellite phone," Lott said to Julia as she climbed the stairs ahead of him. "And your gun."

She glanced back at him and then nodded.

Lott made it back downstairs first, shivering even though he had on dry pants and socks and shoes and a thick shirt and a knit sweater. He started some hot water for tea and stoked the fire in the big stone fireplace.

He laid his phone on the table beside his holstered gun.

Julia came down wearing jeans, a thick sweater, and she had dried her hair and pulled it back. Her face looked white and she clearly was as chilled as he felt.

She put her satellite phone and gun on the kitchen table next to his and they both stood there silently waiting for the tea water to heat. There was nothing either one of them could say.

This situation was so strange, Lott was convinced that they were in shock from what they had found, as well as in mild shock from the cold and the exercise.

Finally, as the water started to boil and he turned to get them mugs, Julia said, "We might be contaminating a crime scene here."

"I doubt it," Lott said as he poured them tea. "Besides, it's too late now. We already did that."

"That it is," Julia said, taking the tea from him and warming her hands on the mug. "That it is."

CHAPTER THIRTEEN

May 14, 2015
9 P.M.
High Mountain Valley
Near the Central Idaho Primitive Area

AFTER GETTING a few sips of the hot tea down him, Lott dug out some crackers from a bag he had brought and some cheddar cheese he had stored in the fridge and cut up the cheese for them to use as a snack.

After the cold and the workout they had had, they both needed something to keep them going.

As he started to warm up, a few more pieces were coming clear and making this puzzle even more bizarre.

If that were even possible.

He and Julia needed to talk about what they were going to do next.

"Well," Julia said, "at least we know it wasn't Willis Williams who did this."

Lott shook his head. "I don't think we can rule him out in the slightest."

Julia looked up at him, clearly puzzled. "Why do you say that?"

"None of this makes any sense at all," Lott said. "And the puzzle piece that bothers me the most is where is Trish's car."

Julia sat back, clearly her detective brain coming back strong as the tea warmed her up.

"Someone drove her up here already embalmed and dumped her in the lake?" Julia asked. "But why?"

"And being embalmed, they clearly didn't want her found," Lott said.

"So us spotting her was an accident," Julia said. "But I still don't see why?"

"With her car gone," Lott said. "We wouldn't have looked for her here, in the lake. We would have searched that cliff face we drove down and hundreds of other miles of highway and never found a thing."

"She would have just vanished," Julia said, shuddering slightly.

"Just as all the women associated with Willis Williams have done over the last decade."

"Oh," Julia said.

For Lott, having Trish dead was slightly better than having her just vanish. But only slightly. At least with a person vanishing, there was always hope they might show up alive.

Lott needed to get Julia back thinking as a detective again.

"Remember where the road in here came up over that slight rise and we could see the lake and this house below us?" he asked.

"You think someone embalmed Trish," Julia said, "put her in her car, and pushed it off the edge up there and into the lake?"

Lott nodded. "A window must have broken or a door came open in the fall into the lake and Trish floated out of the car. Otherwise we never would have found her. Ever."

Julia looked at Lott and he could tell she was thinking the same thing he was thinking.

"You think there are other bodies in that lake?" Julia asked, now following his thinking completely.

"It's a long shot," Lott said, "but I think we need to have divers check it out, at least to see if there is anything down there at all. And find Trish's car which I bet anything is down there."

"And we can't have Williams know we are even here or looking," Julia said.

Lott agreed with that as they both took some crackers and cheese, and he put the teakettle back on the burner to warm up more water.

"I have another problem I can't figure out," Lott said. "Trish does not fit Williams' normal victims."

"Too old," Julia said.

Lott nodded. "Exactly. The woman who disappear have always been thirty or under."

"So why do you think this might be Williams?" Julia asked.

"Because it fits," Lott said. "You never investigated the monster, but I did. I know his profile from front to back. He

was born and raised in Seattle and until the age of ten his father was a mortician."

"Oh, shit," Julia said.

"So Trish might have discovered something or seen something she wasn't supposed to see just by living here."

Julia nodded. "Likely and possible knowing Trish. Remember that single chair out there on the lawn. She would have been able to see the road above the lake from there."

Lott hadn't thought of that, but it made sense.

"So she reported what she had seen to someone in McCall," Julia said, "and that got her killed."

"If we are right, my gut sense is that the reason there are no abductions and disappearances near McCall," Lott said, "where Williams has a home and always goes to within a week of an abduction, is that McCall is where he plays with and kills his victims."

Julia nodded. "And that would be possible if he has help in the local law enforcement."

"This is all speculation," Lott said. "Just trying to put pieces together in some desperate fashion, make some sort of sense of an event that makes no sense. But if I'm right…"

He let that fade off into the faint crackling of the fire and the steady pounding of rain on the deck outside.

Julia picked up her holstered gun and slipped it on her belt, then went and made sure every door was locked.

Lott put his gun on his belt as well.

Then she came back. "We're going to need to be very, very careful if we are right."

"Very careful," Lott said.

He had no doubt that this was going to be a very long night.

CHAPTER FOURTEEN

May 14, 2015
10 P.M.
High Mountain Valley
Near the Central Idaho Primitive Area

JULIA WATCHED as Lott talked to Fleet over the satellite phone. She had never been so relieved in all her life when Fleet answered. This house was so isolated, it scared her far more than she wanted to admit. Over the years she had faced down the worst scum of humanity. But here, isolated and out of her element like this, she felt terrified.

And she could tell Lott wasn't much more comfortable with it than she was.

Lott first asked Fleet if the phone line was completely secure and Fleet had assured him it was.

The next question Lott asked Fleet was if he knew where Williams was.

Fleet listened for a moment, then said, simply "Shit!"

Lott had Fleet hold and told Julia that Williams was in Seattle and another young blonde girl had just gone missing that morning.

"He's on his way to McCall in a few days," Julia said.

Lott nodded and went back to talking with Fleet, explaining everything they had found. And detailing out their theory and how critical it was to keep all this deadly silent.

Then Lott nodded and said, "We need some research. Very secret and careful research."

Julia watched as Lott nodded.

"First," Lott said, "we need to know, deep background, through any sort of shield, who actually owns this piece of property. Who runs it? Who rented it to Trish?"

"Second, we need to know if Williams or any of his companies has any connection to the mortuary business, or casket manufacturing or transportation, or anything like that. Again, super careful."

Lott nodded. Then he said simply, "Thanks. See you then."

He put the phone down on the table and took a deep breath.

"Two helicopters coming in before dawn, as soon as they can see well enough to land."

Julia felt very relieved to hear that. "Eight hours from now."

Lott nodded. "He's bringing an FBI agent and her team that he can trust, a forensic unit for Trish, and a dive team."

"So do you think anyone is coming up here in the meantime?" Julia asked.

"I don't know the answer to that," Lott said. "But I don't think we should take any chance at all. If someone on some sort of video feed saw us find Trish, they might already be on the way."

"You think this place could be wired in some fashion?" Julia asked. "That's a long way for that kind of communication."

Lott pointed to the satellite phone. "I've looked and haven't seen anything, but that sure doesn't mean there isn't something here somewhere."

"Agreed," Julia said, nodding. "We take no more chances."

"Get packed and put on another layer of clothes," Lott said as he took his phone and she picked up hers and they both headed upstairs.

Julia knew they just didn't dare take chances. Not with what happened to Trish. And if Lott and the other members of the Cold Poker Gang were correct, they were now facing one of the smartest and richest serial killers in modern times.

And that just scared her more than she wanted to admit.

Ten minutes later, she heard Lott go back downstairs and start putting out the fire in the fireplace and shutting off lights. If someone did come over that ridgeline above the lake looking for them, that someone would see a dark building.

Julia knew that they needed to make it look as if they were leaving, heading to find help, which would be a logical thing for them to do after finding a body like they had.

Julia headed down with her bag and another quilt. Lott grabbed two pillows from the couch and they shut off lights.

He stuffed two bottles of water and some of the crackers and cheese into his bag, then pulling the door closed and locking it, Julia put the key back under the mat.

Not the visit with an old friend she had hoped for.

The air around them was bitingly cold and Julia could see her breath in the faint light. At least it had stopped raining.

Five minutes later, they had their stuff in the Jeep and Lott, with Julia spotting him with a flashlight, backed the Jeep as far as he could into the trees beside the garage without turning on the lights. From the front seats they could see the road coming in, but in the dark the Jeep would be very difficult to see.

With luck, anyone watching, if there was anyone watching, would think they had left. If not, they had a defensible position.

Julia climbed into the Jeep and Lott went out from under the trees slightly and called Fleet back.

She could hear him talking in the still night air.

Lott quickly told Fleet what they had done. "Bring in some scanning equipment as well. We need to know if we are being watched. It's going to make a difference on what we do next."

Julia watched as Lott nodded and then came back and climbed in the Jeep. She had turned off the interior light so it didn't go on every time the door opened or closed. The heater had the Jeep warming up quickly so he wiggled out of his still damp ski parka and tossed it in the back.

"Fleet's bringing scanning equipment," he said to Julia and she nodded. "Told us to stay safe. Help is on the way."

She just nodded, staring out at the dark night and the road up the hill. "How can a place that looked so beautiful during the daylight feel so threatening at night?"

Lott looked out over the steering wheel and across the dark open parking area to the black mountains beyond, just shaking his head.

Julia knew that he had no way to answer that.

All she knew was that this was going to be a very long night.

CHAPTER FIFTEEN

May 15, 2015
6 A.M.
High Mountain Valley
Near the Central Idaho Primitive Area

JULIA HAD LEANED against him, dozing. The faint sun was just starting to color the very tops of the hills, but it was still pitch black around them.

During the night they had taken turns watching the road, munching on the crackers, and dozing. They had talked some, but mostly about possible plans.

They were both in agreement that if this did have something to do with Williams, if Trish's death helped stop Williams, she would not have died in vain.

They were also both convinced that she had seen something from that lawn chair and had gone in to report it to the county sheriff and that had gotten her killed. So more than likely the sheriff and other law enforcement officials were on Williams' payroll.

Lott had no idea how they were going to prove any of this, if it were true.

About an hour ago, Lott had gone out in front of the Jeep again and called Fleet while Julia stood guard, her back against the garage watching the parking lot and the road, her gun drawn.

Fleet said that he had had two of his best people on cracking who really owned the cabin and the land along the lake. It turned out it was a Williams' holding company four companies deep.

And Williams also had shell companies that not only owned the mortuary in McCall, but a casket manufacturing and shipping company in Seattle.

"See you in an hour," Fleet had said.

Lott had gone back to the car and Julia had joined him.

"Looks like we're going to find a lot of bodies out there in that water," Lott said, not really sure if he should feel excited or really sad.

"What?" Julia asked.

"Williams owns this land," Lott said, "the McCall Mortuary, and a casket manufacturing and shipping company."

"Oh, shit," Julia said, staring off into the dark.

That was all they had talked about.

He convinced Julia thirty minutes later to doze leaning against him and she did. Under different circumstances, he would have loved that.

Now, as the early dawn light hit the tops of the hills, Lott could hear a faint rumbling sound.

He nudged Julia and she came awake.

They both grabbed their guns and went out into the freezing night air. Julia vanished back near the garage and he went out and up the hill slightly behind the base of a large pine. He tried not to breathe too hard for fear that someone would see his breath in the faint light. He could feel his fingers going numb as he held the gun up, ready for anything.

The rumbling sound got louder and louder until it seemed to shake the entire forest around him.

Both Lott and Julia had decided to stay in place, hidden, until they saw Fleet. Williams was more than rich enough to send in a helicopter as well. And if he had heard the conversation Lott had had with Fleet, a helicopter in quickly might be the only way to deal with this mess.

The valley around Lott was now shaking and pine needles were falling from the tree over his head. It was like a thumping sound, but he couldn't see anything.

Suddenly, like a bad science fiction move, the first helicopter turned on bright floodlights about a hundred feet over the large parking area.

The light was so bright, Lott had to turn his head slightly to let his eyes adjust.

The helicopter expertly landed to one side of the wide parking area.

The helicopter was large and looked almost like a National Guard military-style chopper. How was that possible? What kind of pull did Fleet and Doc have, anyway?

97

A second helicopter, much smaller, that looked like a private helicopter, came in for a landing on the other side of the parking lot, much closer to the Jeep and where they were hidden.

Both helicopters cut engines, but the sound of them slowing down still seemed to shake the trees and the valley. Those landings must have been heard thirty miles away.

The door to the smaller helicopter slid open first and Fleet stepped out. He was still dressed in a silk business suit, dress shoes, but no tie. Not wearing a tie had to be a first for Fleet.

In all his life, Lott had never felt so relieved to see someone.

Lott holstered his gun and climbed down the slight slope, brushing off pine needles from his hair and sweater as more men poured from the two helicopters.

Julia came around from the back of the Jeep, smiling.

She came over to Lott and put her arms around him and hugged him.

He hugged her back and that felt flat wonderful.

Then together, arm-in-arm, they moved toward Fleet as the noise of the helicopters finally died off into the still dark trees.

Fleet smiled and shook Lott's hand, then gave Julia a hug.

"I'll tell you," Fleet said, "I need to call your daughter and Doc before they both have a fit. Never seen two people as worried as they were. They are almost to Boise as we speak. And Andor is having a fit down in Las Vegas as well."

"Talk about worried," Lott said, laughing, the tension slowly draining. "You should have seen us about eight hours ago."

"This place is damned creepy at night," Julia said, her arm still around Lott.

They headed back up the steps toward the lodge. A number of men with high-level equipment were scanning the grounds and the area.

Two other men from the larger helicopter came up to Lott and Julia. "Detectives, where is the body you found?"

Lott pointed past the home to the shed down by the edge of the water.

Both men nodded and carrying bags, headed there at a brisk walk.

"FBI forensic field team," Fleet said, explaining them as the two men walked away.

Fleet pointed to the other group doing the scanning. "FBI surveillance team. The best. Another branch of them are also watching Williams as we speak."

"What about the poor girl adducted in Seattle?" Julia asked.

"With your lead on the embalming," Fleet said, "and my people tracing the ownership of the casket manufacturing and shipping company, they found her after Williams had already got her ready to ship to McCall. The FBI replaced her out with a dummy and the casket is on its way to McCall as Williams scheduled."

"She was alive?" Julia asked a fraction of a second before Lott could.

Fleet smiled. "She was alive. Heavily sedated, but very much alive."

Julia started to cry softly and then said, "Thank you, Trish."

Lott knew exactly what she meant. Her friend might be dead, but her death had saved another life. And who knew how many others.

Lott hugged Julia with one arm as Fleet went on.

"That has not been announced yet in any fashion because the FBI want to really make sure this Williams guy goes down for all of his crimes. In all three states. And they want who has been working with him as well. They haven't even told the local Seattle police yet for fear of a leak to Williams."

"A trap?" Lott said, surprised. "They are setting a trap?"

"That's the plan," Fleet said, "if we find here what you are afraid we are going to find."

"Can we help?" Julia asked, her voice intense.

"They tell me that is also the plan," Fleet said, smiling.

And Lott loved the look of that smile.

CHAPTER SIXTEEN

May 15, 2015
6:30 A.M.
High Mountain Valley
Near the Central Idaho Primitive Area

JULIA WAS VERY RELIEVED that the FBI surveillance had found no sign of anything being broadcast from around the house or the valley in general. So in theory, for the moment, Williams didn't know they were on to him.

If they actually were. All this might be a wild goose chase, but no one seemed to be treating it that way.

And the information had saved his latest target, which just made Julia smile.

The morning sun still hadn't hit the tops of the peaks around the valley, so it felt more like the middle of the night than the morning. The air had a hard, crisp bite to it and the rain from the night before had made everything slick, especially the log stairs leading up to the house.

Julia and Lott had both held onto each other while climbing those, and Julia had no idea at all how Fleet made it up them in his slick leather shoes.

Both Julia and Lott only had on sweaters with shirts under them, so they were both starting to get cold as they stood with Fleet talking about the events.

Fleet didn't seem to notice the cold air at all, even though he was only dressed in a dark silk suit and a dress shirt.

After about ten minutes, the three of them had made it up to the front porch of the large log home. Julia unlocked the front door of the lodge again and let in the surveillance team to do a sweep as they waited on the porch.

After ten minutes, the team came back out and said, "All clear. No bugs at all."

Lott and Julia and Fleet headed inside and Lott went right to the fireplace to start back up a fire while Julia put on water for tea and turned on lights.

"I have breakfast coming in shortly," Fleet said. "I figured you two would be hungry."

"Very," Lott said as Julia realized she was hungry after all.

Julia moved over and stood at the kitchen window near the dining room table for a moment, watching as the two men worked on Trish's body just outside the shed, clearly doing preliminary tests.

As a detective, she had watched that process many times. She knew what they were doing.

Along the end of the lake another group of agents were setting up their gear for the dive into the cold water. She did not envy those divers at all in that dark, cold water.

Julia could see four other agents walking slowly up the road toward where the road came into the valley, looking for where a car or cars might have gone over the edge.

They had extremely strong flashlights that they mostly trained along the edge of the road and sometimes down into the water.

As the fire got going and Lott came into the kitchen area, two men and a woman came in, all carrying equipment.

The woman looked at Fleet. "We're going to need to set up here in the living room area."

"Anything you need, agent," Fleet said.

The woman put down the case she was carrying, nodded to the two men, and came over toward them. She was tall at maybe six feet, had on dark jeans, a dark stocking cap over short brown hair, and a heavy jacket with FBI on the front and back.

She had the jacket open exposing a brown sweater with a tan blouse under it. Her eyes were dark and very intense.

The FBI agent extended her hand to Julia, pulling off a thin glove as she did so.

"Detective Rogers I presume. I am FBI Special Agent Carol Munn."

Julia shook her hand, smiling. "Thank you for coming in so fast and on such short notice."

Agent Munn just smiled and nodded at Fleet. "Tough to say no to this man, even in the middle of the night. Especially with the information you two found."

Agent Munn turned to Lott. "Detective Lott, a pleasure."

"I assure you, Agent Munn, the pleasure is all mine."

"Long night, huh?" Munn asked, laughing lightly.

"Very," Lott said, smiling.

Then Agent Munn turned back to Julia with a serious look on her face. "I am very sorry to hear about the loss of your friend."

"Thank you," Julia said, nodding.

There was nothing else she could say.

"Fleet mentioned you might have a plan for us," Lott said after a moment.

"We do," Agent Munn said, nodding. "Fleet and I and your daughter came up with the basics of it earlier this morning. But first I would rather see what we find here."

Julia nodded. "Makes sense."

"You know Annie?" Lott asked.

Julia glanced up at him. She could tell that Lott was surprised.

"I worked with her and Doc on a couple of cases over the last year," Agent Munn said. "They are an amazing couple."

"That they are," Julia said, smiling up at Lott who just looked surprised.

"Agent Munn," one of the agents setting up equipment in the living room said. "We may have found something."

She turned and went back into the living room, pulling off her jacket as she went and tossing it to one side in a chair.

On one laptop screen an image was flickering and then settling as someone on the other end stopped moving the camera.

Julia and Lott and Fleet followed Agent Munn, standing back behind the couch, but still able to see the computer screen in front of the one agent who was sitting on the couch, the laptop on the wooden coffee table.

It took Julia a moment to understand what she was seeing. When she did, she looked out the window toward the road.

There, the four agents looked like dark shadows in the slowly increasing light. They were up about a hundred feet above the water. A bright light was being shown down at the ground where they were.

"There are dozens of different tire tracks going over the edge here," someone said who was up on the road. "Some old and weathered, some newer."

There was intense silence in the living room broken only by the popping of the fire.

"Secure that location completely," Agent Munn said to the agents on the hill. "Then continue your search."

"Understood," the agent who had been talking said.

"Tell the dive team what they may be in for," Agent Munn said to the other agent not behind the computer.

He nodded and went out the door.

Julia glanced up at Lott, who looked puzzled as well. Julia knew why.

"Agent Munn," Julia said, "none of the women who disappeared, besides my friend, had a car in this area."

Munn turned and looked at Julia, then Julia saw the understanding hit Munn's face.

"I'll get my people on that," Fleet said. "That kind of research in a small area like McCall as to who is buying cars is safer coming from my people."

Agent Munn nodded. "Thank you, Fleet."

Then Agent Munn smiled at Julia. "Very good thinking, Detective."

All Julia could do was nod.

They may have found a serial killer's body dump. And if that were the case, down in those smooth, black waters out there were many, many innocent women who had died horrible deaths.

If they were out there, at least their families would now get closure.

Part Four
THE SET UP

CHAPTER SEVENTEEN

May 15, 2015
7:15 A.M.
High Mountain Valley
Near the Central Idaho Primitive Area

LOTT WASN'T SURE if he could eat even though he was hungry. Not with what was going on outside. The divers were just getting ready to go into the water.

But when a tall guy with dark hair, a light flight jacket, and a golf hat brought in six large boxes of fresh doughnuts, a couple thermos of coffee, what looked to be a form of egg sandwiches on muffins, plus orange juice, Lott changed his mind.

Fleet thanked the guy, said he would set things up, and asked the guy to bring up the rest as soon as he could.

"There's more?" Julia asked, shaking her head as she dug into sacks and boxes.

"About three times this much," Fleet said.

Fleet had clearly brought enough food for all the agents working out there in the cold and the three in the living room.

Both Lott and Julia helped set up the kitchen counter and the dining room table with all the food as Fleet made a satellite call back to his people in his office in Boise working on computers to get them searching for who had bought a lot of used cars in this area.

And under what name.

Then he handed the phone to Lott. "Your daughter wants to talk with you. They just arrived at their Boise offices."

Lott laughed and took the phone.

"Out on a date and you send the FBI," Lott said to Annie over the phone, winking at Julia, who laughed.

"Dad, stop fooling around," Annie said. "Are you and Julia all right?"

"We're fine," Lott said. "And it is wonderful to hear your voice. I want to thank you and Doc and Fleet here for rushing to the rescue. It was a long and scary night last night, I must admit."

"Had us scared to death as well," Annie said. "I know this Williams psycho. Worked two of his cases, remember. He's capable of anything."

"We're fine," Lott said. "Honest. And Fleet and Agent Munn here are taking good care of us. So what's this plan I've been hearing about?"

"We'll wait and see if what you think is there in the lake is actually there," Annie said. "Doc and I are going to meet you at the Cascade airport later today and we can talk then."

Lott remembered Cascade. It was a nice town about thirty miles to the south of McCall. They had gone through it on the way to McCall.

"Sounds like a plan," Lott said. "Except I need one more favor of someone very young."

"What's that?" Annie asked.

"Actually, it's two favors. We need a ride out of here through the air and someone to drive our car back out."

Annie laughed. "Roads that bad going in there?"

"Oh, you have no idea," Lott said.

Beside him Julia just nodded in agreement.

In the background behind Annie, Lott could hear Doc laughing so hard it sounded like he might bust a gut. Doc knew central Idaho and had spent his summers

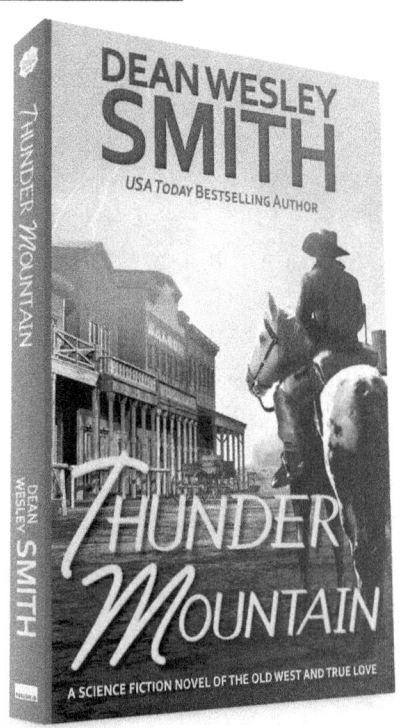

in here and on the River of No Return rafting since he had been in college.

"Have Doc drive you in here some day," Lott said, shaking his head at the laughter in the background.

"Not a chance," Annie said. "I've seen those mountains, been down the rivers with Doc. Don't worry, Fleet can give you a lift to Cascade and we'll get someone in there to drive the car out."

"Thank you," Lott said.

"Yes, thank you," Julia said loud enough for Annie to hear over the phone.

"And tell Andor we are all right, would you?" Lott said.

"I will, Dad," she said. "See you soon." Lott could tell that Annie was barely containing her laughter as well as she hung up.

"Doc and Annie are laughing at us flatlanders," Lott said, smiling at Julia.

"I'm with you two," Fleet said. "I'd rather just pay for that car and let it sit than drive it out of here myself."

"We'll get an agent to drive it out," Agent Munn said from the living room, laughing.

"Thank you," was all Lott could say.

CHAPTER EIGHTEEN

May 15, 2015
7:30 A.M.
High Mountain Valley
Near the Central Idaho Primitive Area

JULIA TOOK A CUP of coffee and one of the fresh doughnuts. She wasn't sure if the coffee would help her stomach, but for the moment she needed to stay awake and alert and strong coffee with a little cream had helped her do that for years on the job.

Especially when Jane had been young and sleep had been a luxury.

Lott did the same, only he added a little sugar to his coffee and took a doughnut with a cream filling.

"Going to pay for this later I'm sure," he said.

"After the long night," Julia said. "We can afford a little price to stay alert."

"Agreed," Lott said, smiling and sipping his coffee.

Julia did the same, letting the wonderful smell and taste kick back some of the tiredness.

She had just finished her doughnut and half her coffee when one of the men who had been working on Trish's body came through the door. He had removed his forensics overalls and his gloves. He was fairly young, not more than thirty, with dirty blonde hair and pimples on his cheeks. He had on the standard FBI dark jacket and dark jeans and tennis shoes.

Agent Munn stood and came over to him and Julia and Lott and Fleet joined her.

"You have a preliminary report, Doctor?" Agent Munn asked.

The doctor, who was clearly also an FBI agent, nodded to Julia and said simply, "I am sorry for your loss, Detective."

Julia was surprised. Clearly everyone knew on this team.

She nodded back as the young blonde doctor turned to Agent Munn.

"As was evident, the victim was embalmed. All organs were removed and her blood replaced with standard embalming fluid and a hardening agent of some sort, which kept down all decomposition. We should be able to trace the fluid back to an exact mortuary because of the special mixture used."

"Good," Agent Munn said, nodding.

Julia was very glad to hear that. That kind of evidence in a trial was very, very difficult to refute in court.

"There are no indications of any kind of injury," the blonde doctor said. "More than likely the victim was drugged and the cause of death would be bleeding out on the embalming table."

Julia just shook her head at that and Lott put his arm around her to hold her.

"There is one more thing," the young doctor said, glancing at Julia as if afraid to say anything because she had been friends with Trish.

"It's all right," Julia said. "I'm a retired detective. I've been around a lot of death over the years."

The young doctor nodded his thanks, then turned back to Agent Munn. "The victim was sexually abused after she was embalmed. Possibly a number of times."

Julia felt her stomach just tighten up and Lott's arm held her tighter, something she really appreciated.

"We might be able to get DNA samples," the blonde doctor said. "Since they closed her up after abusing her. Usually water would wash that away, but in this case it might be possible. We are loading the victim into the helicopter now and I suggest we get the body to a facility quickly to pull tests."

"Will another hour make a difference?" Agent Munn asked.

"I don't think an hour would matter," the doctor said.

"Then stay around a little longer. If what we are afraid of happens, you're going to need to go and bring back a large team."

"Understood," the young doctor said.

He nodded to Julia and then turned and left.

"I'm sorry you had to hear all that about your friend, Detective," Agent Munn said to Julia.

"I'm not," Julia said. "It seems we're going to have a lot of evidence to catch this sicko."

Agent Munn nodded and turned back to the living room.

Lott eased Julia back into the kitchen area and took her cup and freshened it with hot coffee.

"I'm all right," Julia said as he handed the cup back to her.

"Well I'm not," Lott said. "I'm angry and disgusted and want more than anything to just put a bullet in some sick human's head."

"Well," Julia said, smiling at the man she was coming to love, "I'm all for that as well. That's what I mean by all right."

Lott laughed and Fleet just shook his head.

"How you detectives ever sleep at night is beyond me," Fleet said, "with all the sickness out there in the human population."

"It was our job," Lott said.

"It was a good job," Julia said, nodding. "I'm just glad I can still play a small part."

"I don't think putting these pieces together on the most notorious serial killer of our time is a small part," Agent Munn said as she came into the kitchen and took a doughnut with chocolate frosting out of one of the boxes of doughnuts covering the counter.

"Divers are going in," the agent behind the computer in the living room said.

"You sure you want to watch this?" Agent Munn asked as Lott and Julia started with her toward the living room.

"We have no choice," Lott said.

Agent Munn nodded and went in and sat beside the man at the laptop. She had known exactly what he meant.

"Well, I have a choice," Fleet said. "I think I'll just stay out here with the food."

Agent Munn smiled.

Julia quickly turned around and went back and kissed Fleet on the cheek. "Thank you. For everything. And I am sure my friend Trish would thank you as well."

Fleet just blushed.

Julia smiled at him and turned back to the living room. Lott was right. She had no choice.

She had to see what was down there.

CHAPTER NINETEEN

May 15, 2015
8 A.M.
High Mountain Valley
Near the Central Idaho Primitive Area

LOTT STOOD BEHIND the couch that faced the fireplace, his arm around Julia, behind the FBI tech at the laptop computer on the wood coffee table.

Outside the large picture window that looked out over the lake, the sun still was a long ways from hitting the valley floor, but the mountains were bright. From what was on the screen, the light was enough to see clearly in the lake water.

The screen showed one diver's camera and a second laptop set up beside the first showed the second diver's camera.

"Bottom is sloping away sharply," one diver said.

"Visibility about forty feet," the other diver said.

On the screens beside the images, Lott could see each diver's vital signs, their air supply, their temperature, heartbeat, and so on. All were in normal levels.

"Bottom is leveling off some at sixty feet," the lead diver said. "Nothing so far but logs and mud bottom."

Lott was surprised he didn't see any fish. More than likely the divers breathing sounds would have scared them out of camera range.

The bottom of the lake looked more like a desolate alien landscape than anything that could be nearby. The light coming down through the water was dim, but each diver had bright lights on both sides of the cameras on their helmets that seemed to make the bottom of the lake seem even stranger and covered with shifting shadows.

It looked more alien if that was possible.

Another voice came over the link.

"You are still a football field's distance from where the car tracks are leaving the road above the lake. Stay on your heading and you should come to the area below the car tracks."

"Copy that," the first diver said.

Silence filled the living room as everyone watched the two screens except for Fleet. He stood in the kitchen staring out over the lake and watching the scene on the shore of the support divers.

Lott glanced out the front window. The extra crew out there had inflated a large raft with a small motor on one end and another diver was standing by near the raft in full dry suit, clearly in case of any emergencies.

On the screen the alien-looking landscape continued flowing smoothly past the cameras.

The vital signs of the divers showed no variations at all.

Lott had stood on the shore while divers had looked for bodies in golf course ponds and twice on the shore of Lake Mead. He never understood how anyone could be a recovery diver. They couldn't pay him enough to do that job, especially considering the conditions the divers often found the bodies.

"We're approaching something," one of the divers said.

"You are almost to the area where the car tracks go over the edge," a third voice came in.

Agent Munn leaned forward and Lott held Julia even tighter. He could feel her tensing up.

On both screens, shadows started to appear out of the gloom ahead.

At first it seemed like large rocks sticking up out of the mud at various angles, but as the divers moved closer, it became clear the shapes were that of cars covered in layers of sediment.

Some cars were piled on top of others.

"Oh, shit," one of the divers said. "We have an entire junkyard down here."

The intense silence in the living room felt to Lott like it could be cut. He wasn't sure he was even breathing.

Beside him Julia just stood like a stone pillar.

"Let's go left around the pile," the lead diver said. "Get an idea how big it is."

"Copy," the second diver said.

As far as Lott was concerned, they seemed to swim for a very long time before finally passing the huge mound of wrecked cars.

"There's Trish's car," Julia whispered, her voice breathless.

It was clear which car she meant. It was upside down and the driver's door was open. From what Lott could tell, it was a BMW. And it had very, very little lake silt on it.

Trish's car was clearly the newest addition to the pile.

"I'm going to go see if I can see inside one of the cars," the lead diver said.

The camera got closer and closer to a driver's side window on what looked like an old Ford hatchback of some sort.

Lott and Julia both sort of leaned back. Lott wanted to look away, not see what the diver found, but he couldn't make himself.

He had to see.

The driver took a brush from his belt and carefully and slowly brushed back the silt on the window, sending it swirling into the water around him.

Then, as the diver moved up closer to the cleared window, the bright lights of his camera filled the inside of the car as if it was daylight.

A young woman's white, peaceful face stared back at them.

Lott had no doubt that face would haunt his nightmares for years to come.

"Jesus," the guy behind the computer said, leaning back away from the screen.

Lott and Julia both eased back as well, as if getting away from the computer would help what the diver was seeing.

The girl was nude, strapped into the driver's seat, and didn't seem to be more than thirty.

Her long hair floated around her head.

She seemed almost peaceful sitting there.

The diver moved back to a place where he and his partner could see the entire pile.

"There have to be at least forty cars here, if not more," the diver said.

Agent Munn glanced back at Lott and Julia. "We suspect Williams of over forty women's disappearances in the three states. It seems we found the women."

"Now we just have to trap the bastard who did this," Lott said. "Make sure he is tied to every one of those women's deaths."

"We'll get him," Agent Munn said, nodding as she stared at the image of the piles of cars on the lake floor. "We'll get him."

CHAPTER TWENTY

May 15, 2015
9 A.M.
High Mountain Valley
Near the Central Idaho Primitive Area

TRISH'S BODY, along with the FBI forensics team lifted off in the large helicopter, leaving most of the FBI agents in place.

Julia watched the large helicopter disappear up and over the tall ridgeline and turn south toward Boise. The next time she would see Trish, it would be in a proper funeral.

But first they had to capture her killer.

Julia knew that the FBI would be processing all this data, including the bodies, in a private lab in Boise that Doc and Annie were setting up at the airport. They could take no chances that any of this might leak out, and with William's money, having spies in the police and FBI would not have surprised any of them.

So they were taking extra precautions.

That was also why most of the agents here would stay here in this contained valley until Williams was trapped and arrested. No calls out allowed in any fashion.

Julia and Lott and Agent Munn were also becoming convinced that Williams had not killed Trish. She was not his type and he had not been close to McCall when she vanished.

More than likely Trish had seen something, reported it to the wrong person in McCall, and gotten killed because of it. And her body had been handled as if Williams were there.

When Trish was killed, Williams had been in Seattle and nowhere near his home in McCall, Idaho. Chances are, Williams didn't even know about Trish's death.

Julia and Lott and Fleet and Agent Munn all headed down the long wooden stairs from the house to the parking lot and the helicopter Fleet had arrived in. The morning had warmed up some, but the sun still hadn't reached the valley floor.

"I'm arranging to have more food sent in this afternoon," Fleet said. "And other supplies. Your people are going to need it."

"Thank you," Agent Munn said. "I'll be back shortly as well and we'll get set up for a long stay here. This lake and the road above it is a huge crime scene."

"That it is," Lott said, glancing back at the valley as he and Julia got their things from the Jeep. Then Lott handed Agent Munn the Jeep keys.

"Can't begin to tell you how happy I am we are not driving out of here," Julia said.

"I should feel insulted," Lott said, smiling at her, "but I completely agree. In fact, I was thinking that if we did have to drive out, you could do it."

"Not a chance in hell," she said, laughing. Just the idea of that made her stomach twist into a slight panic.

Five minutes later they lifted off, going mostly straight up, since the valley was so narrow. Trish had ridden in her share of helicopters before, mostly police and a couple of television helicopters. Never one this nice.

They all had helmets on with sound-deadening abilities and a communication system so they could hear each other clearly.

Julia and Lott sat in the seats behind the two pilots, with Fleet and Agent Munn behind them.

As they lifted off, Julia could see all the activity going on below. Tents were being set up along the shore of the lake and agents were coming and going from the house.

Other sets of tents were being constructed near the shed.

The one lone lawn chair still sat just above the water line, empty. More than likely sitting in that chair had gotten Trish killed, but Julia still hoped they would leave the chair right where it was.

As the helicopter climbed above the ridgeline, Trish could see that just a ways down the narrow road into the valley, some boulders had been rolled out into the road, blocking the road into the lake completely. Two agents stood to one side.

Agent Munn pointed to the boulders. "If anyone tries to come into the valley by car, the agents will hide at first and then take whoever it is into custody and hold them until we have gotten everyone rounded up.

"Great thinking," Lott said, and Julia nodded.

Julia knew that keeping a lid on an operation this size was going to be hard,

but they only had to do that for another day or so. If Williams followed pattern, he would head to McCall a couple of days after his latest victim went missing. That had happened yesterday.

And Julia was very glad the FBI had found and rescued that poor woman.

No one had put Williams pattern together because, as the reports said, Williams had always made it a point to tell the police where he was going and when. He loved taunting them like that.

As the helicopter gained even more attitude and turned west, the fantastic beauty of the Idaho wilderness came into stark relief under them. The extremely high, snow-covered peaks lined up like huge, sharp rows of teeth going into the distance as far as Julia could see.

All the mountains were covered in dark pine trees, rocks, and bright white snow in the clear morning sunshine.

It all looked stunningly beautiful and amazingly dangerous.

"See that sort of gash in the mountains to the east?" Agent Munn said, pointing out the window near Lott. "That's the main Salmon River, also called The River of No Return."

"That's where Doc spends his summers," Lott said, shaking his head. "He really is crazy."

"Your daughter spends most of the summers now in there as well," Fleet said, laughing. "I think they're both crazy."

Julia just looked out at the vast rugged wilderness below her and agreed. It was stunningly beautiful on a warm May morning, and more dangerous than any criminal on the streets of a major city.

CHAPTER TWENTY-ONE

May 15, 2015
9:30 A.M.
Cascade, Idaho

THE HELICOPTER touched down near one end of the Cascade airport, near a group of what looked to be private buildings and hangers. Cascade was tucked to one side of a wide valley, near a tall concrete dam that seemed to back up water for many miles behind it.

The town looked to be a combination of a tourist town and farming town and Lott figured it couldn't have a population of locals of more than three thousand. But since it was clearly a winter and a summer resort, it was set up to handle a lot more.

The airport was out in what looked like an open meadow across the main two-lane highway from Cascade. Buildings and farms dotted the flat fields and the mountains they had just come over loomed to the east of the big valley like a wall.

Doc and Annie climbed out of the front of a white Cadillac SUV as the helicopter landed. They then stood there, waiting for the engines to shut down, and Lott and Julia to get out, before coming forward.

The morning was still cool, but much warmer than in the small mountain valley they had just left.

Annie had on a dark jacket, jeans, and had her long hair pulled back. Doc seemed completely in his element here as much as in a casino in Las Vegas. He had on jeans, tennis shoes and a dress shirt under a light tan jacket. Doc just radiated confidence, no matter where he seemed to be.

Lott had to admit, after last night on guard in that car in those remote mountains, he was damned glad to see Doc and Annie.

And from the hug Annie gave him when they got out into the cool morning air, she was glad to see him as well.

Then, as Annie hugged Julia, Doc shook his hand and smiled. "Not a fun night in the mountains, huh?"

"I think from now on I'll leave the mountains to you two," Lott said.

"I'll agree to that," Julia said.

"I have always said that," Fleet said.

Lott and Julia and Annie laughed.

Agent Munn just shook her head. "Don't look at me. After we get this sting set up, I'm heading back in there for the night."

"Not looking forward to it?" Doc asked.

"Not with all the ghosts in that little valley," Agent Munn said.

"You found the cars?" Annie asked and Lott realized no one had called them and told them, since they had been on the way to Cascade from Boise.

Agent Munn nodded. "Divers think there has to be at least forty cars down there, more than likely all with embalmed bodies. We're getting makes and models and vin numbers first to trace before we even start the body recovery."

"I'll get someone on tracing where the cars were bought after I get the vin numbers," Fleet said.

Doc nodded, then turned to Agent Munn.

"The warehouse in Boise going to be enough room?" Doc asked, looking worried.

"More than enough for the next three days or so," Agent Munn said. "Thank you for doing that."

"Anything," Doc said. "You know that."

Fleet nodded in agreement.

"Thank you both," Agent Munn said.

"Now," Doc said, "let's get to the cabin and get these two into some fresh clothes and get some food and do some planning."

They all headed toward the big white SUV. Fleet and Agent Munn climbed into the third seat. Lott sat with Julia on the second seat, with Annie and Doc in the front seats.

"You have a cabin up here as well?" Julia asked as Doc got them onto the two-lane highway and headed north.

"Just a little place on the lake," Doc said. "Across from the Tamarack Ski Resort."

"Why am I guessing that "little place" won't really describe this cabin on the lake," Lott said. He knew Doc and Annie and they didn't hesitate in going first class all the way.

Annie laughed and turned and winked at her dad. "It won't."

"My family and I love it up here in the summer," Fleet said. "I promise, it doesn't feel remote at all."

"Paved road, neighbors, running water, and telephone reception," Julia said.

"All that," Doc laughed. "And so much more."

Lott was going to need that, and a good nap at some point.

Beside him Julia reached over and took his hand and then smiled at him.

Lott smiled back. "We'll get the bastard," he said softly, leaning into her and gently squeezing her hand.

"I know we will," she said. "How can we not with this team?"

CHAPTER TWENTY-TWO

May 15, 2015
10 A.M.
A home across the lake from the Tamarack Ski Resort,
Near Cascade, Idaho

THE CABIN was as Lott had expected. Not a cabin at all, but a huge, modern mansion sitting on a slight rise looking out over an expansive blue lake that seemed to almost shimmer in the morning sun. On the far side of the lake was a massive lodge and ski runs cut out of the trees above the lodge. There was still some snow near the tops of the ridges, but not much.

The cabin had a huge green lawn and flowerbeds around the bases of pine trees. The lawn sloped down to the lake and a large ski-boat sat at the long wooden dock.

The road in, as promised, had been paved and they had passed dozens of other similar mansions along the water. The cabin, as Doc called it, was only about five miles off the main highway and about fifteen miles from McCall.

The house came to life on its own as they entered. A massive gas fireplace that dominated the living room sprang to life as lights came on, clearly triggered by motion sensors.

The place had six bedrooms up a wide wooden staircase and a huge main area that had an open feel of kitchen, large dining table, and vast living room all combined. Everything was done in wood tones, including the wonderful-looking couches and chairs around the fireplace.

Two-story-tall windows opened the living room up to look out over the lake, making the inside feel almost like a patio.

"Wow," Julia said, looking around.

Lott had to agree. "Wow" expressed seeing this place perfectly.

"No wonder you and your family are comfortable here in the summer," Lott said to Fleet.

"The kids really love the lawn and the lake and the boat," Fleet said.

"I've really got to learn how to play poker," Agent Munn said as she looked around, shaking her head.

Lott and Julia were shown to guest rooms up the wide wooden staircase by Annie, and both given time to take showers and change clothes while lunch was prepared.

Lott had started to feel extremely rummy and tired from lack of sleep and the helicopter and then the car ride, but the shower refreshed him. And getting into clean clothes helped as well.

Now some lunch and a good cup of coffee and he might almost feel half human again. But there was no doubt he was going to need a good night's sleep tonight. He was just too old to be staying up all night. Those days of doing that on stakeouts were long past him.

Julia looked just as refreshed as he felt when she came down the stairs a few minutes after he had joined the other four in the kitchen. Lott had taken a chair at the brown granite kitchen counter facing into the kitchen and Annie was working on sandwiches.

Doc stood to one side watching and drinking a Diet Coke out of a bottle.

Some sort of chicken soup cooking in a large pot on the stove smelled wonder-

ful, and Annie was just finishing making them all sandwiches from fresh French bread and turkey.

Fleet was helping Annie as much as he could, which made Lott smile, since Annie moved so fast on things like this, it made anyone near her look like they were just moving in slow motion. She had been that way as a kid as well.

As Julia joined them, pulling up another stool beside Lott, Agent Munn, who had stepped into the living room to talk, hung up her phone and turned to Fleet. "About thirty of the makes and models and vin numbers of the cars are being sent to you now."

Fleet nodded and moved from the kitchen and into the living room area to use his iPad and then make a call.

When he came back a moment later, after Annie had given both Lott and Julia fresh cups of coffee, Fleet said, "That's not going to take long to trace. Even being careful."

"How much you want to bet none of them were bought around here," Doc said.

"No bet," Agent Munn said.

Lott agreed. This was too small an area, too many small towns to have someone buying that many cars even over years, and then having the cars vanish.

They were talking about the wonderful view and Annie was about to serve up lunch when Fleet's phone beeped and he glanced down at it. Then he answered it, staying at the edge of the kitchen counter instead of moving away, which meant it was news for all of them.

No one spoke as Fleet quickly wrote down a few names and something else Lott couldn't read from where he was sitting. Then he listened for a minute and then scribbled down more notes.

"Thanks," Fleet said finally and clicked off his phone.

Then he looked at Lott and Julia and smiled. "Every car was bought from the same used car dealership out on the old Boulder Highway in Las Vegas."

Lott was stunned. "Las Vegas?"

"You are kidding?" Julia asked.

"I'm not," Fleet said. "They were all bought by a man by the name of Mack Regan from Boise. All were paid for with cash."

"I know that name," Doc said.

Fleet nodded. "A shiftless private detective who manages to skate around the law more than inside it. Red hair, balding, bad teeth, worse breath."

"Plays private games around Boise," Doc said, remembering and clearly disgusted. "Never seems to be short of money."

"The one and the same," Fleet said, nodding.

"Anyone know where he is now?" Lott asked, feeling suddenly worried.

"We need to get him under wraps quickly," Julia said.

"I agree," Agent Munn said.

Fleet smiled. "Mack Regan booked a one-way flight to Vegas yesterday and bought another car with cash just about an hour ago. He reserved two nights at the Golden Nugget downtown and the car he bought is now parked in valet parking for the night, so doesn't look like he's headed north until tomorrow morning."

"I don't have anyone down there I can completely trust," Agent Munn said, looking worried.

"We do," Lott said, smiling. "Let's send Andor and the rest of the gang to sit on him for a few days. Make sure he and that car never move until we get this all settled up here."

"Can you do that?" Agent Munn asked.

Lott and Julia both laughed.

Annie smiled and nodded as well. "Five or six retired detectives out to solve cold cases. Trust me, you don't want to get in their way. They can do it and be trusted completely."

"And Mack Regan won't like it one bit," Lott said, smiling.

"Good," Doc said.

CHAPTER TWENTY-THREE

May 15, 2015
11:30 A.M.
A home across the lake from the Tamarack Ski Resort,
Near Cascade, Idaho

AFTER LUNCH, the conversation quickly turned to the upcoming plan. Julia had been worried about it because she knew that they couldn't tip off Williams in any way until he arrived. They had to catch him in the act, if they could, and have all his help rounded up before then.

It needed to be like a perfect trap play on the poker table. The other player needed to have no hint at all that they were on to him and held the winning cards. That was the only way this would work.

Julia only had one worry. They had no idea how Williams got from his mansion on the west side of the lake to the mortuary in the downtown area without being seen. That bothered her, but it seemed to be a problem they could deal with after finding out exactly who was helping Williams.

"So who do you think your friend Trish would have reported what she saw to?" Agent Munn asked, pushing her empty bowl that had been filled with a chicken noodle soup away.

For Julia, that soup and the soft-bread sandwiches had been perfect. She felt full and for some reason protected.

"Knowing Trish," Julia said, remembering her bright smile and light, fun attitude, "the first cop she saw."

"As you come into town from the mountains, just past the old golf course, the county sheriff's office is right there on the highway," Fleet said.

Julia had no doubt that Trish would have just turned in right there.

"That would be the place," Julia said, nodding. "If Trish saw a car go over that road's edge and into the water, she would want to report it as soon as possible and to the right people. I'm amazed she didn't call me when she got into town, to be honest."

"I have no warrants or probable cause to get taps on the county sheriff's phones and computers," Agent Munn said.

"I know some people," Fleet said. "It will get done. Including all his financials. See if any extra money is pouring in over the years."

"Don't tell me about it," Agent Munn said, smiling.

"We will leave no trace," Fleet said. "Just background your people can rediscover later under warrants."

Agent Munn nodded.

"And the mortuary Williams' holding company owns," Doc asked. "Who runs that?"

"Don't know yet," Fleet said. "I will have my people digging into that as well this afternoon and evening. Again tracing the money."

Julia nodded. "So there was a mention of a plan."

"A decoy plan, more than anything else," Agent Munn said. "We were thinking you two, as friends of Trish, could go in and check with the sheriff about her being missing. See what he says."

"He'll take a report and ignore us," Lott said.

"Not sure what that's going to do," Julia said, puzzled. "Lott is right, he'll ignore us."

"I doubt he will," Agent Munn said, "if you tell him you are headed up to Trish's place and plan on staying there for a week or so to wait for Trish to come back? He must know there's a body dump coming."

"You think he might move on us at that point?" Julia asked.

"If he doesn't know you are detectives, yes," Annie said. "If he thinks you are just two retired friends of Trish and Trish was your only family, he'll stop you."

"Assuming," Agent Munn said, "if he is the one working with Williams. If he is working with Williams, he won't be able to take a chance of anyone like Trish seeing a car dumped into that lake."

"We can be monitoring the phone and computer lines to make sure no warning goes out to Williams," Fleet said. "We'll block anything that he attempts to send."

"And we can have you wired as well," Agent Munn said. "And have agents ready at a moment's notice to back you up."

"My gut sense is that he'll try to lure us to a private place later in the day to clear out the problem we are causing?" Julia asked.

"More than likely," Agent Munn said, nodding. "Again, if we have the right man."

"And he will call the mortician and give him a warning as well," Annie said. "Which will tie the two of them together."

Julia looked at Lott who shrugged.

"I've done stings like this a dozen times over the years," Lott said.

"So have I," Julia said. She didn't say that they always scared her to death. With Trish dead, she wanted to make sure the bastard who killed her was locked up for good. And for that, she would do damn near anything.

"So sleep on it for the night," Agent Munn said, standing. "I've got to get back to the lake."

"I'll keep my people digging and looking for other possible suspects as well," Fleet said. "I'll drive you back to the airport. They should have the helicopter serviced and supplies for your people loaded by now."

"Thank you," Agent Munn said, first to Fleet, then to Doc and Annie. "We couldn't be doing this without you."

"If it puts away a monster," Doc said. "It will be worth far more than we are doing."

Agent Munn turned to Lott and Julia. "Think about it."

Julia shrugged. "No need to think about it. We'll see you in the morning."

Lott nodded. "We're ready when you are."

Agent Munn nodded and then left with Fleet, leaving Annie and Doc standing beside the kitchen counter and Julia and Lott still sitting.

"You two go do what you need to do," Julia said to Doc and Annie. "I have just about enough brain left to do the dishes before a nap overtakes me."

She stood and picked up her empty soup bowl and headed for the sink.

"I'll help," Lott said, moving with Julia to start the cleanup.

Both Doc and Annie nodded and took out cell phones and went into the living room. Both clearly very focused.

Julia glanced up at the wonderful, but clearly tired face of Lott. How had she gotten so lucky as to find a man like him?

After this was all over, they needed to take this trust and friendship and affection to the next level, of that there was no doubt.

She motioned that he should come down closer to her as if she was going to whisper something in his ear.

She then just kissed him. Square on those wonderful lips of his.

Before he could react in any way, she pulled back, smiling.

"Thank you," she said. "For being you."

Lott smiled at her. "Whatever I did, I'm going to have to figure out how to do more of it."

She laughed, and the two of them turned to clean up the kitchen together. And that felt wonderful to Julia.

Natural and perfect in the middle of all the ugliness they had faced at that lake.

CHAPTER TWENTY-FOUR

May 16, 2015
7 A.M.
A home across the lake from the Tamarack Ski Resort,
Near Cascade, Idaho

LOTT FELT almost human after a nap, a fantastic dinner with Annie and Doc and Fleet and Julia, and then a long night's sleep. The image of that dead woman in that car hadn't really haunted him much, but Lott had no doubt that once they got

Williams put away, the image would come back when Lott least expected it.

He had that problem over the years with different cases and often woke up Carol in the middle of the night shouting. She always managed to calm him down and get him back to sleep after a short cup of hot chocolate.

And she never asked what had given him the nightmare. And he had never shared. There was no way he had ever wanted to bring the horror he saw on the streets into his home.

Julia was already sitting at the dining room table talking with Annie and Doc when Lott managed to get showered and downstairs. Julia looked radiant and smiled at him when she saw him coming down the stairs. He wouldn't mind seeing that smile a lot more in the mornings, of that there was no doubt.

Julia was dressed in jeans, a dress blouse, and a thin gold necklace. She had her hair pulled back off her face.

Annie was in her standard blouse and dress slacks, and had a suit jacket hung over the back of her chair. Doc just looked like Doc, with jeans and a dress shirt with the sleeves rolled up.

The sun hadn't hit the mountains across the lake from them, making it seem like it was still dark outside. The smell of coffee filling the wonderful home was like a welcome glove around him.

Annie got up from the table and kissed him on the cheek as he came toward the table, then pointed to the chair next to Julia. "Sit. I'll get you a cup of coffee the way you like it. Breakfast will be as soon as Fleet gets back from picking up Agent Munn at the airport."

Lott went over and sat down next to Julia. She touched his arm and said, "Good morning. Feeling better?"

"I'll let you know after the first cup of coffee," Lott said. "But I think so."

She laughed as Annie slid the cup in front of him and sat down.

The coffee smelled even better coming right off the cup and he sipped at the hot liquid, letting the taste just flow through him.

"Doc and Annie were just telling me their history," Julia said, "and how Doc and Fleet made so much money."

"I honestly don't know how we got so rich," Doc said. "That was Fleet's doing. I just played poker."

"But I didn't know you were involved with capturing the White House Chief of Staff's killer," Julia said. "And it was on that case that you two met?"

"It was," Annie said, leaning over and kissing Doc.

Lott had been on the edges of that investigation as well. It had been a traumatic time, especially since the guy had also killed Doc's father.

Before Julia could ask another question, there was the sound of footsteps on the porch and Fleet and Agent Munn came in, bringing with them a bitingly cold draft of air from the still mostly-dark morning outside.

Fleet looked to be his normal self, with a silk business suit and an open collared dress shirt under it. But Agent Munn looked exhausted and slightly rumpled in her black slacks and dress blouse and FBI dark jacket.

"Coffee?" Annie asked.

"Please," Agent Munn said, sitting at the kitchen table where Annie told her to sit.

Julia got up and went into the kitchen area clearly to help Annie with breakfast. Lott loved the fact that those two liked each other so much. And that Annie was encouraging him to move on after the years of being alone.

"Okay," Annie said as she worked on cracking some eggs, clearly running the show as she tended to do. "We all need details. Who wants to go first? Fleet?"

Lott watched as Fleet nodded, giving Agent Munn some time to sip the coffee Julia had brought her.

"My people looked into all the phone calls Williams made near ten different women's disappearances. Not once did he call his car man in Las Vegas. So we're clear to get that guy stopped."

Lott nodded. Last night he had talked with Andor and got him all prepared and how no one, not even the Chief, could know what he and the rest of the Cold Poker Gang were going to do.

Andor guaranteed that no one would know until it was all clear. Then they would haul the car man's ass down to the station. They all should be in position now.

"Let me take care of this before the guy hits the road and we lose him," Lott said.

Everyone nodded and Lott took his cell phone and called Andor.

"Yeah," Andor said, his voice gruff, exactly how he always answered the phone.

"Detain the bastard," Fleet said. "Williams made no contact with him before every murder, so he is just a part of the puzzle. Keep that part in Vegas."

"We're set," Andor said. "He doesn't know it, but his room reservation has just been extended."

"Perfect," Lott said. "Thanks. Just make sure that bastard makes no calls to anyone. I'll call you when we have Williams contained."

"You got it," Andor said and hung up.

Lott hung up and nodded to the group that had been listening to the call. "One piece down."

"Second part," Fleet said. "The driver bringing the casket in from Seattle. It seems there is no regular driver, so my sense is this is just a regular delivery. There are two other caskets besides the transport casket in the delivery order."

"We'll contain him anyway after the delivery," Agent Munn said. "Without anyone seeing it happen."

Lott nodded. "Two pieces down."

"We are going to have to detain the mortician at about the same time the driver arrives," Doc said. "We can't take a chance on the guy opening the casket and finding a dummy in there."

"We checked all phone records over the past year," Fleet said. "Including outgoing calls from towers that might have been made on a burner phone. No outgoing calls to Williams have ever been made from that mortuary. It seems this system just functions without communications between the parts."

Lott nodded. That made sense.

All the women Williams had taken had just vanished without a trace or a crime scene or any evidence in the slightest. Now Lott was starting to see why.

Agent Munn nodded to Doc's statement about needing to take the mortuary right after the truck driver left. "Here's what I think we should do," she said. "We have eyes on the truck and when it approaches the mortuary, we'll need people inside to hold the guy."

"His name is Wade Andrew," Fleet said. "He has run the Lakeside Mortuary for over fifteen years. He gets some very large amounts of money from varied sources that all looked legal on the surface, but led back to Williams when we dug."

"Perfect," Agent Munn said, nodding. "My people will be able to find all that when we have the right warrants, correct?"

"Easily," Fleet said, smiling.

"I'd like to be one of those to go in," Julia said. "More than likely Andrew was one of the sickos who hurt my friend. I would love to be a part of that takedown."

"As would I," Lott said. "We can go in just ahead of the truck arriving, posing as a couple thinking about making arrangements."

"I'll go in as their daughter," Annie said. "That way you don't have to have so many agents out in the open."

Agent Lott nodded. "Doc, you and I can be surveillance, making sure no one else goes in while that truck is there."

"And no one sneaks out, either," Doc said, smiling.

Agent Munn nodded. "We detain the mortician in his own building until after we take Williams. That way no one sees anything suspicious."

"You going to need us to stay in there?" Lott asked.

Agent Munn shook her head. "I have two men I can trust to sit on him. We'll do official arrests on all of these pieces of the Williams puzzle at once. We have more than enough to do that now."

Lott liked the idea of that a great deal.

"So how bad is it at the lake?" Doc asked.

Agent Munn's eyes got distant. "We have pulled twenty-eight women from the cars so far, all embalmed and naked and strapped into the driver's seat. It's taking time to get the rest because cars are piled on one another down there and we have to pull them aside. We think the total, counting your friend, will reach just under fifty."

Lott was stunned. That was more than anyone thought. They were shutting down a major serial killer.

If they did this right.

And didn't get killed in the process.

CHAPTER TWENTY-FIVE

May 16, 2015
8:30 A.M.
A home across the lake from the Tamarack Ski Resort,
Near Cascade, Idaho

FOR THE NEXT HOUR over breakfast, they worked out the details on how they were going to shut down the mortuary, then set the trap for the sheriff, assuming he was the one involved.

Julia was convinced he was and so was Fleet. It seemed the sheriff lived far, far higher than his salary. He had told a number of people it was old family money that supplied the beautiful home on the lake, but Fleet could find no old family money. Only money coming through shell corporations from Williams, which had convinced Agent Munn as well. But she couldn't act directly on that information because she had no probable cause or warrant to get the information. That was going to be up to Lott and Julia to get the probable cause.

Julia knew they were going to have to bluff the sheriff into action. Both she and Lott were great bluffers at the poker table. She was convinced they could get him to act and show his hand in doing so.

So with two hours until the delivery truck with the three caskets arrived at the mortuary, Doc and Annie and Lott and Julia headed for McCall in two cars. Right before they left, they had gotten word that Williams had announced to the cops following him that he was going to head to McCall.

Julia's stomach twisted. Williams would be here by late this afternoon.

It was all going to go down today, one way or another.

Fleet stayed with Agent Munn to supply information where needed and remain in the background. His silk suit was just a little too noticeable in May in the tourist town.

The four of them ended up eating a sort of small second breakfast at a wonderful restaurant in downtown McCall that was on a second floor of an older building and looked out over the lake. The restaurant was only two blocks from the mortuary and the view was amazing. The morning had no wind and the huge lake was as smooth as glass. The mountains on the other side of the lake reflected in the mirror-like blue surface.

If Trish hadn't died here, Julia had no doubt she could have come to love this little town. She sure understood why Trish had come up here.

The smell of bacon and fresh bread made Julia slightly hungry, even though they had just eaten. She decided to have a glass of orange juice and some toast anyway to go with her cup of coffee. Better to keep refreshed.

The others did basically the same thing, drinking coffee and eating a light continuation of breakfast.

Doc glanced around, but there was no one sitting close to them. Then he said in a soft voice, "You can see Williams' mansion along the lake from here. See the point of land sticking out into the water on the far shore. He owns that entire

piece of land and his place it tucked along this edge of that point."

Suddenly Julia knew another part of the puzzle.

An important part.

"What stage is the moon tonight?"

Lott glanced at her, clearly puzzled.

Doc and Annie looked puzzled as well.

"I'll ask Fleet," Doc said, hitting a button on his phone.

After a moment Doc said, "Is there a moon tonight?"

Julia watched as clearly Fleet on the other end looked that up. Then Doc said, "No. No moon at all."

Julia nodded. "Have Fleet look at the disappearances and trips to McCall and I'll bet he'll find they are all on nights of no moon. And all during the late spring, summer, and fall, when that pass is clear of snow."

Doc repeated that to Fleet and sat there silently.

Lott looked puzzled, but sat beside her saying nothing.

After another moment Doc said, "You are right. Why?"

Julia pointed out over the lake. "Because on a dark night, without running lights, in a black boat and dressed in black, no one would be able to see Williams leave his home and come across the lake to the mortuary. And then return."

Lott smiled and shook his head. He took her hand and squeezed it.

Doc repeated that to Fleet, then said, "Tell Agent Munn we are going to need a couple boats on the lake, running dark and way out from the shore after Williams gets to the mortuary, in case Williams slips from the mortuary after he is confronted."

He listened to what Fleet said. "They will, I have no doubt."

Then he hung up.

"He said be careful. Both he and Agent Munn are convinced it will all happen today and tonight."

Lott nodded.

Julia agreed completely. By sometime this afternoon, Trish's killer would be facing justice.

And by tonight, the killer of a lot of other women would be facing the same thing.

If they did this right and could pull off a great bluff first, and a great trap second.

And do it without anything alerting Williams that his system had broken down.

Part Five
THE PLAY

CHAPTER TWENTY-SIX

May 16, 2015
9 A.M.
McCall, Idaho

"TRUCK IS fifteen minutes out," Agent Munn said in Lott's ear. Actually, he and Julia and Annie were all wired up with almost invisible communication links that if even noticed looked more like a hearing aid stuck deep in the ear.

Lott and Julia and Annie were all ambling down the rough sidewalk beside McCall's main road, headed for the mortuary. The morning air still had a bite to it and the traffic on the main two-lane highway that ran through town was consistent.

All three of them had their service guns and badges on them, but well-hidden. Right at this point, Lott was very happy that the Las Vegas Chief of Police had allowed them to keep their badges and guns and work unofficially.

Granted, they were way out of jurisdiction, but considering they were working with the FBI at the moment, that made no difference.

And besides, Williams owned the police here, from everything Fleet had found. Or at least Williams owned the sheriff.

Lott forced himself to take a deep breath and let his nerves calm. The smell of pine trees, even in the middle of the small town, was strong, combined with some fish smells from the lake. He really liked it here.

"Ready?" Annie asked as they neared the two-story blue mortuary building sitting on a small rise above the shore of the lake. From the outside, the building looked more like an old remodeled church than anything else, only without a tall steeple.

"Ready," both Lott and Julia said at the same time.

From the floor plans that Fleet had found, the office, viewing room, and main chapel were on the main floor.

A small one-bedroom apartment filled the street side of the second floor, allowing the tall ceilings of the chapel on the main floor to open out over the lake.

In the basement area was the cold storage and embalming rooms, along with another office. A door opened to a path on the basement level that led out to the lake and a nearby dock.

Casket storage was off the viewing area on the main floor and a large door opened to a driveway beside the chapel that allowed caskets to be rolled in and out easily. Lott had no doubt that would be where the delivery truck would roll up.

The building also had a casket-sized freight elevator for raising and lowering caskets with bodies in them from the embalming area up to the chapel area.

Lott turned and went up the sidewalk toward the large wooden double front door. Lott pulled the door open and held it for Julia and Annie.

His stomach was twisting more than he wanted to admit. It had been a long time since he had been up front going into a dangerous situation like this. And it had been a long time since he had felt this kind of fear and heightened senses that went with this kind of operation.

Inside, there was faint chapel music playing in the background and the inside was lit with dim lights and the heat was a little too high, giving the place a stuffy feel.

A fake smell of lilacs filled the air as well.

"Truck five minutes out," Agent Munn said in their ears.

As the door closed behind them, a man came out of the office to the right, smiling. He wore a gray suit with a matching gray tie, black shoes, and a fake rose pinned to his lapel. His hair was thinning and he combed it back up and over the thinning spot.

Lott stepped forward, a massive fake smile on his face, his hand extended. "My name is Rick Guiss."

"Wade Andrews," the man said, shaking Lott's hand.

Lott felt so disgusted, he almost pulled his hand away and hit the guy right there. But somehow he managed to keep his poker face and turn slightly. "My wife Betty and my daughter, Betty-Anne."

Both Julia and Annie just nodded, but didn't step forward to shake the pervert's hand. Lott didn't blame them in the slightest.

"We're here to do a little shopping for caskets, set up some services for the two of us. Betty-Anne here insisted we get this out of the way."

"And a very smart thing to do," Andrews said, nodding.

"Truck has arrived," Agent Munn said in their ears at the same moment a slight ding echoed through the mortuary.

Andrews nodded to them. "If you'll excuse me for just a moment, that's a delivery I need to take care of. Would you like to wait in my office?"

"If you wouldn't mind," Lott said, smiling, "we'd just like to kick a few tires on some caskets."

"Dad," Annie said, playing along and hitting him on the shoulder slightly.

"This is serious business, dear," Julia said, giving him a fake stare to behave himself.

They had played it perfectly so far.

"Be my guest and feel free to look around," Andrews said. "Chapel is through those doors and the showroom for various caskets is through the doors to the left of the chapel. This delivery will be bringing in a couple more caskets as well."

Andrews nodded and turned toward the delivery door on the far side of the casket showroom.

"Cameras," Lott whispered without pointing to the cameras fairly well hidden in both corners.

Now Available
from all your favorite booksellers
in trade paper and electronic editions.

Both Annie and Julia nodded slightly, pretending to look around.

"No one else is in the building," Agent Munn said in their ears. "We now have the camera feeds blocked and all communication from the mortuary cut off. Just let them get that casket into place with the dummy in it and the truck gone and you can take him."

Lott liked the sound of that a great deal.

They went toward the casket showroom. At one point Julia pointed to some flower arrangement picture and then whispered to Lott. "I didn't see any sign he was carrying a piece."

"Let's not take any chances," Lott whispered.

Julia nodded and they went into the casket showroom filled with six caskets, all different colors and polishes. Three had their half-lids open, the other three were closed.

The wide doors on the other side of the room were standing open and Andrews and a truck driver were carefully wheeling one golden-toned casket in the door.

Lott knew, from the description, that was the one that was supposed to have the girl in it. Thank heavens they had rescued her in Seattle. Now there was no body there, just a dummy.

"Where do you want this one?" the driver asked.

Lott had no doubt that one question might clear the driver of being a part of this.

"On the elevator," Andrews said.

The two moved the large golden casket directly to the elevator and Andrew hit the down button before going back to help the driver wheel out the other two caskets into the showroom.

Then as Lott was pretending to study one of the mahogany caskets, he saw Andrew sign for the delivery and thank the driver.

Lott turned his back to Andrews for a moment and whispered, "Fleet, Andrew signed for the delivery. That has to be a hell of a paper trail if he has been doing that for years."

"Perfect," Agent Munn said.

Andrews came toward them, smiling after he closed the large doors and bolted them. Annie had moved to the left of the room, Julia to the right of Lott.

Lott hated the sick look the man had and just pretending to be nice to the guy was about as hard as anything he had ever had to do.

"Seeing anything you like?" Andrews said, stopping directly in front of Lott.

Both women eased over behind him, still both pretending to look at caskets.

"Actually," Lott said, "this will be a hard choice."

"Truck is away," Agent Munn said in their ears.

"But I have one thing I've really wanted to do when I came in here," Lott said.

"Yeah, me too," Julia said, laughing.

Julia's laugh sounded odd and Andrews turned slightly toward her just as Lott kicked Andrews as hard as he could right in the groin.

Lott knew that the trick to such a kick was to pretend that the target was about halfway up the spine, which then meant the foot hit the actual target with full force.

Lott felt his foot and upper shin connect perfectly with Andrews' soft genitals.

The force of Lott's kick almost lifted the man off the ground.

Andrews went down hard on the thin, blue carpet, trying to breathe and holding his crotch.

Annie and Julia were on Andrews instantly, expertly yanking his hands behind his back and zip-tying them there. Then they quickly searched him as he struggled to catch even the slightest bit of air.

"He's clean," Annie said after patting down his pants cuffs.

"Target is down," Lott said. "Send in the guards."

"Perfect," Agent Munn said in his ear.

Lott reached down and yanked the red-faced man to his feet. Andrews still hadn't caught his breath and any movement seemed to be sending waves of pain through him.

Good, as far as Lott was concerned.

As Lott held Andrews between the caskets, facing the two women, Julia said, "That was some kick."

"Thanks," Lott said, smiling.

"How exactly did you do that?" Julia asked, smiling.

Lott laughed. "I just pretended I was trying to kick a spot about halfway up his back."

Then, as Lott held Andrews, Julia said, "You mean like this?"

And she kicked Andrews in the groin even harder than Lott had done.

Andrews went instantly back to the floor in a silent scream.

"That was for Trish, you sick bastard," Julia said, almost spitting on the man on the carpet.

Annie just laughed and shook her head. "You know, you two are made for each other."

"We think so," Julia said, smiling at Lott and winking.

CHAPTER TWENTY-SEVEN

May 16, 2015
9:15 A.M.
McCall, Idaho

"AGENTS AT the service door dressed in electric company uniforms," Agent Munn said.

Lott moved over and unlocked the service door the caskets had come through, then stepped back so no one outside could see him if they happened to be looking.

Julia and Annie went up front to make sure the closed sign was up and the lights across the front were shut down. It would look like Andrews was gone at the moment, which is what they needed, since the mortuary was on the main road and a lot of traffic passed the building.

The two agents lifted Andrews from the floor and quickly taped his mouth shut. Then one told him he was under arrest for murder. One agent carefully read Andrews his rights while Lott and the other agent listened.

Then as Julia and Annie came back in, the agent asked Andrews if he understood his rights.

Andrews nodded.

"He nodded affirmative," one agent said.

"Perfect," Agent Munn said over the com link. "Get him on ice and don't let him even move a muscle until this is finished."

"Copy," one agent said and they hauled Andrew roughly up the stairs to his own apartment where the agents would hold him until everything was done tonight.

"Remember," Agent Munn said through the com link, "we don't have a search warrant yet. So we need to get on to the second part of this to get that warrant."

All three of them knew she was right. With the casket delivered there, they clearly could have gotten one, but at this point, they didn't want to take any chance at all in alerting Williams.

But Lott really, really wanted to see what was in the basement. But they had the sheriff to take care of first. And this was going to be the tricky part.

Then they could come back.

They headed out the front door of the mortuary, making sure that the door was locked and all the closed signs were in place. It took them only a couple minutes walk to reach the white Cadillac SUV in the ski-shop parking lot.

Doc was in the driver's seat, Annie climbed into the other front seat beside him and he leaned over and kissed her.

Agent Munn and Fleet were in the back seat, so Lott and Julia climbed into the middle seat.

"Anyone have a sanitary wipe. I had to shake that pervert's hand."

Annie laughed. "And great job there, Dad," she said, digging into the glove box and handing him a Wet Wipe.

"I loved the kicking the casket tires," Julia said, bumping Lott's shoulder.

"How did you take him down?" Agent Munn asked. "We heard no struggle at all."

Annie and Julia laughed.

"At my age, I sometimes have muscle spasms in my legs," Lott said. "This one was a pretty violent spasm, on the scheme of things."

Agent Munn and Doc broke into laughter, but Fleet looked confused.

"After we searched him and had him standing again," Annie said, turning slightly and winking at Julia, "Detective Roger's leg also had a violent spasm. It must have been something we ate at breakfast."

"Just our advanced age," Julia said, smiling.

Both Doc and Agent Munn were laughing so hard, Lott thought Doc might fall out of his seat.

"Do you mean you kicked him in the nuts?" Fleet asked, looking almost horrified.

"Not intentionally," Lott said, turning to smile at Fleet. "Muscle spasm is all."

Fleet just shook his head and turned to Agent Munn. "Are the communications links down at the moment?"

"They are," Munn said, nodding, still grinning from ear-to-ear.

"Then I have some more information about the sheriff," Fleet said. "He is the one who hires our friend in Las Vegas for the cars. I have traced the money finally on that."

Lott nodded.

"And the sheriff gets all his money from a Williams holding company that is three levels deep, but Williams has nothing to do with any of it. No trace at all that Williams even knows about the money, and it will be hard to trace, to be honest."

"Damn," Annie said.

"What about deputies?" Lott asked.

"The second in command is living well, also in theory on an inheritance," Fleet said. "Still digging on that one."

Lott could feel his stomach twisting. They needed something to tie Williams into all of this. Or far too much would rest on Williams showing up at the mortuary. And since he had a company that owns the mortuary, his presence could be explained away as well by a good attorney.

Right now all they had was a lot of circumstantial evidence, much of which had been obtained without a warrant. Unless the women's bodies had evidence that attached Williams in some way, and Lott doubted Williams would be that careless.

"We need to flip the sheriff," Lott said. "Get him to turn on Williams."

"And get Andrews at the mortuary to flip as well," Munn said. "Then if we catch Williams in the act in the mortuary, we'll have him rock solid."

"We trap the sheriff as planned," Lott said, glancing at Julia. "Get him to think he's going to lure us to kill us. And then we make him think he's going to go down for all the murders."

There was silence in the big car.

Lott turned to Julia. "You ready?"

"As I'm ever going to be," she said, smiling at him.

Agent Munn handed them both new Idaho driver's licenses. "Just in case," Agent Munn said.

Lott's license said his name was Rick Guiss. Julia was Betty Guiss. They lived in Boise.

"The blue sedan beside us is your car," Munn said. "I already have agents in place on both sides of the sheriff's office. He is in his office now."

"And we won't be far away," Annie said.

"Shall we go catch a bad guy, Mrs. Guiss," Lott asked, smiling at Julia.

"I think we should, Mr. Guiss," Julia said, laughing.

And with that they climbed out of the car and moved to the blue sedan and crawled in. This time they weren't going up against a mortuary owner, but an armed sheriff.

There were so many more things that could go wrong, Lott didn't even want to think about them all.

CHAPTER TWENTY-EIGHT

May 16, 2015
9:45 A.M.
McCall, Idaho

JULIA FELT SCARED to death as they climbed out of the sedan in the side parking lot of the sheriff's office. It had concrete block walls painted off-white, a shingled pitched roof, and the entire building seemed to sprawl fairly deep away from the road. From what she could tell, the back side of the building consisted of jail cells with thick metal screens over the windows.

The parking lot beside the office was small and a couple of white with black letter patrol cars were there. It hadn't occurred to Julia to ask how just how many deputies the sheriff had.

The front was glass doors and a wooden secretary's desk sat to one side of a small entry room. The desk was empty and didn't look like it was ever used. A dozen vinyl-cushioned metal chairs filled the small room with a few magazine racks that had some very old magazines in them, most of them gun or hunting magazines of some sort.

The door on the right was standing open showing a hallway leading to some office. As the glass front door closed behind them, a bell went off in the back.

A man about forty with broad shoulders and dark hair came into the hall from an office near the end and smiled. He was wearing a tan uniform and a gun on his hip.

"Hi, folks. Come on back," the officer said.

"You are coming in loud and clear," Agent Munn said in their ears. "And we heard whoever that was as well. All communications from the building have now been cut off."

Julia was very glad to hear that. They had both left their badges and guns in the car just in case the sheriff had a good eye for such things.

The man waited for them as they moved down the cement block hallway with worn linoleum on the floor. The other two offices they passed looked like they were used regularly, but at the moment no one was in them. The hallway smelled of burnt coffee, something most police stations smelled like at one point or another.

As they got closer, the man in uniform smiled and indicated they should come into his office, then turned and led the way inside.

Julia had no idea if this man was a deputy or the sheriff. They were about to find out. But they knew that the sheriff was in the building somewhere.

Julia went in first as the man in uniform went around behind the desk and indicated they should sit in the two chairs facing him. Over the years, Julia had done the same thing with numbers of people who came into the station in Reno. Did they all feel this scared?

She and Lott both sat and the man said, "I'm Sheriff Blake. What can I help you with on this fine spring day?"

They had their man. Now to set the trap.

Lott introduced them both as Julia sat watching Sheriff Blake's face. Then Lott

said, "We're from Boise and are here to look for our good friend, Trish Vittie."

At Trish's name, Julia saw the sheriff's eyes squint just slightly. On a poker table, that would have been enough of a tell to cost the sheriff a lot of money. In this office it was crystal clear.

"What seems to be the problem?" the sheriff asked. "Why are you looking for her? Has she gone missing?"

"She usually contacts us about once a week," Julia said, staying on the script they had worked out. "We are her only real family. And we haven't heard from her for a few weeks so we're worried."

The sheriff acted concerned and took out a pad as he would have been expected to do. "Do you have her address and I can send a car past her home."

"She lives in an isolated cabin up in the mountains," Lott said. "No real address, but we know it's on the other side of something called Lick Creek Summit. We've never been up there, but she sent us a map and it looks very isolated."

"So maybe her car broke down and she can't get out," the sheriff said.

"Possible," Julia said. "That's why we are going up to her place this afternoon. And if she's not there, we're going to stay for a week or so. She told us where the key is. But we wanted to check in with you first to make sure you hadn't heard anything."

When she had said they were planning on staying for a week or so, the sheriff's eyes squinted even more. He had a really bad tell. And he didn't much like at all that they were going in to the lake.

He stood. "Let me check to see if her name has come through any accident or hospital reports."

"Thank you," Julia said and Lott nodded.

The sheriff left and turned to the back of the building. At this point Sheriff Blake was playing his part perfectly. They had rattled him, of that there was no doubt.

But what was he going to do next? That was the question. If he really worked for Williams as it seemed, he couldn't take the chance that they would be in there for another body dump, not after Trish clearly reported the last one and it cost her life.

Now they just had to sit here, being bait on the end of a hook, and wait for the fish to bite.

CHAPTER TWENTY-NINE

May 16, 2015
10:05 A.M.
McCall, Idaho

LOTT SAT PATIENTLY beside Julia in Sheriff Blake's office. They didn't talk, but just waited as any good couple would do in this situation, hoping that law enforcement might help them.

"He tried to call the mortuary," Agent Munn said in their ears. "We let that call go through since no one is home there."

Lott looked at Julia and nodded. That linked the sheriff with the mortuary. Perfect.

"You have your agents in place?" Lott whispered.

"We do and they can be through the door in a matter of seconds," Agent Munn said.

"How many others besides the sheriff in the building?" Julia whispered.

"Jailer in the back, no one else," Agent Munn said. "All are on patrol."

"Be ready," Lott whispered. "This guy is already rattled. I think we can break him here."

"You sure?" Agent Munn asked.

"I'm sure," Julia whispered. "He clearly has never been confronted like this before. We're going off script to shove a stick in this hornet's nest."

"We're ready," Agent Munn said.

Finally the sheriff came back in and sat down, shaking his head. "Good news is that there are no accident reports on her and the hospital shows no one admitted by that name."

"That is good news," Lott said and Julia nodded, playing along with the script. But right there Lott decided it was a fine place to leave the script completely. "But did you also check the morgue?"

Sheriff Blake actually jerked slightly on that.

Lott had dealt with a lot of criminals and this guy was going to fold like wet tissue paper, of that there was no doubt.

"I had a horrid dream," Julia said, "that my friend was embalmed and floating on a smooth lake surface."

"She woke up screaming," Lott said, smiling at the sheriff.

The poor guy seemed to suddenly be sweating a little. This guy would have been the worst poker player in recorded history.

"Why would my friend be embalmed and in a mountain lake, sheriff?" Julia asked, staring at Sheriff Blake, her voice intense.

"We're moving in," Agent Munn's voice said in their ears. "We're coming in silent, so keep going."

"That is a good question," Lott said to Sheriff Blake. "How did our friend end up embalmed in a lake?"

The sheriff sputtered, then shook his head, but he had broken out in a sweat. The man knew something bad was happening to him and he had no idea what to do about it. Or how to stop it, so he tried to stay on a normal conversation. "That is an amazing dream."

"And I dreamed her car was there as well," Julia said, staring at Sheriff Blake. "On top of a large pile of older cars, all with embalmed women in them."

"This is too crazy," the sheriff said, standing and pulling his pistol and aiming it at them.

Lott and Julia both stood and stepped back. The sheriff clearly had not drawn his gun in a very long time and it was clear he had forgotten to put a clip in. He was so flustered, he didn't even realize that.

"Outside in the hallway," Agent Munn said in their ears. "We're holding here."

"No need for the gun, sheriff," Lott said to let the agents outside know what was happening.

"Who are you two?" Sheriff Blake demanded.

"Friends of Trish Vittie," Julia said. "As we said. But we are not sure why you had to kill her and all those other women as well."

"Who said I killed anyone?" Sheriff Blake demanded. "You two are nuts."

"Oh, we know you killed Trish," Lott said. "And we'll be pinning all forty or fifty or so murders on you as well. DNA you know, inside the bodies will be preserved in that cold water."

Lott doubted that would be possible, but he was wagering Sheriff Blake didn't know for certain that was the case. It was just another part of the bluff.

And from the look of how Blake went almost white and started sweating even more, he knew he had left DNA in many of those women.

"You have fun with the dead women?" Julia asked. "You and Andrews liked killing them all and then having sex with them?"

Lott smiled at Sheriff Blake. "We have your guy who bought the cars in Las Vegas. He's singing like a bird about you paying him a ton of money to get them. You know, the cars at the bottom of that lake with all the bodies in them?"

"I didn't kill anyone," Sheriff Blake said, almost whining like a child. He was now sweating even harder.

"You and Andrews are going down as two of the greatest serial killers of all time," Julia said. "Andrews is already singing as well, blaming it all on you. Death row won't take long for you two."

"It wasn't us," Sheriff Blake said as two FBI agents stepped into sight in the hallway, rifles aimed at the sheriff.

"Please put the gun down now, sheriff," Lott said, indicating the FBI agents. "It's over."

The sheriff put the gun slowly on the desk, his hands shaking. His face was totally white and he was sweating so hard, it was starting to stain his shirt.

The two FBI agents came in and quickly cuffed him, said he was under arrest for the murders of at least forty women. Then holding him there like that, one agent read Blake his rights.

When they were done, Lott looked at Sheriff Blake. "You said it wasn't you that killed all those women, yet we know it was. You killed them and Andrew embalmed them and you both got your sick jollies with the bodies before dumping them in the lake."

"I didn't kill them and Andrew didn't embalm them," the Sheriff said, looking panicked. "I swear. That was all Willis Williams doing."

"Yeah, right," Julia said. "And how do we prove that?"

For an instant the sheriff looked even more panicked. Then his eyes brightened and he said, "Williams kept all their clothes, their jewelry, everything. He called it his trophies. We only got rid of the bodies, nothing more."

"Where does he keep all that?" Lott asked, stunned.

"Damned if I know," Sheriff Blake said. "He took it all with him every time in a black bag."

The FBI agents pulled Sheriff Blake from his office, put a piece of tape over his mouth, and instead of turning toward the front door, turned toward the cells in the back. The sheriff's office was on lockdown until Williams arrived in town and showed up at the mortuary. And the sheriff was going to get to experience one of his own cells for a short time.

"You get all that?" Lott asked into the air.

"Loud and clear," Agent Munn said. "Loud and clear."

Part Six
THE SHOWDOWN

CHAPTER THIRTY

May 16, 2015
5:20 P.M.
McCall, Idaho

JULIA FOUND HERSELF walking along the beautiful mountain McCall Lake as dark settled over the water. The main part of town was just behind them, the dark mortuary ahead of them.

She was walking hand-in-hand with Lott, the man she was coming to love more and more each day. And she wished like anything this could have been under different circumstances, because it felt so right.

Maybe at some point she and Lott could go up to Taos and walk along the lake there. That would be perfect, especially on a beautiful spring night as this was.

The warmth of the day hadn't yet left the air and the smell of pine trees and steaks cooking at a nearby restaurant were like a comforting blanket.

She felt very rested because after the sheriff was tucked away, she and Lott and Annie and Doc and Fleet had gone back to Doc's house on Cascade Lake.

She and Lott had stretched out on couches in front of the fireplace and both taken short naps. She could have gone up to her room, and he could have gone to his room, but it seemed they wanted to stay close to each other at the moment.

She really wanted to stay close to him a lot more when this was finished. He seemed to be a rock to her worry, even though she could tell, and he had said, he had been scared to death a few times, especially when Sheriff Blake pulled his gun.

But knowing the FBI agents were right outside the door had helped calm them both.

Fleet had said that he and Agent Munn had search warrants ready to file for the mortuary, the sheriff's office and home, and Williams' home on the lake as soon as Williams ended up at the mortuary.

As soon as they arrested Williams, search warrants would be issued for his other homes in Boise, Seattle, and Las Vegas.

They had had to file the search warrant for the mortuary first, but Fleet and Agent Munn were positive that Williams would not find out about it before he did his boat trip across the lake.

They had had a nice early dinner that Annie and Doc had cooked, then had all headed back into McCall.

Just at dark, Julia and Lott had headed down the beach to go in the back door of the mortuary and get set up for Williams' arrival.

Williams had been in his home on the lake for four hours now and hadn't made a call or taken an incoming call.

"This has been a nice walk," Lott said.

"It has," Julia said, squeezing his hand. "Let's do it again without half the world listening and a serial killer on the loose."

"Deal," Lott said, glancing around to see if anyone was watching.

Julia knew that a number of FBI agents were watching, but she couldn't see any of them.

They went up the back steps to the mortuary from the beach as if they belonged there and went inside.

The room was a stark, white room with three metal embalming tables lined up. Shelves filled with various supplies filled the right wall and the concrete floor was washed down and clean. But the place still smelled of a slight rotting flesh covered with the odor of disinfectant.

The gold casket sat on the lift to the back of the room and a door to the right led into a small office there, which also had a shower and bathroom. Stairs from the upstairs were against the left wall with the door closed at the bottom.

The larger freezer door on the left of the lift was to a cooling room. Julia didn't want to know if any townspeople were in there at this point. They were going to have to find another mortuary starting tomorrow.

Julia had watched numbers of autopsies as a detective and it was always the smell that got her the worst. The smell in this place wasn't much better.

Agent Munn greeted them.

"How's Andrews holding up?" Lott asked.

"Pleading for a doctor and a deal," Agent Munn said, laughing. "He has also said, while being recorded, that Williams did the murder and the embalming, confirming the story the sheriff said."

"The rats are jumping this ship," Lott said. "Did you ask him how he leaves the lights in the mortuary and the back door open or locked for Williams.

"Andrews said the upstairs lights are always off," Agent Munn said. "These lights are on, back porch light is on, back door is unlocked."

"So we're set," Lott said.

"And where is the victim?" Julia asked.

"Andrew said they leave her in the casket on the lift, and leave her alone with Williams," Agent Munn said. "They are always upstairs when he arrives and never saw the victims alive. When Williams calls for them a couple hours later, she is dead and embalmed."

Julia was so glad they had rescued the girl in Washington.

A moment later, Annie opened the back door and came in and shut it behind her.

"Nice smell," she said, waving her hand in front of her face.

"So now we are completely set," Lott said.

Agent Munn nodded. "My people will tell us when he arrives and goes in the back door here. It will take them about fifteen seconds to get to the back door to block it."

"So now we wait," Lott said. "How about we do that upstairs in the dark in those comfortable chairs in the waiting room?"

"I agree," Julia said, having no desire at all to stay in this smell or this room of death. "It's just barely dark out there. It might be hours."

At that very moment a voice came through their communication links in their ears. "Williams just left his boat dock, no running lights, wearing black."

"How about fifteen minutes," Agent Munn said, smiling. "Report when he lands."

"Copy," one of the agents said.

She went over, made sure the back door was unlocked, then the four of them stood there, waiting.

CHAPTER THIRTY-ONE

May 16, 2015
5:40 P.M.
McCall, Idaho

LOTT COULDN'T BELIEVE they were about to capture Williams. And they had built a very, very strong case against the killer already. A case so strong, not even a good lawyer was going to get him off.

Lott really wanted to see the smirk on the man's face just disappear. That smug you-can't-catch-me attitude had been more than he could take, especially when it came to that young married college girl named Carrie Coswell.

Carrie had just vanished seemingly into thin air while jogging and everyone knew that Williams had done it, but there hadn't been one shred of evidence that he had. Lott and Andor had been the lead detectives on the case and had wanted to just smash the smirk from Williams' face.

Now Lott knew that Carrie's body would be found in that lake, in a car, and now Williams would go to jail for her death. And Carrie's family could finally get some closure.

"You all right?" Julia asked, taking his hand.

"Just thinking of one of this animal's victims is all."

Julia squeezed Lott's hand and smiled at him. "We almost got him. Almost."

They stood there, waiting. Lott figured it would take Lott about twenty minutes, going slow, to cross the distance from his place to the dock near the mortuary.

After fifteen minutes, Lott glanced at his watch.

Julia was looking nervous as well.

"Why do I feel this isn't going to work as planned?" Lott said.

He turned to Agent Munn. "Have your people check for any kind of signal along the shore out to the lake in case we have a leak somewhere."

"Do it, folks," Agent Munn said.

After a moment one agent came back. "We have a state police car in the Shore Lodge parking lot, its lights going as if it has pulled someone over. That's it."

"Someone check it," Agent Munn said. "Everyone else remain in position."

Three more minutes went by until an agent came back. "The State Police Car is empty. Its headlights were on high-beam aimed out over the lake, the bubbles going."

"Find out who was driving that car," Agent Munn ordered, clearly very, very angry.

"Those of you at Williams' home, close in and secure the place and secure him if he comes back to that dock."

Lott knew he wasn't coming back to the dock. He had been warned off. And knowing Williams, he had a plan and a way to escape. But if they acted quickly enough, with enough force, they might be able to catch him.

"We need to lock down every road in and out of this town," Lott said. "No one in or out without eyes on them. And Williams will be in disguise."

"Do it, people," Agent Munn said. "Get the State Police to help as well and find out who was driving that patrol car and get that person rounded up as well."

"His name was Ben Stephens," one of the agents came back. "He's gone missing and is not responding to any calls."

Lott glanced at Julia. It felt as if he had been smashed in the stomach. Not Ben.

Anyone but Ben.

That wasn't possible.

Not with his family and kids. Ben wouldn't do something like this.

Then Lott heard what he had just thought.

"Fleet," Lott said. "Are you monitoring this?"

"I am," Fleet said, his voice low and clearly as shocked as Lott was feeling.

"Ben wouldn't do this," Lott said, "so his family, his kids, must be threatened. Get people to his house in Boise as fast as you can. Tell them to go in silent and armed."

"On it," Fleet said.

Lott just stood there in the smell of death in the basement of the mortuary, holding Julia's hand. Now they had one of the world's richest men on the run.

And one of the world's most dangerous killers.

CHAPTER THIRTY-TWO

May 16, 2015
6:10 P.M.
McCall, Idaho

JULIA AND LOTT caught a ride with Annie out to Williams' home along the lake. Doc and Fleet had sprinted for the airport to contain Williams' plane and to make sure no one rented him anything.

Fleet had downloaded a floor plan for the big mansion for him and Annie on a tablet as they went into the beautiful, but sterile place.

Wood and stone and glass, along with mostly bright white furnishings and carpet and counters and cabinets made the home feel far, far from a home on a mountain lake. It felt more like the inside of a hospital to Julia.

"This is like looking inside a snowstorm," Lott said, looking around.

Julia could not agree more. It was awful. The worst design she had ever seen.

Why would you have white kitchen counters, white tile on the floor, white carpet in the living room with white furniture?

As they went from room to room, nothing changed.

The place had no color at all. Just white and glass and white stone.

The FBI had already secured the home and were now patrolling around the edge of the entire lake, both by boat and by land. But as Agent Munn had told them, it was a very large lake. Almost fifty miles of shoreline and coves and hidden homes. They just didn't have enough manpower in here to do that as well as set up roadblocks on the roads.

And it would take time to get more people, time that allowed Williams to escape.

Fleet had a horde of computer people searching for any record that Williams or one of his many companies owned another property around the lake, but so far that had been for nothing. Just this one huge property that jutted out into the lake.

They looked around, and all of them looked for any kind of secret room that wasn't on the plans, but one clearly didn't exist. That was easy to see with the open floor plan. The FBI would bring in sounding equipment to see what was under the building, but Julia doubted they would find anything at all.

"We're missing something," Julia said. "He would know we would find more property if he owned it here."

Lott and Annie both nodded.

"So he wouldn't really leave this place," Julia said. "And this would be where he would keep his trophies from all his kills."

"I agree," Lott said. "But there is nothing here. And they have searched the out buildings and the empty boat house."

Julia suddenly remembered what she had seen that had been bothering her. She turned to Annie. "Do you have an aerial shot of this property during the day taken recently?"

"I'll download it to your tablet," Fleet said in their ears. He had blocked them from all the chatter from the FBI, but kept the five of them hooked together.

A moment later the aerial image appeared with property lines marked in green dashed lines on both sides. The main house was clear, as was the dock and the outbuildings and boat shed.

Julia looked around the end of the point and studied the trees along the far side of the property.

"There," she said, pointing to what looked like a faint roofline hidden under the trees. "I'm betting he's there."

"Agent Munn," Fleet said. "Need you and a couple agents at the house at once. We have a lead."

"Copy," Agent Munn said. "Ten minutes out."

Julia looked at Lott who nodded.

Julia knew that she was right, they had a very dangerous killer trapped in that small area. And when that happened, lots of things could go very wrong.

She had once had a bullet smash the bones in her leg in just such a situation.

CHAPTER THIRTY-THREE

May 16, 2015
6:30 P.M.
McCall, Idaho

LOTT AND JULIA and Annie were just inside the sliding glass doors that led out onto a wide porch over the boathouse and dock. This was as far as they could get outside the house. Lott was convinced the white on everything would give him a headache in short order; they at least had managed to find a warm spot to stand and could face out at the dark night and the trees.

The three of them were studying the various ways to get to the hidden building on the far side of the property when Fleet contacted them again.

"You were right about Ben's family," Fleet said in their ears. "His wife and kids are all right, but scared to death. The two men who were holding them are down, shot in a firefight with the Boise police. One is dead, the other isn't talking."

Lott looked at Julia and shook his head. Ben would have never done this without that kind of major threat to his family. Thank heavens they were all right, but now they needed to figure out where Ben was.

"Any idea where Ben might be?" Fleet asked as Lott tried to puzzle out that same question.

"He doesn't drink, he doesn't smoke, he loves law enforcement and his family," Lott said.

"And he would have to just wait this out, hope we took down Williams, before he dared try to rescue his family," Julia said.

Lott nodded, then suddenly realized what he had said and where Ben would hide. He would hide right in plain sight, close to where he left his car, but where no one who knew him would look for him.

"He's in the bar at Shore Lodge," Lott said. "He will not be armed and once he learns his family is free, he's going to be willing to help. Actually, he's going to be so angry, he's going to demand to help."

"Doc and I are one minute from there," Fleet said. "We'll pick him up if you are right."

At that moment Agent Munn and two other agents in black FBI jackets came into the house and through the living room to them.

"Good job on saving the State Police officer's family," Munn said.

"We knew him," Julia said.

"My partner and I trained him in Vegas," Lott said. "We knew he wouldn't have done anything like that without a threat on his family."

Agent Munn nodded. "So what kind of lead do you have?"

Annie showed the agents the overhead view of Williams' property. And pointed to the almost hidden roofline on the far side of the ridge near the lakeshore.

"Agent Munn nodded. "I think you are right. Logical."

She quickly got two of the FBI boats to converge on the other side of the Williams' property. "Come in dark and quiet," she ordered them.

She nodded and turned to Lott and Julia and Annie and the other two agents. Then she waved over another agent on duty on the door.

"We might have our suspect trapped in a hidden building on the property," Agent Munn said.

She showed them Annie's pad and the image. She pointed to a place on the road that went past the property. Then she turned to two agents. "You two go up on the road and get hidden there in case he comes out of the brush that way."

They both nodded.

Lott liked how Agent Munn was thinking. And she wasn't calling for more help, which might tip off Williams if he was listening in.

Agent Munn turned to the agent who had been on the door. "Take one of the agents who is down on the dock and both of you move around the lake shore slowly. Make no sounds and stay out of sight."

The other agent nodded.

"No contact. We can't tip Williams off in any way."

All three agents nodded.

Then she turned to Lott and Julia and Annie. "Detectives, the four of us are going over the ridge by land and going to come in on the building from there."

Lott nodded, as did Julia and Annie beside him.

Lott again felt his stomach twist at the fear and the excitement of actually being back on the job once again.

CHAPTER THIRTY-FOUR

May 16, 2015
6:45 P.M.
McCall, Idaho

LOTT, GUN IN HAND, moved as silently as he could along the trail through the tall pine trees. The night was pitch black and the air had a cold, crisp bite to it.

He had a small flashlight that gave off just enough light so that he could see the ground in front of him. Someone had kept this part of the forest cleared of any deep underbrush, but everything was covered with pine needles and small branches that seemed to crack or rustle with every step.

A trial led from the porch into the trees and toward the small ridge that ran down the center of the property down to the lake. Agent Munn was on that trail, moving slowly.

All of them were moving slowly, checking for any kind of alarm or trap that might have been set.

Julia was to his left, Agent Munn on the trail to his right, and Annie on the other side of Agent Munn.

"In place," the two agents up on the road said.

Otherwise all the chatter was coming from agents in different areas around the lake, at roadblocks, and so on. Fleet had taken Lott and Julia and Annie off just the private links with him and hooked them back into the major FBI link system.

Lot had to admit, the FBI were doing an amazing job of locking down the small town in a very short time, from what he heard.

As they crested the small ridge, Lott could see the faint glimmering of the black surface of the lake down a gentle slope through the trees. The night was unbelievably still and he wanted to hold his breath to try not to make any sounds.

And could swear his old heart was going to beat right out of his chest with every step.

"In place," a different agent said. Lott figured that was from the boats on the lake.

If they were wrong about Williams being in this building, then they had wasted a lot of critical time.

All four of them moved down closer to the dark building, mostly dug into the side of the hillside between two large trees. It was amazing Annie had seen anything at all here, and brush had been allowed to grow up between the building and the lake edge, so it couldn't be seen from the lake at all.

As Lott got closer, he could tell the building was made of cement blocks and painted brown to match the surrounding forest. And it was much larger than it seemed from the glimpse in the picture.

Since the back of the building was dug into the hillside, there was no back entrance at all, or side entrances.

Agent Munn moved along the edge of the building and looked around front. No front windows, just one metal door that looked more like it belonged on a utility shed or pump house than anything else.

Could they have been wrong? Was this a well house or something else like that?

Annie and Julia and Lott fanned out around the front of the building entrance, guns drawn and covering it. Lott took a position just to a side of a large pine tree so he could duck for cover if he needed.

Agent Munn glanced around, nodded, then went up from the side, turned the handle and pushed the door open.

Nothing.

She eased forward, without poking her head around the corner and shone her light into the room.

Pumps and other machines sat in there from what Lott could see.

But that didn't mean that Williams wasn't still hiding in there.

Lott came up to the door quickly, followed by Julia and Annie.

Without a word, Agent Munn went inside, going one way, gun drawn, Lott went in going the other, Annie and Julia followed.

It took them only a few seconds to clear the large pump house.

Williams was not here.

CHAPTER THIRTY-FIVE

May 16, 2015
7:05 P.M.
McCall, Idaho

JULIA COULD NOT BELIEVE that they had been wrong. She had been so convinced that Williams would have been in here, finding only pump and well equipment stunned her.

There just was nothing but some basic ground equipment and tools and supplies. No sign at all that Williams had even set foot in this building ever.

They had all four holstered their weapons and were standing near the door sort of in stunned silence when something in the upper corner of the back wall caught her eye.

She instantly recognized it and turned away.

"Well, we were wrong about this one," Julia said, easing Lott toward the door. "We're wasting time here. Let's head back to the house and decide where to go next."

Agent Munn nodded and led the way out of the building. Julia followed her quickly outside and before Agent Munn could give the call for the other agents to stand down, Julia grabbed her arm and shook her head. She indicated they should all be quiet.

Lott was about to pull the door closed and Julia, out of any camera angle, waved that he not do that.

Lott acted instantly, bent down to pretend to pick up something, and then left with the door standing open.

They moved back flat against the concrete wall.

"Cameras," Julia whispered.

Instantly all four of them were searching the edge of the eaves on the building, the trees, anything for any sign of cameras.

Nothing that they could see.

"Camera inside upper corner on the left," Julia whispered. "My gut sense tells me there's a hidden bunker behind that back wall."

"Nice spot, Detective," Agent Munn whispered.

Lott squeezed her hand gently and smiled.

"There is no need to whisper, Agent Munn," a man's voice said.

Julia glanced around, but could not see where the voice was coming from, but Lott, Agent Munn, and Annie instantly froze into guns drawn position.

It was clearly Williams and he was clearly watching them and listening to them.

"All agents," Agent Munn said, "Converge on my position."

Julia just hoped that would be fast enough.

CHAPTER THIRTY-SIX

May 16, 2015
7:10 P.M.
McCall, Idaho

LOTT COULDN'T BELIEVE that Williams was taunting them at this point. He had to know he was trapped like an animal in a hole.

But just the sound of the man's voice sent chills down Lott's back. And made him angry. The images of that dead woman sitting in the car floated back like a ghost and he shook it away.

As Williams had spoken, all four of them had eased away from the wall and farther apart, each seeking some cover in the trees.

"Detective Lott, you two are sure a long ways from home. What brings you out of Glitter Gulch to the beautiful mountains of Idaho?"

"Tracking you down," Lott said, his voice angry as he motioned for everyone to ease back farther from the building.

"And who is the detective with you with the sharp eye?" Williams asked. "I don't think I've had the pleasure."

"Detective Julia Rogers," Julia said into the air. "Your goons killed my best friend Trish."

"I have never had the pleasure to meet a Trish," Williams said.

"We know," Lott said as Agent Munn indicated they should keep him talking and all of them should keep easing back to find cover. From what Lott could tell, more than a dozen agents would be here in minutes.

"Sheriff Blake and Andrews killed her because she saw the last body dump," Julia said. "She was living in the home on the lake where you stashed all your victims."

There was silence. Finally Williams said, "So you have the killers. Why are you hounding me?"

"Because we have tracked all the mortuary trucks you used to transport your victims," Lott said. "The last poor woman was rescued in Seattle before you left the city. She can identify you easily."

There was again silence.

Lott glanced at Agent Munn who nodded and indicated help would come pouring in within two minutes.

"Come on, Williams," Lott said. "You know you want to let us in there to show us your trophies."

Williams laughed. "No one but me will ever see these wonderful prizes I have accumulated over my lifetime. They are my intimate moments with women of my dreams."

"That's just sick," Julia said.

Williams laughed. "Detective, each person has their own ways of finding love in the world. Too bad you didn't know about your husband for so long?"

Julia's eyes went wide and she glanced at Lott.

Lott was stunned. Clearly Williams had known about what they were doing for some time.

What the hell was happening here?

They hadn't been trapping Williams, he had been trapping them, cleaning up his messes as he went along. More than likely that entire building was rigged to explode.

Lott waved Agent Munn and Julia and Annie back and pointed to the lake. Then he mouthed the word, "Run!"

"And you know what, Detective Lott?"

"What?" Lott asked, backing up slowly as Agent Munn, Annie, and Julia turned and ran for the lake edge down the shallow slope.

"No one will ever know for sure if I was killed here or not," Williams said. "Isn't that just ironic? No real trace will ever be found."

"It doesn't have to end this way," Lott said, still backing slowly up.

Williams laughed, the pure evil sound echoing through the dark trees. "Detective, it was always meant to end this way. You detectives just don't ever see the long game, do you? You are all the same."

"Williams…" Lott started to say, but was cut off.

"Detective," Williams said. "You bore me. Goodbye."

Lott turned and sprinted to the edge of the lake as Julia, Annie, and Agent Munn went into the water and ducked under.

The explosion smashed Lott in the back and he flew down into the water and the blackness that cold brought with it.

CHAPTER THIRTY-SEVEN

May 16, 2015
7:15 P.M.
McCall, Idaho

LOTT CAME AROUND quickly as Julia and Annie pulled him from the freezing cold lake water and up onto the shore. He tried to blink the water from his eyes, but everything was bright golden from the huge fire.

"Dad!" Annie said, leaning over him. "Are you all right?"

Annie's face was close on the left, Julia's on the right.

"With my two favorite women on the planet this close, how could I not be all right?"

They both laughed and Julia kissed him on the cheek. "Can you stand?"

"Getting tougher with every year," Lott said, smiling, "but I think so." He had no doubt he was going to have a very sore back, and one knee felt like he scraped it on some rock or something, but otherwise he seemed to be all right. Damned lucky. At his age he didn't bounce when he fell.

They helped him up as the water drained from his clothes. He leaned on Julia as they turned around and looked back up at the burning building and the trees around it, some of which were burning as well. The crackling and popping echoed through the night and beyond that sirens were wailing.

He knew he had to be numb and in some shock, because he couldn't really feel the cold.

"He wasn't in there," Lott said as they stared at the fire that seemed to be burning hotter by the moment.

"What do you mean?" Agent Munn asked, standing beside them on the edge of the water. She was as wet as he was, her hair plastered to her face, her FBI jacket hanging soaked on her shoulders.

"He so much as told me so," Lott said. "He said we never play the long game. He said we would never find his remains in there."

Agent Munn nodded. "From the way it's burning, he may have been right."

"This was planned ahead," Munn said.

"How did he know me?" Julia asked. "Shocked me down to my poor soaked feet."

"He set up Trish to be found," Lott said, looking at Julia, the woman he loved. "And for Sheriff Blake and Andrews to take the fall for him. He wanted this to end now so he could move on. The challenge of beating us again and again was over."

"There is no way he would kill himself in there," Annie said. "I agree."

"So where is he?" Agent Munn asked.

"He's close," Lott said. "More than likely in a car near the edge of town. He was talking with us. And I think after we get into some dry clothes and get something hot to drink, I'll bet Fleet and his people can help us find out where exactly he is."

"Did I hear my name taken in vain?" Fleet asked as he and Doc and Ben ran along the beach to them.

They all looked worried and were moving as fast as they could. Around the fire other FBI agents were swarming the area now.

"You all right?" Doc asked, moving quickly to Annie.

"Thanks to Dad," Annie said, giving Doc a very wet hug. "We got out of there in time."

Lott turned to Ben. "Glad to see you're all right."

"Thank you all for believing in me and saving my family," Ben said. Lott could see the pain in his eyes. "I didn't know what else to do."

"You're going to have to answer some questions and face some consequences you know," Agent Munn said, patting Ben on the shoulder.

"I know. And I will face them. I'm just glad you got him."

"We didn't get him," Lott said. "This was just to let him think we did."

"What?" Fleet and Ben both asked at the same time.

Lott was now starting to really feel the cold and Julia was shivering.

"He set all this up," Lott said, "including Trish's death and we went right along with it. He led us to the bodies, everything."

"How do you know?" Fleet asked.

Lott turned to Ben. "I assume this is the only time he has threatened you in the slightest. Right?"

Ben nodded slowly. "I wanted to get the bastard as much as you all did. I was in Vegas when one of the women went missing there, remember. I hated how that bastard taunted us. But I had no choice when he sent pictures of my wife and kids tied up and a man standing there with a gun at their heads."

"You were needed to make us think he had been warned away. He was never on that boat."

Ben nodded. "So this all was his exit strategy. Everything?"

"Everything," Lott said, agreeing.

Lott pointed to all the FBI agents watching the fire. "And we played right into his plan as he knew we would."

"Damn it all to hell," Agent Munn said, shaking her head and heading up the hill to some other agents there.

"He taunted me right before the explosion, said we never play the long game," Lott said. "So now it's time we figure out his long game and surprise him. But first we need some dry clothes and something very warm to drink."

"Oh, yes, please," Julia said.

CHAPTER THIRTY-EIGHT

May 16, 2015
7:30 P.M.
McCall, Idaho

JULIA COULDN'T believe how cold she had gotten in the night air while wet from the icy lake water. She and Lott, walking arm-in-arm had taken only a few minutes to get back to the cars in front of Williams' house and into Doc's big Cadillac SUV, but by the time they got there, they were both staggering slightly.

Julia could feel her energy draining away because of the cold. They all would be in serious trouble if they didn't get warm quickly.

Agent Munn had come along after reassigning agents back to watching the roads and other agents with the fire department that was arriving to put out the fire.

Doc had the car going and the heat up quickly, but even the warm air filling the car didn't take off the chill. She had to get out of the wet clothes and quickly.

"Let's get to Shore Lodge," Doc said. "We'll get a couple suites there and get you all into warm showers. Ben and Fleet can head toward Cascade to get fresh clothes for everyone."

"I think Ben needs to stay here for the time being," Agent Munn said, her teeth chattering slightly.

"I agree," Ben said. "I need to stick close so I can be questioned and detained for my actions."

"When the time comes," Agent Munn said. "Right now we need all hands on deck, but I don't want to be getting too loose about it."

"Thank you," Ben said, nodding. "I'll help where I can. I'm just glad my family is safe."

Doc got them suites quickly at Shore Lodge and this time they went to the left past the desk and up a flight of stairs.

She still leaned on Lott and he leaned against her, but both of them were shaking they were so cold. Doc opened one door and indicated Lott and Julia should go in there.

"Clothes and some hot coffee and tea and hot chocolate coming quickly," Doc said. "Then he opened the door to the next suite and let Annie and Agent Munn in.

"Back shortly," Doc said, closing the door behind Annie. Then he and Fleet and Ben headed almost at a run down the hall back the way they came.

Julia smiled at Lott and closed the door. "Looks like we're sharing a suite."

"Seems people see more about us than we even admit to ourselves," Lott said, smiling.

Then he pointed to the bathroom. "Toss out two towels and don't be too long in the shower."

"You could always join me," she said, smiling at him as best she could considering how cold she was.

"Oh, trust me, I would love to," he said. "But going from freezing cold to boiling hot might be too much for my system."

She laughed and stripped out of her wet coat and tossed it into a pile near the bathroom door. Then she kicked off her soaking wet and muddy tennis shoes and soaking socks and tossed them on her coat.

Then she went into the bathroom, turned on the hot shower, and went back out with two towels for Lott.

He was already mostly undressed, standing there only in his wet pants.

She was stunned how a man his age, who had just gone through an explosion and who was freezing, could look so damned good.

She tossed him the towels. "I'll be fast."

"You had better be or I'm going to climb in there with you," he said.

"That is not an incentive to hurry," she said, laughing and turning away.

CHAPTER THIRTY-NINE

May 16, 2015
7:45 P.M.
McCall, Idaho

LOTT MANAGED to get himself naked and toweled off pretty well and then had a towel around his waist when Julia came out of the bathroom. Getting out of the wet clothes and dried off had helped the chill some, but not all the way.

She had a towel wrapped around her and her skin looked almost pink from the warm water. She was drying off her hair as best she could with another towel.

"All yours," she said, smiling at him as he stared at her.

"You are really the most beautiful woman I have ever seen," he said. He was stunned. He loved her as a person, but now he was seeing the more personal side of her and discovering she was even better looking than he realized.

She beamed and seemed to get a little redder in the face. "I'd kiss you after such a nice comment, but chances are your skin feels cold and slimy and I'm just not into that."

"Hold that promise of a kiss," he said, moving past her and into the steaming hot bathroom. "I'll be all hot and squeaky clean in a minute or two.

She laughed as he closed the door slightly and then stepped into the shower, letting the hot water take away some of the aches.

Finally, after he had rinsed every bit of the lake water from his hair and body and soaped twice, he turned off the shower and used another fresh towel to dry off.

Then wrapping the towel around his waist, he opened the bathroom door. "Want to share a hair dryer?"

"Perfect," she said, coming back in and standing beside him as he first did a quick run on the dryer through his hair, then handed it to her.

He stood there staring at her as she used her fingers as a comb through her long hair. Her body moved perfectly under the white towel and he wanted to watch this sort of thing every morning.

There was a knock at the door. He kissed her on the shoulder and went back out into the living room area of the big suite and opened the door, making sure his towel wasn't showing anything that shouldn't be shown.

Doc and Ben came in carrying trays of hot drinks and a couple of boxes of hot food and pastries. The wonderful smell of hot chocolate hit Lott instantly as Doc passed him.

"Fleet says he's ten minutes out," Doc said. "So we'll set this up here and when he gets here with the clothes we'll all meet in here to figure out where we go next."

"Hot chocolate and a doughnut first," Lott said.

"Double that," Julia said, coming out of the bathroom holding her towel up to make sure it stayed in place as well.

Ben worked quickly to pour them both hot chocolates out of a large thermos while Doc poured a cup of coffee from another one and grabbed a breakfast pastry for Annie and headed next door.

A moment later he was back pouring another hot chocolate and grabbing a doughnut for Agent Munn.

Lott let the hot chocolate take the last of the chill from his back and stomach and then a bite of the cake doughnut made his stomach really happy.

Julia smiled at Doc and Ben. "Thank you."

Then with her doughnut in one hand and her hot chocolate in the other, she headed back to the bathroom and closed the door to work on her hair some more.

"Hope putting you both in here together was all right," Doc said, smiling at Lott.

"Just perfect," Lott said.

And it had been.

CHAPTER FORTY

May 16, 2015
8:30 P.M.
McCall, Idaho

JULIA COULD NOT BELIEVE how much better she felt after a shower, some hot chocolate, a doughnut, and fresh, warm clothes. She couldn't remember being that cold in a very, very long time. There was a reason she liked Las Vegas so much. It was warm.

She sat next to Lott on the couch in the large suite. Annie sat in a cloth overstuffed chair and Doc had pulled up a chair from the small table and sat beside her.

Fleet sat at the small table near one wall, his laptop in front of him, his fingers seeming to not stop moving.

Agent Munn and Ben sat facing Lott and Annie. All of them had hot drinks and Julia was working on her second doughnut. Doc had ordered in pizza and it would be here shortly.

"So how come we're not all panicked to catch Williams now?" Julia asked, looking around at the fairly relaxed group drinking hot beverages.

"Because he's going to believe we think him dead and is heading out of the area," Agent Munn said.

"And that's the problem Williams has," Doc said, smiling. "There are just very few ways out of this area."

"Only three," Fleet said, "and two I am convinced he would never take."

"Three?" Julia said, surprised.

"Besides flying," Fleet said, not looking up from his keyboard, "which we have covered, yes only three. The major highway outside the hotel here is the only north-south road in the state. It's only two lanes, so that is two of the three ways. And about twenty miles to the east of here there is another road that leaves the highway and goes back toward Boise and Oregon."

"He wouldn't go that way," Ben said, "and he wouldn't go back toward Boise because too many people have the chance of recognizing him."

"So he's headed north," Julia said.

"How long until he can actually get off that road in any real fashion?" Lott asked.

"The road merges into the highway coming in from Missoula, Montana," Ben said. "About three hours from here."

"If he left right after the explosion," Fleet said, "He would be just over an hour along the road."

"He would know he was putting himself into that bottleneck," Annie said.

"He flat does not think we survived the explosion, or that he has anything to worry about," Lott said. "He has steered us like cattle in chutes and believes there is no way we could ever be ahead of him."

"So before we talk about how we find him," Agent Munn said, "I think Ben needs to leave us."

Ben nodded. "I completely understand, Agent Munn."

She nodded and stood and Ben stood while Julia and everyone watched. She knew this was the right thing, but from the looks on Lott's and Fleet's face, it hurt them.

Agent Munn opened the door to the hallway where two of her agents stood. She indicated that Ben turn around. She was handed cuffs by one agent and she put Ben in cuffs, then nodded to the two men. "Watch him closely until this clears."

Both men nodded.

Ben glanced back at the room. Julia could see the hurt in his eyes, but the strength as well. "I'm sorry for the part I played in this."

"All of us were duped up to this point," Lott said.

"You'll be fine," Fleet said, "and your family is in a safe place, so no worries there. This will be over soon."

Ben went out the door and let the two agents take him down the hallway.

Agent Munn closed the door and came back and sat down. To break the silence she asked, "So how do we find Williams? That's some stretch of road and even at this time of the evening there are going to be cars all along it."

"We got him," Fleet said, looking up from his computer and smiling. "He's just passing through the little town of Riggins driving a pretty standard dark blue Ford sedan. And unless he really wants to trap himself up in dead-end roads along the River of No Return, he's continuing on the main highway."

"There is no real way off that road there," Doc said, laughing. "River of No Return on one side, Hell's Canyon on the other."

"How did you do that?" Lott asked Fleet a half second before Julia could. "How did you find him?"

She was stunned that Fleet had been able to find Williams so easily, even with the limits on the road.

"Once I turned my people on Williams' finances to look for money he was funneling away from his businesses, the trails went cold quick. We could find nothing," Fleet said, smiling. "Everything

looked as if he was going to kill himself in that building."

"I'm not following you?" Julia said.

"Williams had his fingers and ownership in hundreds and hundreds of companies all over the world," Fleet said. "And many, many of the companies were almost impossible to track back to him. He had many good people working for him who knew how to cover ownership tracks through offshore accounts and such,"

"But when you have a large web," Lott said, sitting forward on the couch, "and suddenly there is a very black hole in the middle of the web, you know something is there, but not able to be seen."

"Exactly," Fleet said. "And in many of his shell companies, money tended to vanish into official and then not-so-official offshore accounts and then vanish completely."

"I don't want to know how you did any of this tracking," Agent Munn said, shaking her head.

"No worry," Doc said. "None of us but Fleet and his people understand any of it anyway.

Fleet laughed. "Not even so sure I do, to be honest. But we found a way to trace just one of those accounts and discovered another web, almost as large as the first web, with hundreds of companies, some standard, some shell, some holding companies, but with a different named spider at the core."

"And all working with no contact at all with the other web?" Julia asked.

"Nothing but the money trails," Fleet said. Then he hit a key on his computer and turned the laptop around.

Meet Jefferson Last."

Lott was stunned. The image on the screen could be identified as Williams, maybe. The same eyes, the same basic smirk, but this man had silver hair combed back, and his cheekbones were higher and more pronounced and his nose was smaller.

"Oh, my," Julia said.

"Williams after some surgery I'm sure," Fleet said. "This picture was clearly Photoshopped. And there is no evidence anyone has ever seen Mr. Last. But one of his companies rented the car he is driving. And since it is a rental, there is a tracking signal on it. That's how I know where he's at exactly."

"So how are we going to get him?" Julia asked.

Doc smiled at her. "I have just the plan."

"As long as it doesn't include a cold dive into a freezing lake," Julia said, "I'm in."

Annie and Agent Munn and Lott all completely agreed to that.

CHAPTER FORTY

May 16, 2015
9 P.M.
White Bird, Idaho

LOTT WAS STUNNED from the air that he could see the ruggedness of the wilderness they were flying over. The snow-topped peaks seemed to glisten in the moonlight and the dark shadows of the canyons looked like deep and very dangerous lakes.

It had taken them all of fifteen minutes to get to the small McCall airport and be picked up by the chopper.

In Doc's helicopter, Lott and Julia and Annie sat in the center seats. Agent Munn, Fleet, and Doc sat in the seats behind them.

The FBI chopper with men that Agent Munn trusted completely had left just ahead of them.

Lott was surprised at how fast the trip went as they were dropped off in a field just up a narrow valley from a small town called White Bird. The FBI chopper was already there. It couldn't be seen at all from any place along the highway.

Lott could see that the highway passed about a hundred feet above the lower part of the tiny town at the bottom of the steep valley and then wound its way up the side of a very steep hill.

FBI helicopters coming in from Spokane had already reached the top of the summit. They had borrowed the use of a large semi-truck and had it pulled off to one side waiting. When they got the signal, the truck would be positioned blocking the road as if it had an accident.

Agents with rifles would be stationed in hiding above the area behind the truck. They planned on letting Williams just pull up behind the truck and stop. On one side it would be straight up, on the other side was a drop of over a thousand feet.

The agents that had gotten there slightly ahead of them had set up three cars from local residents. One was a large Ford Bronco, another was a Chevy pickup with a load of hay in the back, and the third was an older style Jeep.

Lott decided he was best suited to drive the Ford Bronco, since a bunch of years back he had had one. Julia got in the passenger side.

Agent Munn and one other agent got in behind them.

Doc got into the pickup with Annie and Fleet.

Three other agents piled into the Jeep.

"He's coming by in about two minutes," Fleet said into all their communication links.

They pulled where he wouldn't see them in a turn-out, but where they could get onto the road behind him. The Jeep with the agents stayed down hidden in the town and would come on last.

Lott turned off the Bronco, shut down the lights and the four of them sat there silently for a minute until Fleet said, "Here he comes. Dark sedan."

Everyone in the Bronco ducked so the car looked empty. Then when Lott saw the sedan was past, he started up the Bronco and climbed up onto the highway. He slowly gained speed, letting the sedan get a ways out in front of him.

There were no other cars on the road. Seemed that very few people drove this twisty north-south highway at night.

Behind the Bronco, Lott could see the pickup come up onto the road and then a few moments later the Jeep.

"Last car ahead of Williams has passed the truck," Fleet reported. "Truck is getting into position."

"The driver going to be able to get out of there?" Julia asked.

"An agent is driving," Agent Munn said.

"Truck is in place," someone reported.

Once again Lott could feel his stomach starting to clamp up from the excitement of all this. Williams had played them for a very long time and thought them too stupid to figure him out. He was going to be in for a very sudden surprise.

The road, the higher they climbed, got slightly more frightening. Not like the gravel road they had first driven, but even though this road was paved and three lanes wide, two going up, one coming

down, with guardrails, Lott felt more like he was piloting an airplane that was slowly climbing instead of driving. Nothing but space and stars and snow-capped peaks could be seen to their right.

Ahead, Lott could see the blinking warning lights of the truck and Williams slowing down to stop near the truck.

Lott slowed down behind him, finally coming to a stop near the bumper of the brown sedan. Lott put the Bronco in park and set the parking brake.

Around the truck, a man who looked like he was the driver was inspecting something near the front of the cab. The truck looked like it had almost rammed into the hillside.

The other two cars behind him pulled up and stopped, one in the center lane and back twenty paces, while the Bronco and Williams' car were in the outside right lane near the guardrail.

"Everyone in position?" Agent Munn asked.

"Ready," were the responses quick and short.

"On my mark we move," Agent Munn said.

A two count, then she said, "Now!"

Extremely bright lights from the hillside above and the top of the truck hit the sedan as Lott clicked on the bright lights on the Bronco and went out the driver's door and to the ditch on the inside of the road, his gun drawn.

He could see that Julia went out on the passenger side, holding her position, with her gun drawn, using the door as a shield. The agent behind her went out and took a position using the rail as a form of shield.

The truck driver pulled a gun and ducked in behind one wheel of the big truck, aiming back on the sedan and Agent

Mann followed Lott from the Bronco and to the ditch.

Behind them the agents spread out while Fleet and Doc stayed crouched in their rig.

"Williams," a very loud speaker shouted, echoing over the valley. "Please open the door and keep your hands on the wheel."

Nothing.

"Williams," Agent Mott said, "you have no place to run this time."

Nothing.

"I doubt he even has a gun in there," Lott said.

"Can't take the chance," Agent Munn said.

"Let me try to egg him out," Lott said. "But be ready for him to try to make a run for it."

"Go ahead," Agent Munn said. "We either arrest him or kill him and I honestly don't care which at this point."

After seeing the woman embalmed and floating in that car, and digging Trish's body out of the lake, Lott didn't much care either.

"Hey, Williams," Lott shouted to the car, standing up near the edge of the road and lowering his gun to his side. "Now who is boring? We're getting tired out here."

Williams rolled down the window, his hands not visible, and looked across the road to Lott.

Lott had been, for a moment, afraid it would be someone else in the car, but it was actually Williams.

In the flesh.

They had finally cornered the bastard.

Lott didn't let himself smile, kept his poker face on solid.

"I'm surprised the four of you survived that blast," Williams said. "Very impressive, Detective."

"We knew you weren't in there," Lott said. "And we knew you weren't coming to the mortuary either. "We rescued that poor state cop's family the moment he turned on the lights. What an amateur play. We expected more of you."

Williams said nothing, so Lott went on.

"You thought you were playing us, but we played you the entire time," Lott said, lying. "We were just waiting for you to make a boneheaded mistake like this one, show yourself, and make it easy for us to trap you or kill you. And what kind of stupid name is Jefferson Last, anyway?"

Williams seemed to jerk at that.

Lott smiled. The bluster was completely gone from the man.

"And it was very nice of you to lead us to your body dump," Lott said. "And show us exactly who was working with you. They are singing like songbirds on a beautiful day, by the way. They don't much like you."

Williams jerked at that as well.

"You know," Lott said, "if you hadn't decided to move on and push all that money into Jefferson Last corporations, we never would have trapped you like this."

"Who says I am trapped, Detective?" Williams asked, turning to really stare at Lott.

Lott suddenly knew what Williams had done. He had rigged the car to explode just in case. He liked that kind of dramatics it seemed. And Lott had a hunch Williams would take himself out this time.

"I suppose you could take the easy way out, give up the fight, lose the game," Lott said, "by letting us kill you, or you blowing yourself up with that rigged car."

Again Williams jerked.

Bluff called. Lott had hit it right on the head again.

"Not fun having someone ahead of you, is it?" Lott asked, laughing. "So how about you take the fight to the courts, see if you and your team of lawyers are smart enough to beat a few dumb cops and prosecuting attorneys."

Williams just sat there, saying nothing.

"Don't think you can beat us, do you?"

Williams sat staring forward.

"Then pull the trigger on that bomb," Lott said, "if you think you can't beat us yet again. This is getting boring."

Williams sat for a long moment and Lott just let him.

Finally Williams lifted his hands slowly to the steering wheel. "Come and get me, Detective."

"You really do think I'm that stupid," Lott said, laughing. "I'd suggest you blow yourself up right now, or just make a sudden move and let us all put a few hundred bullets into your pathetic body. Great target practice. You clearly keep underestimating us and that won't get you a win in court."

"I'll walk free," Williams said. "You watch, Detective."

"Maybe in hell," Lott said, laughing.

"I swear, Detective," Williams said, "You can really get on a person's nerves."

"I've been told that," Lott said.

Williams reached for the door handle and pushed the door open.

Then suddenly Williams' face went white and he scrambled to do something under the dash.

"Down everyone!" Lott shouted and dove for the weed-choked ditch.

And for the second time, an explosion triggered by Williams smashed into Lott's back.

A moment later, but what seemed like an eternity, he heard Agent Munn shout to see if everyone was all right.

Lott could barely hear her, his ears were ringing so loud.

But all he could do was smile, because burning in the brush against the hillside about ten feet in front of him was what was left of Willis Williams.

And never had Lott seen such a perfect sight.

A moment later, an angel appeared over him, looking very, very worried.

She asked if he was all right. Lott rolled over slowly onto his back in the weeds and he reached up and indicated she should come closer.

She leaned in, even more worried.

Then he kissed her.

He planned on doing that a lot more very shortly.

CHAPTER FORTY-ONE

May 17, 2015
9:20 A.M.
McCall, Idaho

JULIA SMILED at the wonderful man asleep in her bed.

The suite around them was wonderful and Doc said she and Lott could use it as long as they wanted.

The sun was already up and full and she had ordered them both room service breakfast.

After the explosion on the hill and the death of Williams, they had spent some time giving statements, then promised more today and for the next week or so.

They had flown back to McCall, and Doc had suggested they just stay in the Shore Lodge suite for the night, since Lott was again covered in dirt and mud from the ditch.

They both liked the idea.

Lott had gone into the shower after they got back to the room to get clean and she had decided they had waited more than long enough. She took off her clothes and joined him, helping him wash his back.

And then he helped her.

Then together, they tumbled into the soft featherbed and made love in the most wonderful and slow way.

After so many years, she couldn't even believe that was possible for her. But it clearly was.

Then they had gone out for a late dinner with Doc and Annie and Fleet, then had come back and fallen asleep in each other's arms.

It had felt so natural.

The sun through the drapes woke her and she had gotten up, ordered breakfast, and then gone back to bed.

Now she lay there staring at Lott. She couldn't believe it, but she had fallen in love again. She had thought that part of her life was over. But it clearly wasn't.

She touched him gently, just wanting to feel his skin. Then she cuddled against him, her body pressed against his.

Lott smiled and turned slightly so he could look into her eyes. "Even though I hurt in more places than I care to think about, that feels wonderful."

She laughed. "We are getting a little old to be blown up twice in one day."

"Anyone's too old for that," Lott said.

"Have I ever told you I love you, Detective," she said, smiling at him.

"You haven't," Lott said, smiling back at her. "And I love you as well, you know that, Detective?"

"I do," she said.

She kissed him.

He kissed her back.

And then for the next thirty minutes, until breakfast arrived, they did some pretty amazing things for two retired detectives.

~

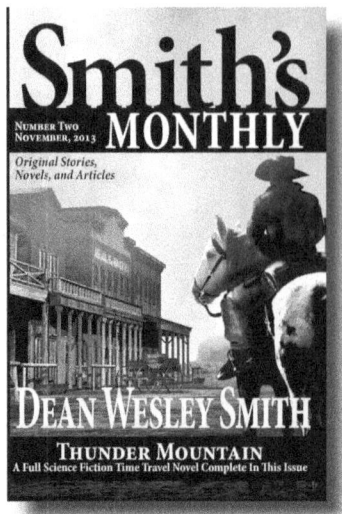

#7... April 2014   *#8... May 2014*   *#9... June 2014*

Poems by Dean Wesley Smith

Being Young

A young woman,
maybe twenty-two,
bent over
without a thought
and without bending her knees,
to pick up a dropped water bottle.

An elderly woman,
slumped over in a wheelchair,
watched,
sadness for lost years
filling her eyes.

Human aging isn't measured by years,
but by lost freedoms
taken from the human body.
The old woman
in the wheelchair understood that.
The young woman
was still decades from catching a clue.